SAVING WHAT'S MINE
Men of Maddox Security

LOGAN CHANCE

Copyright © 2025 by Logan Chance

All rights reserved.

No part of this book may be reproduced in any form or by any electronic or mechanical means, including information storage and retrieval systems, without written permission from the author, except for the use of brief quotations in a book review.

Cover Design by Kim Lehnhardt

For my Greedy Girls—Kim L., Valerie, Lorey, Kim S., Tiffany, Rochelle, Maria, Stacey, Lisa H., Kasey, Lisa A., Maritza, Amy, Julie, Shaunna, and Kim G.

The Men and Women of Maddox Security

Dean Maddox- Owner of Maddox Security. A total badass who's completely in love with his wife, Sophia. (You can read their love story in Stolen By The Boss)

Isabel Maddox- Dean's younger sister. She runs the business with her brother. She takes care of the day-to-day running of things.

Ranger Cole-ex-Navy SEAL and one of Dean's top security specialists. He specializes in negotiation tactics. Hard working, and loyal to those around him.

Lincoln Zane- ex- Navy SEAL. He's been working for Maddox Security since its creation. Specializes in communications and leadership. Don't let his quiet demeanor fool you, Lincoln cares deeply for those he's sworn to protect.

Orion Locke- Orion's got his own style of security and has been working in the law enforcement field since he turned eighteen. A complete loner, he takes his job seriously.

Boone Porter- A man who thrives off the grid. Ex-military, and a pure mountain man. He's skilled with his hands, and bush crafting skills.

Asher Hawke- the newest member of Maddox Security, and the youngest. He's eager for a chance to prove himself worthy of being one of the elite Men of Maddox Security.

MADDOX SECURITY

Please Read before Continuing

The first chapter of this book is a meeting of the Men of Maddox Security. Each book will showcase this SAME meeting, but from each hero's perspective in their book.

So, in this book the meeting will be shown from Orion's point of view.

In the next book, Guarding What's Mine, the same meeting will be shown from Boone's point of view.

Etc...

About

When life hands Orion Locke a new assignment, it's not just any routine security detail—he's tasked with protecting Briar Green, a quirky bird handler with an even quirkier pet bird named Jeb. Between dodging the advances of a persistent stalker and Jeb's constant chaos (seriously, who knew a bird could have *that* much attitude?), Orion's life takes a nosedive into feathers, flirty banter, and flying distractions.
Briar isn't your typical damsel in distress. She's independent, headstrong, and far too comfortable with letting Jeb run wild. Orion's job was supposed to be simple: protect her from the shadows and maintain a professional distance. But as danger gets closer, so do they, and suddenly keeping his heart safe becomes harder than dodging Jeb's random flying attacks. Will Orion be able to save Briar from her stalker before she drives him completely bananas? Or will the real challenge be keeping his feelings caged?

Chapter 1

Orion

I smack the snooze button again, the soft thud of it echoing in my dimly lit room.

Shut the fuck up, motherfucker.

Seriously, who in their right mind thinks nine a.m. meetings are a good idea? Certainly not me. My body feels like lead, weighed down by the exhaustion from yet another late night spent indulging in my secret obsession—magic tricks.

Yeah, I'd never tell anyone I'm into sleight of hand tricks. Especially the men I work with at Maddox Security. I'm sure the guys would love to rag on me for that. I'd probably never hear the end of it, and listen... I'd rather keep this shit to myself.

However, my fingers have a natural agility. They move with a kind of fluidity over the cards, shuffling and flipping them effortlessly. It's not just a party trick; it's skill, discipline, finesse.

Few people can handle a deck the way I do. There's only two things I'm really, *really* good at. Fucking and cards.

The alarm shrieks again, more demanding this time, yanking me out of my daydream. I groan, throwing my rumpled dark-blue comforter to the floor in frustration.

Fine, I'm getting up.

I rub my eyes, the clock flashing an accusatory 8:20 a.m. Ten minutes to get out the door. Fantastic.

I leap out of bed and stumble through my morning routine like a man possessed. A wrinkled t-shirt is the first thing I grab from the pile of semi-clean clothes on the chair in the corner of my room. Not ideal, but it'll have to do. At least Dean, my boss, doesn't believe in suits and ties for these meetings. It's one of the few things I appreciate about him.

However, what I don't appreciate… Dean's obsession with holding early-morning meetings. He's one of those "stick to a schedule" types, convinced that knocking out meetings at the crack of dawn somehow frees up the rest of the day for productivity. Maybe for him, but for me? I'd prefer an extra hour of sleep.

I guess it also goes to say the majority of the men who work for Maddox Security are ex-military. They're used to this shit, and sure, when I worked SWAT, I got up early for work… but it's been a while.

My phone buzzes on the nightstand, a text from Boone popping up. "Don't be late. You know Dean will notice." Great, just what I need. As if the anxiety about the meeting wasn't enough, I now have Boone in my ear reminding me of Dean's eagle-eye for tardiness. I throw on some jeans, grab my keys, and dash out the door, hoping I can make it downtown in record time.

Dean Maddox is the head of one of the world's largest security firms—though calling it a "security company" hardly does it justice—and has a reputation for taking on the most challenging cases, the ones other firms shy away from. It's also how he met his wife, Sophia. They had to pretend to be married for a case, and somewhere along the way, Dean fell hopelessly in love with her. Their unconventional love story is one for the books, but right now, I need to focus on making it to that early meeting.

I race across town in my SUV, tires screeching as I speed through the traffic lights. Bursting into the conference room, I'm a groggy mess, barely able to keep my eyes open.

"Why do you schedule these meetings so early in the morning?" I grumble, collapsing into the nearest chair.

Dean, Boone, Ranger, and Lincoln turn to look at me, their expressions a mix of curiosity and amusement. It's as if I'm some peculiar artifact they can't quite place. Maybe they've never been this tired before.

"It's nine a.m. I wouldn't exactly call this early," Dean chuckles, his gray eyes assessing me.

"Someone had a rough night," Boone observes, his grin widening as he leans back in his chair.

If he only knew. I let out a groan and rest my head on my arms, desperately trying to stay awake while I wait for the last person to arrive.

A few minutes later, Asher, the newest member of our team, strides into the room, clearly apologetic. "Sorry I'm late," he says, offering Dean a quick nod.

"Thanks for being here, everyone," Dean begins, flipping through a stack of papers with practiced efficiency. "I know the past couple of months have been challenging with my search for Bishop Blackstone. I want to extend my gratitude to each of you for your invaluable contributions in locating him."

As Dean speaks, I stifle another yawn, wishing more than anything for this meeting to be over so I can crawl back into bed and catch up on some much-needed sleep. The room's early morning light feels harsh, and the comfort of my bed seems like a distant dream.

"I know Isabel has been a tremendous help, and I'm incredibly lucky to have such an awesome sister," Dean says, his tone filled with genuine appreciation. He glances at Lincoln, who's watching him, before continuing, "Now, I have some assignments that have come up, and I want to assign each one."

I force myself to focus, mentally kicking myself for not grabbing a coffee before the meeting. If only I had gotten up a bit earlier, I might have had the chance.

"Ranger, let's start with you," Dean says, sliding a thick file across the polished wooden desk. "The G-Summit Meeting is this weekend, and this is Tory Ann."

Ranger picks up the file and begins flipping through the papers, his brow furrowing in concentration. "Is she attending the summit?"

"No, she's not," Dean replies, shaking his head. "Her father, the world-renowned scientist Frederick Malser, will be a keynote speaker. He'll be there, and he'll have his own personal security detail looking after him."

Ranger looks up, curiosity piqued. "Why not have his own security team watch over his daughter as well?"

"Frederick has received several threats regarding his speech at the Summit," Dean explains, his voice steady. "He's adamant about keeping his daughter's presence in town a secret. He wants everything to remain under the radar and is even hesitant about some members of his own security team."

The room falls silent as everyone absorbs the information. I shift in my seat, mentally reviewing my to-do list. This is going to be a long day, but at least it's starting to take shape.

"That sucks," Ranger mutters, glancing down at the file in his hands with a frown.

"You'll take her to the safe house: SEASHELL, and keep her there until the Summit is over," Dean instructs, his tone allowing no room for an argument.

I let my gaze drift out of the conference room window, where the morning sun casts shimmering reflections over the ocean. The rhythmic pull of the waves lulls me into a semi-trance, momentarily pulling me away from the meeting's intensity.

"Orion," Dean continues, snapping me back to attention, "Briar Green's the daughter of socialite Minnie Green. Briar's been dealing with a persistent ex-boyfriend who's been stalking her. Her mother insists on having security for her while we work on getting a restraining order."

I shake my head, trying to clear the fog that seems to be enveloping my brain. I wish I could just shake off the exhaustion and focus.

"Ex-boyfriend?" I ask, my voice tinged with frustration. "Can't I just take him out back, scare him half to death, and call it a day?" I reach for the file Dean slides toward me.

"It's not that simple," Dean replies, his expression serious.

I flip open the folder, and my breath catches. The photo inside nearly leaves me speechless. "It never is," I mutter under my breath, staring at the striking green eyes gazing up at me from the picture. Damn. I've never seen anyone so stunningly beautiful in all my life. Her eyes are a mesmerizing shade of emerald, framed by thick lashes that curl just right, almost too perfect to be real. They seem to shimmer with a life of their own, pulling me in, and for a second, I forget where I am.

Her face is a dream, delicately sculpted like something out of a Renaissance painting. Full lips are perfectly balanced in shape and color, curving into a subtle, confident smile that seems to challenge the world around her. She's magnetic, radiant, and the kind of woman who'd turn heads wherever she goes without even trying.

Despite my best efforts to focus on Dean as he assigns the next task to Boone, my gaze keeps drifting back to Briar Green's photo. There's something about her that's impossible to ignore, a quiet intensity in her beauty that leaves a *fucking* mark.

Listen, I love a pretty lady, sure, but there's something about Briar that's *different*. Dating women isn't really high on my priority list of things to do. Relationships are something I never indulge in. Ever. Now fucking women, whole other story, however, looking at Briar's picture right now has me rethinking my fucking priorities.

I hate to admit it, but I can understand why her ex-boyfriend can't let go. She's a fucking knockout.

Dean's voice cuts through my thoughts, "I want everyone to know I'm here if you need anything." His words pull me abruptly from my fixation on Briar.

I force myself to refocus on her file, skimming through details about her job at the Saint Pierce Zoo, where she works in the aviary.

I'm not the type to fall for someone at the mere sight of a photograph. Yet, as I stare at Briar, something within me shifts. A primal urge begins to stir. A rush of molten lava surges through my veins. A fierce, possessive rage ignites in my gut, compelling me to protect this woman with every ounce of my being. It's as if my body has decided on its own that her safety is now my only responsibility, no matter what.

I glance at the name of the ex-boyfriend, Jason Baker, and an intense wave of hatred washes over me. It's not just dislike; I feel a deep, visceral anger, and I silently hope that by the end of this job, I'll have the chance to confront him one-on-one and make him understand just how much I despise him.

My thoughts shift abruptly as I read through the rest of the file. I'll also be spending time alone with Briar. I scan her address and the contact number for her parents. They want me to meet her at her job and then bring her to my place. My place?

The meeting wraps up, and I grab the file, heading out of the room with it clutched tightly in my hands.

"Asher, can you hang back a minute?" Dean calls out as I shut the door behind me.

Boone turns to the group. "We all need to catch up soon. It was a blast last time."

My foggy brain struggles to reconcile the idea of a fun night with the guys and the serious task of protecting Briar. I just stand there, half-listening as the guys chat about planning another get-together.

"Maybe once I'm done with this assignment, we can do a guys' poker night," I suggest, trying to sound casual.

"I'm down with that," Ranger replies, his trademark cocky attitude evident in his voice. "Of course, I want to play again."

I can't help but smile slightly at this. Motherfucker stole all our money last time we had a poker night. I still remember losing three hundred bucks to that card shark.

Ranger's laughter cuts through my thoughts. "I'd love some more free money," he jokes, his eyes sparkling with amusement.

"No way. I'm not playing poker with this guy again," Lincoln mutters, barely above a whisper. Lincoln's the giant silent type—one of those stoic figures who keeps to himself. I don't know him well, and honestly, neither does anyone else. "Besides, my job isn't exactly a walk in the park."

Ranger gives Lincoln a friendly slap on the shoulder, his grin widening. "I figured as much when Dean brought you in before everyone else. Must be a tough gig."

Lincoln merely nods, his expression unreadable. He sighs deeply. "It's Isabel. Dean's sister. She's being threatened."

That jolts me fully awake. Isabel is like family to us—one of the guys, really. We'd all put our lives on the line to protect her, just as we would for each other.

"Who's behind it?" Boone asks, his voice tight with the same fury I'm feeling.

Lincoln shrugs, his face a mask of frustration. "Not sure yet. Dean's got some leads. My job is to keep Isabel safe while he sorts it out."

"Good luck with that," I say with a forced laugh. "I'm sure she's thrilled about this." Knowing Isabel, I'm sure she's not. She's a tough chick, a real badass, like her brother.

Just then, the sharp click of Isabel's heels echoes through the hallway. The sound sets my nerves on edge. I imagine her frustration at being shielded, and I'm not keen on sticking around for the inevitable confrontation.

"Isabel on your six," Boone says before bolting toward the elevator.

I quickly hit the elevator button, eager to escape before the real fireworks start. I've got to get to the Saint Pierce Zoo and focus on my own assignment.

Chapter 2

Briar

"Did you hear?" my best friend, Heidi, says, her eyes scanning my face.

I brace myself, already guessing what's coming. "If you're about to tell me they filled the bird trainer spot with an outside hire, I might just scream."

Heidi's face falls flat. "Okay, I won't tell you then." She starts tapping away on her phone, obviously scanning the dating app she's on.

I slump into the chair in the break room of the Saint Pierce Zoo Bird Aviary. This place—the largest open-air Asian aviary in the Western Hemisphere—is where I've dreamed of working as a bird trainer for as long as I can remember. It's an important role here; training some of the rarest birds in the world for the zoo's educational shows is a big deal.

I've been chasing this job for a year, only to be consistently overlooked. Right now, I'm stuck with cleaning cages and handling other menial tasks that the zookeepers usually avoid.

"I can't believe they hired someone else," I mutter, the disappointment heavy in my voice.

Heidi tucks her phone into her handbag and settles down beside me, her big brown eyes locking onto mine with a mix of sympathy and determination. "They're idiots," she says, her voice firm. "Briar, you're one of the best bird trainers I've ever seen. I mean, who else would take in a rescue parrot and teach him how to speak?"

I nod, the mention of Jeb, the Congo African Grey parrot I've been working with, tugging at my pride and frustration. "Jeb's great and easy to train, but yeah, I don't understand it either."

Heidi leans in closer, her expression serious. "Listen, maybe you need to sit Marcie down and tell her how you really feel."

I shake my head vehemently. "I can't do that. No way."

Marcie's my boss, the head of what Heidi sarcastically calls the 'grunts,' and one of the toughest women I've ever met. She's the no-nonsense, doesn't-take-shit-from-anyone type. I once asked her for a day off to go to the beach, and she told me the beach wasn't going anywhere and I could visit it when we weren't in the middle of the busy season.

Since then, I've learned to navigate around her as much as possible, avoiding her like the plague. I've gotten pretty good at it, too. It's not just a matter of preference; it's survival.

"Hey, Marcie wants everyone over by the entrance to the Wings of Asia in ten minutes," Perry calls out as he passes by. He's another grunt worker like me and Heidi, part of our little trio of bird poop warriors. It's not glamorous, but someone has to do the dirty work at the zoo, and that someone is us.

I sigh, grabbing my gloves and standing up from my seat. "This is my life. I've accepted it."

Heidi, always the optimist, stands too and wraps an arm around my shoulders, giving me a reassuring squeeze. "No, it's not. This is just a stepping stone on the way to bigger and brighter things. Trust me. And hey, at least you finally left Jason. That guy was toxic as fuck."

If only she knew how toxic. And how he's still lingering. Just the thought of him sends a bitter taste to my mouth. It's been weeks since I left him, and he's just not getting it. He still messages.

"When we first met, it was… I don't know. Like everything was falling into place," I admit, half to myself, as the memory of Jason's charm flickers through my mind. He had that effortless way of making me feel special, but it was short lived. And then all the red flags started appearing. "I really don't know why I stayed with him as long as I did." I should have left at the first sign.

"But I was so wrong," I continue, my voice hardening as the memories of the lies, the manipulation, and the gaslighting come flooding back. "I never thought I could be that wrong about a person. I mean, I can read birds like nobody's business, but humans? Apparently, I'm terrible at it."

Heidi rubs my back, her expression soft but knowing. "You weren't stupid, Briar. He was just that good at lying."

"I believed every word," I mutter. "Every damn word. He was a manipulator, and I was the fool who trusted him."

Jason had been a master of pretending. He spun lie after lie after lie. I cringe at the thought of how easily he had me wrapped around his finger. Now, I feel like an entirely different person—more guarded, more cautious, and definitely not as naïve.

"Thank God that's over," I lie, shaking off the dark thoughts.

"Damn right," Heidi agrees, giving me one last squeeze before letting go. "Onward and upward, girl. Let's show Marcie that you're meant for more than this grunt work. We'll make sure that bird trainer spot has your name on it next time."

I nod, forcing a small smile. Maybe Heidi's right. Maybe this is just a stepping stone. But for now, it's hard to see past the bird poop and broken hearts.

"I'll never make another mistake like that again. I'm done. I'll never fall for anyone ever again," I declare with finality, feeling the conviction settle deep into my bones.

Heidi's brown eyes widen, her usual easygoing expression tightening with concern. "Well, that's a bit extreme, don't you think?"

"I'm serious," I insist, my voice firm. "I have way too much I need to accomplish before I let another man into my life like that again. And for what? To be completely shattered? Never again." I shake my head, more resolute than ever.

Heidi sighs, her brow furrowing. "You can't let one asshole dictate your future. That's not fair to you, Briar."

"I'm not," I say, my voice softening but still unyielding. "But I'm also not about to pretend like I didn't learn from my mistakes. I trusted him blindly, and it backfired in the worst way. I'd be a fool to do that again."

Heidi shrugs, her playful nature dimming just a little as she considers my words. "I guess I see your point. I just don't want you to shut yourself off from the world because of some douchebag."

I offer her a small, tight-lipped smile. "Trust me, Heidi, I'm not swearing off the world. Just… relationships. At least for a long time." I cross my arms, trying to make the decision feel more empowering than defensive.

A teasing grin pulls at Heidi's lips as she eyes me mischievously. "Well, I've just been asked out by Perry."

I burst out laughing despite myself, the tension in the room easing slightly. "Perry? Seriously?"

Heidi widens her eyes and opens her mouth in mock shock, but the blush creeping into her cheeks betrays her. "I don't like Perry," she says, the denial coming out far too quickly.

I arch an eyebrow, folding my arms as I smirk at her. "Uh-huh. Sure you don't."

Her cheeks flush an even deeper pink, and she swats at me playfully. "I don't! It's just… he's funny, okay? And kinda cute in that dorky, bird poop-cleaning way."

"Uh-huh. Sure," I say, stretching the words out as I give her a knowing look.

Heidi huffs dramatically, but I can see the smile tugging at the corner of her lips. "I swear it's not like that! But hey, at least one of us should be allowed to have a little fun, right?"

I shrug, my smile softening. "If you want to date Perry, you should. Don't let my past relationship deter you."

Heidi laughs, her earlier tension fading as she rolls her eyes. "I haven't said yes yet."

But even as she says it, I can see the glint of amusement in her eyes, and I know she's considering it.

As for me, I'm still committed to my decision—no more falling for smooth-talking charmers like Jason. I've got my work, my goals, and my birds to focus on. Love can wait. Or maybe it's better off not showing up at all.

I laugh, dragging the word out. "*Riiiiight.*"

Heidi rolls her eyes, grabbing her things with a huff of mock indignation. "I haven't."

"Uh-huh," I tease, my grin widening as we leave the break room and head toward the aviary. The air outside hits me like a warm blanket, thick and humid, but the sky is bright and clear, a perfect shade of blue with barely a cloud in sight. "Let's hope we avoid the afternoon showers today."

"Fat chance," Heidi says, glancing up at the sky with a skeptical squint. "You know it rains like clockwork at four p.m. every day."

She's right, of course. Like a daily ritual, the afternoon rain always sweeps through, cooling everything down for a few moments before the humidity comes back with a vengeance. The birds love it—happily flapping their wings in the downpour—but I can't say the same for my hair. I run a hand through it, dreading the inevitable frizz. Not that it matters. It's not like I'm trying to impress anyone these days.

As we stroll through the park, the lush greenery of the aviary stretches out before us, a beautiful oasis of tropical plants and the melodic sound of birds chirping in the trees. This is one of my most favorite places in the entire world. But today, there's a subtle edge to my mood, a nagging sense of frustration that lingers just beneath the surface. Maybe it's the constant rejection for the bird trainer position, or maybe it's Jason still haunting my thoughts despite my resolve to move on.

My phone pings with a text, pulling me from my thoughts. I reach into my pocket and glance down at the screen, relieved when I see who it's from—my mother.

> Mom: Got you someone to watch over you.

I FROWN, quickly typing back, wondering what on earth she means.

> Me: What? Who?

HER RESPONSE IS IMMEDIATE, which makes my stomach drop even further.

> Mom: Security.

"WHAT THE HELL?" I mutter under my breath, stopping in my tracks.

"What is it?" Heidi asks, peering over my shoulder as I stare at the screen.

"My mom…" I hesitate, trying to make sense of the sudden, cryptic message. "She says she's got me a bodyguard. Like, someone to watch over me."

Heidi's brows shoot up. "For what? Did Jason do something?"

"No," I lie, my fingers hovering over the screen. A familiar mix of frustration and anxiety bubbles up inside me. My mom has always been a bit overprotective—especially after what happened with Jason—but this? This is next level shit.

"I mean, it's kind of sweet, I guess?" Heidi says, though her voice is unsure. "Maybe she's just worried about you after everything."

I shake my head, my thoughts racing. "I don't need a babysitter. I'm not some damsel-in-distress."

"I know, but you can't really blame her after everything with your ex," Heidi says, her tone softening. "You know how your mother gets." Heidi's been my best friend for years, and sometimes I swear her and my mother are closer than I am with my own mother.

However, she's right. My mom never really liked Jason, and after everything blew up between us, her protective instincts obviously kicked into overdrive. But this—hiring security? I groan internally, already dreading whatever conversation I'm going to have with her later.

I glance around at the aviary, its peaceful beauty suddenly feeling a little less comforting with this unexpected complication looming over me.

My mother can be a bit... dramatic. I hate that about her sometimes, though I know it comes from a place of love. She panicked the second I mentioned Jason calling and texting me again. He hasn't done anything threatening or dangerous—just his usual desperate attempts to "explain" how he's not a lying, cheating jerk. But my mom? She jumped straight to DEFCON 1.

I roll my eyes at the thought. A bodyguard? Really?

I fire off a quick response, trying to reassure her.

> Me: Mom, I can't have a bodyguard following me around at work. I'll be fine.

I SHOVE my phone into the back pocket of my jeans, feeling the weight of the conversation still hanging in the air. Just another thing to worry about.

With a sigh, I join the rest of the staff, lined up near the entrance to the Wings of Asia exhibit. Marcie, in her usual authoritarian fashion, stands front and center, arms crossed, her sharp blue eyes scanning us like a hawk. As always, she's meticulously put together, her red hair slicked back in a tight ponytail that could probably withstand a hurricane. She's tough, no-nonsense, and always demanding excellence—especially from me.

"Now, we have some VIP parties this upcoming week," she begins, her voice clipped and commanding, "so let's make sure this cage really shines."

It's the same speech she gives before every shift, and yet, the unspoken pressure to make everything perfect seems heavier today. Clean, clean, and more cleaning. That's the core of our lives here in the aviary. No one, especially the high-paying guests, wants to see bird poop when they're marveling at exotic species.

I glance around at the familiar faces of my coworkers, who seem just as thrilled about today's work as I am. Perry stands a little too casually, hands in his pockets, like he's mentally checked out. Heidi is beside me, tapping her fingers restlessly against her thigh. We all know the drill—scrub down the enclosures, polish the windows, make everything sparkle. But even so, Marcie feels the need to remind us. Every. Single. Time.

"And remember," she continues, her gaze sweeping across the group, but landing directly on me, "when someone asks you specifically about the species of bird, or anything more technical, refer them to the zookeepers. Don't try to answer the questions yourselves."

Her words cut right through me, her eyes boring into mine like she's already anticipating that I'll mess up. I bristle under her stare, fighting the urge to snap back. I know she's talking to me. It's like she enjoys putting me in my place, constantly reminding me of the invisible line between the "real" zookeepers and us grunt workers.

As if I don't already know.

I glance down at the gloves in my hand, my knuckles white from the tight grip. I've worked here for three years, busting my ass day in and day out. I know these birds better than most of the keepers. But does Marcie see that? No. To her, I'm just another cog in the cleaning crew, here to handle the dirty work while the real stars answer questions and get all the glory.

I tuck a stray strand of brown hair behind my ear, trying to look as nonchalant as possible. In my own defense, I've only answered a few questions here and there when the tourists asked. I mean, what's the harm? If someone's genuinely interested in learning about the birds, I'm not going to stand there and act clueless. They're here to enjoy their time, and if I happen to know a fun fact or two about parakeets, who am I to deny them that bit of knowledge?

Okay, maybe I know more than a fun fact or two. The truth is, I'm a walking encyclopedia of bird facts. Years of obsession and dedication have filled my brain with more bird knowledge than even some of the zookeepers here. And if I occasionally outshine them with my enthusiasm? Well, that's not really my fault, is it?

I can't help but smirk at the memory of a group of tourists last week, wide-eyed and completely captivated as I talked about the parakeets' natural habitats, feeding habits, and quirky behaviors. The zookeeper on duty had shot me a look that could kill, but it's not like I was trying to show him up on purpose. I just love what I do. I love birds, and I'm not about to let anyone dim my brightness just because I know my shit. And I *so* do.

Still, I give Marcie a quick, tight nod, signaling my agreement. "Yes, Marcie," I say, my voice flat but polite. "I'll keep the bird facts to myself." Even though every fiber of my being rebels against that idea. It feels wrong to hold back when people are genuinely curious, but I know how it works around here.

Play the game, Briar. Just play the game.

I glance around the aviary, taking in the lush greenery and hearing the soft flutter of wings as the birds move through the space. I know every inch of this place, every bird call, every branch in the trees. I've worked so hard to get here, and I'm not going to let a little thing like being "too knowledgeable" hold me back. If they don't want me to answer questions, fine. I'll play along for now. But one day, I'll be the one they come to for the answers.

Marcie moves on to the next set of instructions, oblivious to the internal pep talk I'm giving myself. But I'm not just a grunt worker cleaning cages. I'm a future bird trainer—and a damn good one.

"Also, try not to get in anyone's way. Remember, a hidden cleaner is the best cleaner," Marcie repeats, her usual mantra. We all mumble the words back in unison, like a group of bored school kids who have heard the lecture a thousand

Saving What's Mine

times. With a dismissive wave, she sends us off to do our glamorous duty—cleaning bird poop, but discreetly, of course.

As soon as we break formation, Perry strides past, lobby broom and dustpan swung over his shoulders like some kind of avian sanitation cowboy. "I can't take another day of cleaning parrot shit," he groans, shooting a wink at Heidi, who blushes faintly and pretends not to notice.

"I'm right there with him," I say, more to myself than anyone else. The monotony is wearing me down. Sure, I love the birds, but cleaning up after them day in and day out without any sign of advancement? It's starting to feel like a cruel joke. I know I'm more qualified than whoever they brought in to fill the bird trainer position. I've paid my dues, worked harder than anyone, and yet here I am, scrubbing cages.

As if on cue, the new hire walks in, and my stomach drops.

Speak of the devil.

"Name's Heath Hone, new bird trainer," the new hire says with a smug smile, adjusting his black-rimmed glasses and tugging at the sleeves of his tweed jacket. A tweed jacket? At the Saint Pierce Zoo. In the middle of Summer? In ninety-degree heat. I bite back a snort, but seriously, who wears tweed to a zoo job?

He looks like he belongs in a lecture hall, not among the exotic birds here at the zoo. I can practically feel my blood pressure rising just looking at him. He oozes pretension, like he thinks he's too good for this place already.

Heidi leans in and whispers, "Who wears tweed to work with birds?"

"Someone who clearly hasn't met the humidity yet," I mutter under my breath, crossing my arms over my chest. Heath flashes a too-wide grin, oblivious to the side-eye he's getting from the rest of us.

"Pleasure to meet you all. I've got a few fresh ideas on how to improve the bird training program here. Just wait until you see what I've got planned for the shows," he says, puffing out his chest.

Oh, give me a break. I can't believe this is the guy who got the job I've been busting my ass for. Fresh ideas? Please. He probably learned everything out of a textbook. Does he even know the difference between a True Parrot and a regular parrot?

Perry catches my eye and raises an eyebrow. He can sense my irritation bubbling beneath the surface. I grit my teeth and force a smile, determined not to let Heath Hone and his tweed-jacket arrogance get under my skin.

"Welcome, Heath. We're excited to see what you bring to the team," I lie through my teeth, trying to keep things professional, even though all I want to do is throw him into a cage with the loudest, most obnoxious macaws and see how well his fresh ideas hold up.

This is just another roadblock, I tell myself. I've worked too hard to let some tweed-clad know-it-all stand in my way. My time will come.

Chapter 3

Briar

I grab a broom, ready to sweep out a few of the cockatoo's cages before the park fills up with its usual swarm of visitors. The air smells faintly of eucalyptus and fresh hay, mingling with the familiar scent of the aviary. From my spot in the back, I have a perfect view of the stage where today's bird show is about to start, the very show I'd give anything to be a trainer for.

Jenny, one of the lead trainers, steps confidently onto the stage as the morning sun filters through the canopy, casting a warm glow over the space. Her posture is relaxed, and the crowd immediately perks up at the sight of her. I've always admired Jenny. She's skilled, patient, and knows how to keep the audience engaged with every flip of a wing or screech from the birds. I can't help but imagine myself in her place, commanding the stage, sharing my passion for birds with hundreds of wide-eyed onlookers.

Then, Jenny introduces the new trainer joining her team—Heath. The crowd claps politely, but I know the truth—they're here for the birds, not the staff. I stifle a sigh and lean on my broom, watching as Jenny effortlessly transitions into the real stars of the show.

My eyes light up as she brings out Chester, the Yellow-naped Amazon, who's as mischievous as ever. I can already tell he's up to something. As soon as Jenny tries to settle everyone down, Chester is making a game of it, squawking loudly and darting between the other birds, pretending to cause chaos, but it's all part of the act. His green feathers flutter wildly as he jumps from perch to perch, riling up the other birds, who start chattering and flapping their wings in response. The audience erupts in laughter, and I can't help but chuckle along with them.

Chester is the show's little troublemaker, and he's absolutely brilliant at it. His antics are what makes the crowd fall in love with him every time, and honestly, it's what makes me love him too. Out of all the birds here, Chester has the biggest personality—cheeky, smart, and just unpredictable enough to keep everyone on their toes.

Chester's also the one with the most fans—Chester the Yellow-naped Amazon is practically a celebrity in his own right. Jenny manages his social media, and somehow, Chester has over twelve million followers. People adore him, and not just the locals. Tourists travel from all over the world just to catch a glimpse of him in action. I overhear families talking about how seeing Chester is the highlight of their trip. It's wild to think that a bird can be more famous than most people, but Chester earns it with every mischievous squawk and playful dive off the perch.

I chuckle to myself as Chester cracks another joke, his sharp little beak snapping playfully as the crowd roars with laughter.

My heart swells with pride, but I'm quickly reminded I still have a job to do. I push my broom across the floor of the aviary, sweeping up bits of feathers and stray twigs while glancing up at the show. It's hard to stay focused with Chester putting on his performance, but I force myself to get back to the task at hand.

As I finish up with one of the cockatoo cages, something catches my eye—movement near the restricted area behind the enclosures. I squint, spotting a man slipping around the corner where only staff are allowed. My stomach tightens immediately. That area is off-limits to the public.

I put down my broom and step forward, my heart pounding as I call out, "Excuse me, you're not supposed to be back here."

The man steps out from behind the shade, and my breath catches in my throat as my eyes lock with his cold, familiar blue ones. Jason. My pulse quickens, and a chill runs down my spine. Of all the people I didn't want to see today—or ever—it has to be him.

He's wearing that smirk I've grown to hate, the one that used to make me feel special, but now it just makes my skin crawl. His blonde hair is tousled like he hasn't bothered to comb it, and the slight shadow of stubble on his jaw suggests he's been living in the same state of disarray since we split. But it's his eyes that unsettle me the most—those piercing blue eyes that used to hold charm, now sharp and unreadable.

"I just had to see you," he says, stepping closer, his voice low and uninvited in the otherwise peaceful aviary.

I take a step back, instinctively putting distance between us. "Jason, you're not allowed to be here." My voice is firmer than I expected, but there's a tremor beneath the surface I hope he doesn't catch.

He ignores my words, taking another step toward me, his presence invading my personal space like a thick, suffocating fog. "I know," he says, his gaze never leaving mine, "but you won't return my calls. I *had* to see you."

There's an edge to his tone, something desperate that sends alarm bells ringing in my head. I've been trying to avoid this confrontation for weeks, dodging his texts, ignoring his voicemails. But here he is, standing right in front of me, uninvited and unwelcome.

I glance around quickly, hoping someone might walk by, but the back area is secluded. Just me and Jason.

"There. You saw me." I hold my hands up in a gesture of surrender, trying to convey just how much I want him to leave. "Now, go away."

Jason's face twists into a hurt expression, and he takes a step closer, his eyes narrowing with a mix of frustration and something darker. "Ouch, you're being so rude, Briar. Can we just talk?"

I cross my arms over my chest in a defensive stance. I force myself to meet his gaze, though every second he's near feels like an assault on my sense of safety. "Fine, let's talk. Want to talk about how you lied to me? How you cheated on me?"

Jason's expression shifts, and he moves in closer, grabbing my upper arm with a grip that's firmer than I'd like. Almost painful. His touch sends a shiver down my spine. "No, I don't want to talk about that. I saw you staring at the guy you work with."

"Who, Perry?" I blink in disbelief. "You can't be serious."

"I don't like when you stare at other men. I should be the only one you're staring at." His voice is low, almost possessive, and

I can see the possessive glint in his eyes. It's both unsettling and enraging.

This can't be happening. My gaze drops to where his hand is still clamped around my arm. "Let go of me, Jason."

"Or what?" he retorts, his eyes flashing with a dangerous intensity that makes my heart race. There's something almost menacing in his gaze, and I feel a pang of fear mix with my anger.

"I'll scream," I warn, my voice steady despite the knot of anxiety tightening in my stomach. I brace myself and lift my knee sharply, connecting with his groin in a swift, deliberate motion. He drops my arm, his face contorting into a grimace of pain.

"Goddammit, Briar. You hurt me," he groans, his voice a strained mix of anger and agony.

I take a step back, my pulse pounding in my ears. My hand trembles slightly as I reach for my phone, ready to call for help. The encounter has left me shaken, but I'm resolute. Jason's presence here, his demands, his invasion—none of it will deter me from taking control of my own life.

I scoff, a bitter laugh escaping my lips. "You've more than hurt me. Now leave, Jason. I'm calling security." My fingers fumble as I pull my phone from my back pocket, the screen bright in the dim light of the enclosure.

Jason's face contorts into a mock gesture of surrender as he raises his hands, a smirk playing at his lips. "Fine, I'm leaving." But his eyes, dark and cold, betray his words. The air between us is thick with tension, and I can feel my pulse quicken with unease.

Just as I start to dial, Jason's eyes flash with a dangerous glint. In an instant, he's moving toward me with a force that makes my heart leap into my throat. Before I can react, he's pinned me against the cage door, my phone clattering to the floor. The sharp metal of the cage presses into my back, and I struggle to breathe.

"One last thing before I go," he sneers, his breath hot and foul against my skin. "You'll never disrespect me again like that." Without warning, his lips crush against mine in a forceful, violating kiss. The sensation is painful, like a rough scrape against my dignity and my sense of self.

I squirm and twist, trying to break free from his unyielding grip, but his hold is firm and unrelenting. Panic surges through me, and I push against him with all my strength. Just as I think I'm trapped, a sudden, powerful force yanks Jason away from me. My breath hitches as I see the stranger who's come to my aid.

The beast of a man grips Jason by the collar, slamming him against the side of the cage with a force that makes the metal rattle. Jason's eyes widen in shock and anger.

"You do *not* touch her. Understood? Now, we're going to get to the bottom of why you feel you can stalk her," the stranger growls, his voice low and dangerous.

Jason, stunned and infuriated, sneers defiantly. "Fuck you."

The stranger's grip tightens, and the threat in his voice is unmistakable. *Who is this man? And how does he know about Jason stalking me?* I watch, my heart pounding, as Jason's bravado falters. The sight of him being held back is both terrifying and relieving. I can't help but feel a flicker of hope as the situation starts to turn in my favor.

Before the man can respond, Jason wriggles free and bolts down the path, his heavy footsteps echoing in the empty enclosure. The man watches him go, a storm of indecision in his dark, intense eyes, clearly torn between pursuing Jason or staying behind.

"Thank you," I manage to say.

He turns to me, his expression fierce as he takes in my disheveled state. "Are you okay?" His voice is deep and gravelly, carrying an undertone of concern that seems at odds with his imposing presence.

I blink up at him, taking in the full extent of his appearance. He's older than me, though by only a few years, and his physique is something out of a fitness magazine—muscles rippling under his fitted t-shirt. His face is ruggedly handsome, with sharp features and a strong jawline. His presence is both intimidating and incredibly captivating.

Whoa.

"Wow," I murmur under my breath, unable to hide my amazement. I've never seen a man quite like him in real life. He seems more suited for the movies than for saving people at the zoo. His rugged charm is disarming, and for a moment, I completely forget what he asked me.

He chuckles softly, the sound like a warm rumble. "Are you okay, Briar?"

The use of my name jolts me back to reality. "How do you know my name?"

His gaze remains steady, and he gives a small, reassuring smile. "Your mother hired me to be your personal bodyguard."

"Oh," I say, reaching for my phone and preparing to get back to work before Marcie notices me lingering. "That's all a big misunderstanding. I really don't need a bodyguard."

The man leans in, his presence overpowering and somehow comforting at the same time. "It kind of looks like you do. That asshole is definitely going to come back."

I find myself momentarily lost in his deep, chocolate-brown eyes, their warmth and intensity making it difficult to focus on our argument. "It's fine. I promise. I'm sure my mother will compensate you for your time."

His black t-shirt has a logo that's a circle with the words 'Maddox Security' inside, and jeans, and despite his casual attire, he exudes a powerful aura. He smiles, a small, confident curve of his lips. "I'm not leaving, Briar."

I chew on my bottom lip, conflicted. "Well, my boss won't appreciate you following me around while I work."

The man glances around the aviary, his eyes scanning the surroundings with a possessive expression. "I don't really care."

I let out a soft laugh, shaking my head at his persistence. "What's your name?"

"Orion. Orion Locke." He pulls out a badge and shows me his credentials. I take a quick photo of them and text my mother to verify that this man is legitimate and not some random guy.

When my mother confirms that Orion Locke is indeed the security she hired, I turn back to him with a raised eyebrow. "Like the constellation?"

He nods, his eyes sparking with a hint of something there. Something powerful. Something I can't quite identify. Something dangerous. "Yeah, just like that. My mother was really into star signs and constellations."

"Well, my mother is into over-worrying. I promise you, I can handle myself."

Orion steps even closer, his breath warm and faintly scented, brushing against my skin. His proximity sends a tingle of electricity through me. "I'm sure you can. But you don't have to, now that I'm here."

His closeness and the gentle touch of his breath stir an unexpected flutter in my chest. "Oh," is all I manage to say, caught off guard by the strange but intriguing mix of emotions he evokes.

Chapter 4

Orion

Green eyes gaze up at me, and it's like a cosmic joke. They turn me inside out and upside down all at once. I've never had a reaction to any woman quite like this before. Seeing that man mess with her stirred a rage in me that I'm not proud of —let's just say he's lucky he fled before I had a chance to act on it.

"I can't just let you whisk me away," she says, her tone a blend of defiance and curiosity. There's a spark in her eyes that both challenges and captivates me.

"You can and you will," I reply, my voice steady and confident.

She clutches her phone tighter to her chest, as if it's her shield. "I have a job. I can't just miss work."

"Then I'll be here every day to watch over you," I declare, determined.

She rolls her mesmerizing jade-green eyes with an exaggerated sigh. "Seriously, I can handle myself."

I step closer, closing the space between us until my presence is almost overwhelming. "What if next time there's nobody here to save you? What then, sweetheart?"

Her breath hitches slightly, and I notice the way her cheeks flush ever so slightly, adding a touch of color to her otherwise pale complexion. The intensity of the moment seems to hang in the air, creating a bubble around us that's both tense and oddly exhilarating.

"I don't need a babysitter," she retorts, but there's a softness in her voice that belies her bravado.

I'm so close now that I can almost feel the warmth radiating from her. "Maybe you don't. But sometimes, a little extra protection doesn't hurt."

She looks up at me, her eyes searching mine for sincerity. There's a flicker of vulnerability there, and for a split second, I can see that she's not as invincible as she pretends to be. The atmosphere between us is electric, charged with a mix of frustration, attraction, and something unspoken but palpable.

"Fine," she says after a moment, her voice barely above a whisper. "But you'd better not cramp my style."

A smile tugs at the corner of my lips. "I promise not to."

With that, I give her a nod and step back, though the pull to stay close to her is almost irresistible.

She bites her bottom lip and the action makes me all growly. "Fine."

I step back, giving her some space. "Also, you'll be staying with me."

Her eyes widen. "I can't..." she doesn't finish her sentence, and hopefully it's because she realizes there's no point.

I'm not the type of man to take no for an answer, and I won't let anything happen to her on my watch. Ever. I take my job seriously. Even though she's beautiful, I'd never cross that line. I never sleep with clients. I also don't do attachments. Women are to be enjoyed for one night only, and I'm always out the door before the sun comes up the next morning. I don't do relationships in any way, shape, or form. I'm just not capable of it.

"I'll wait for you to finish work, then we can swing by your place and pick up your things."

Her eyes roam over me, and I puff out my chest a little. I stare at her so she knows I'm dead serious, and once she nods, I cross my arms over my broad chest. "Fine," she says like a defeated little bird. "Just stay out of my way." She steps away from me and picks her broom up.

I give her a quick nod to let her know I'll be watching, then casually wander around the aviary, staying close enough to keep an eye on her but trying to blend in with the tourists. My gaze sweeps the crowd every few minutes, half-expecting that jerk of an ex-boyfriend of hers to pop up. But it's mostly families and bird enthusiasts milling about, so I relax—just a little.

As I stroll through the aviary, I'm bombarded with more bird facts than I ever thought possible. Apparently, cockatoos can mimic voices, and Yellow-naped Amazon birds like Chester are some kind of mischief geniuses. I smirk as Chester entertains another group, causing a kid to break into fits of laughter. I never realized how much went into these shows—or how many kinds of birds there are.

A couple of hours later, as the afternoon sun filters through the trees, Briar finds me by the parrot exhibit. She's got that tired, drained look about her, cheeks flushed from exhaustion. "I'm ready," she says. Her lips are pressed into a firm, stubborn pout, her nose scrunched just slightly in distaste. I can tell she's not happy. But I don't care. I'm here to protect her ass, not become her bestie. And what a fine ass it is, if I'm being a hundred percent honest.

"Great. Let's get out of here," I say, motioning toward the exit. As we start walking, I add, "I'll also need to know your schedule—can't protect you if I don't know where you're gonna be."

She tilts her head slightly, thinking it over. "What do I do with my car?" she asks, a small frown forming on her lips.

"We'll figure it out. I'll drive you back to get it later, or better yet, I'll have someone pick it up for you," I say with a shrug, leading her toward the entrance where the tourists are thinning out.

She doesn't argue, but there's that little spark of independence in her eyes again, like she's not entirely used to someone taking care of things for her. It's kinda cute, honestly. But underneath it all, I can tell she's relieved, even if she won't admit it. She's tough, but everyone needs a little help sometimes, whether they like it or not.

I pull out my phone, sending a text to Riggs, from the BRAVO team and work out the details with him to pick up Briar's car from the zoo.

Normally, on missions, I'd opt for a safe house, but I'm not too concerned about an overzealous ex-boyfriend. The guy's not exactly a criminal mastermind. After going through the file on him, I'm pretty confident he doesn't have the skills to hack into the DMV or track down where I live. He's all bluster and no brains.

If by some miracle he does manage to find us, I'll ask Dean to set us up in a safe house. But until then, I'm confident I can keep Briar safe while this mess gets sorted out. Dean's working on the restraining order and gathering the evidence needed to arrest him. The legal process just takes time.

And let's be real—how many criminals actually respect a restraining order? Not many. So yeah, we're being extra cautious. Keeping Briar close, making sure she's not alone, and always watching. It's my job to protect her, and I don't plan on letting some petty ex get in the way of that.

We walk through the zoo, and past many different animals. I clear my throat, considering how to phrase my next question. "Why do you work here?" I ask her, wondering what would ever make somebody interested in cleaning up after birds.

She stops walking and blinks up at me. "What do you mean?"

"Listen, I know you come from money." Our services aren't cheap and her parents are wealthy. "So, why shovel bird shit for a living?"

"I love birds. One day I hope to be a bird trainer and get to be able to work with the birds directly."

"You love birds, huh?"

Her eyes sparkle as her face lights up into a smile. "More than humans."

I continue walking, checking our surroundings as I do. Always on the lookout. "I get that." Which I do understand. People are messy. People take a lot of work to handle. Birds are probably much easier.

They're little and hang out in cages, how hard can that be to handle.

We make our way to the parking lot, and we wait until Riggs arrives to handle Briar's car.

"She's hot," Riggs says to me before leaving, his eyes roaming over Briar's body. "Have fun with her."

I've always gotten along with Riggs, but right now I'm feeling murderous when he stares at her a little too long. "It's a job," I say, my voice rough and hoarse from anger.

Riggs laughs, slapping me on the shoulder. "Dean's never given me a hot as fuck assignment before."

"Maybe because you suck ass, and he can't trust you to get the job done. I don't fuck clients," I say, which he knows. Everyone knows. It's one of the major rules I've followed since I started with Maddox Security. One I'll never break, no matter how tight Briar's little body is, and how badly she tempts me with every smile she casts my way.

"Hey, neither do I," he hits the key fob on Briar's car and opens the door, "but for her I'd make an exception."

Briar's sitting in the front seat of my SUV, unable to hear our conversation which I'm grateful for.

I glance at her before returning my focus on Riggs. "And this is why I get the hot as fuck assignments."

Riggs laughs as he hops into her car.

The drive is easy, though I'm already mentally mapping out the best escape routes, just in case. Riggs follows closely behind. When we arrive, I park and step out, taking in the building—cozy, with a charming, lived-in vibe. Riggs hands off the keys, and heads to the corner of the major intersections waiting on a pickup.

Briar leads me up a narrow flight of stairs to her apartment.

The second I step inside, a voice calls out from across the room, "Intruder, who are you?"

I freeze, eyes darting around the space, my hand already reaching for my gun in the holster at my hip. "What the—?" I start, trying to locate the source of the voice.

Briar laughs, walking over to a large birdcage near the bay window. "That's Jeb," she says, pointing to a gray-colored bird with a striking red tail. "He's a Congo African Grey. And yes, he can talk."

Before I can respond, Jeb squawks again, louder this time, "Jeb can talk!"

I blink, staring at the bird. "You've got to be kidding me," I mutter under my breath, marveling at the sass radiating from the little creature.

Briar grins, clearly amused by my reaction. "He's quite the character. Likes to announce visitors. Sometimes he even tells people to go away."

"Charming," I say, my eyes still fixed on Jeb, who's giving me a scrutinizing look as if he's deciding whether I'm worthy of being in *his* territory. "I take it I need to win him over?"

"Pretty much," Briar chuckles, scratching Jeb's head through the cage. "He's a tough critic. But if you're nice, he might say something nicer next time."

"Noted," I reply, shaking my head. This job just keeps getting more and more interesting.

I peer at the bird closer as Briar opens the cage, and Jeb climbs onto her finger. "Jeb here is one of the smartest talking birds in the world."

"Jeb smart," he repeats a few times.

"That's very cool." I glance around her apartment, taking in her eclectic style. Her apartment is a cozy blend of mismatched charm. The walls are painted in soft shades of lavender and cream, with vintage posters framed along one side. A mix of mismatched furniture fills the space: a velvet armchair in deep emerald green, a weathered wooden coffee table, and a quirky, overstuffed couch covered in a colorful, patterned throw. "You should get packing."

Briar goes into busy mode as she reaches under her sink. "I'll need to get Jeb's food. I'll also need to pack a few of his medications to give him."

I watch as she prances around the kitchen.

"I sometimes pack some music when we're staying away from home. He gets nervous."

Wait. "Huh?" I ask her. "He's not coming with us, is he?"

Briar stops moving and just stares at me. "Well yeah, silly. I can't leave him here to fend for himself."

I shrug. "Why not? He's a bird. Just toss enough food in his cage while we're gone."

Briar looks horrified at my words. "I know you're joking."

I wasn't.

"The bird will come with us?" I can't understand why I can't wrap my head around this idea, but what do we do with a bird?

"Either he comes, or I stay. Take your pick." She crosses her arms across her perky tits.

I growl under my breath a bit and finally agree to the bird. "I was *not* expecting on protecting a bird as well."

The bird squawks loudly, like he's offended at my words. "Jeb protect Briar."

I smirk, crossing my arms over my chest. "I highly doubt that, bird."

"Jeb protect Briar," he screeches louder.

"You're upsetting him." Briar smiles and it nearly takes my breath away. "You should consider yourself lucky. Jeb's a gem."

I stare at the bird, looking right into his little eyes. "Are you going to pack any of your own things, or only the birds?"

"Of course, silly." She flutters from room to room, packing things into a small suitcase.

Once she's deemed herself and the bird ready, I pack them both into my SUV and head toward my house, driving a little extra around town to make sure I'm not being followed. You can never be too safe.

A little over an hour later I safely arrive at my place, and get Briar and the bird settled. "You'll stay in the guest room close to my room." I'd love to tell her how she'll be staying in my bed with me, but I have to remain professional here.

"I'm going to put Jeb in here with me," she says, unpacking a few things and sliding them into the dresser.

"Make yourself at home. What's your work schedule like this weekend?"

"I have the next two days off, but then I'm in on Monday morning."

"Perfect. Hopefully everything will be wrapped up by then."

She smiles with determined eyes. "Jason wasn't a bad guy when we first met."

I lean against the door jamb to the guest room, crossing my arms over my chest. "They're usually not at first. But there's signs to watch for."

Briar finishes getting the birdcage set up in her room. "Believe me, I know the warning signs to look for now. He used to never let me order my own food at restaurants. He liked having that control."

"Yeah, you should be able to make your own choices." There's different types of control, and the kind of control Jason liked is never the good kind.

"There were other signs. Little things really. He would get angry over the smallest issue. I should have known."

I step closer, dropping my hands. "Don't beat yourself up about it. You got out of that relationship which proves how strong you are."

She smiles at me, her green eyes shining. "Thank you, Orion."

She's close, very close and more than anything I want to kiss her. This would be the moment in the movies where the hero grabs the girl and kisses her deep, and my chest warms up.

Before I can talk myself out of kissing her, the bird speaks up, "Jeb just made a poo," he says, killing the mood completely.

I roll my eyes.

This is gonna be a blast.

THE NEXT MORNING, I wake up to something red hovering above my head. My vision is still blurry, so I rub my eyes, trying to make sense of the sight. *What the hell is that?*

"Jeb is hungry. You feed Jeb now," the familiar, grating voice of Briar's feathered menace squawks.

Groaning, I roll over, burying my face in the pillow. "It's way too early for this shit," I mumble, hoping the bird will magically disappear.

"Oh my god, I'm so sorry!" Briar's voice filters through my sleepy haze, followed by the sound of her snapping her fingers. "Jeb, here."

"Jeb is hungry!" the bird repeats, like some tiny, demanding dictator, and suddenly, with a flurry of feathers, he flies across the room. He lands gracefully on Briar's outstretched hand like this is all totally normal.

I jolt upright. "Holy shit! That thing just flew in here!" I wasn't expecting to wake up to a bird dive-bombing my bedroom.

Briar tries to stifle a laugh, though the amusement dances in her eyes. "I'm so sorry he got in here. I swear, he's harmless... just dramatic."

I shove the covers off, sitting up, trying to get a sense of time. It feels like dawn with how groggy I am, but the light streaming through the window says otherwise. "What time is it, anyway?"

Briar fumbles, her eyes wide as she stares at me. "Um...I, I..." She's flustered.

I glance down, noticing I'm wearing nothing but my black boxer-briefs. "Oh shit," I grunt out. "Sorry." I spot my jeans on the chair by the bed, and slide them up my legs. "What time is it?" I ask again.

Briar leans against the doorframe, holding the bird, who looks annoyingly pleased with himself. Her eyes roam over my chest, and I know she's taking in my tattoos. "Almost noon," she says, breathless. "Are you planning on sleeping all day? Not that I mind, but we were about to make lunch."

I stifle a yawn, rubbing my eyes again. "The bird cooks too? What a multi-talented bird you've got there."

Briar giggles, shaking her head. "Sadly, no. He's more into bossing people around than actually being useful."

"Well, at least he's consistent." I tug on a t-shirt. "Guess I'll join the lunch crowd, then. Unless the bird has more demands before we start?"

The bird lets out an indignant squawk, and I swear I catch a glint of mischief in his beady little eyes.

She laughs. "No silly, I was going to cook something up. I'll need to look in your pantry to see what you have."

I try to remember the last time I went to the store. "I'm sure there's not a lot to choose from."

Her pink lips turn into a sexy pout. "Oh, well then, we'll need to go to the store."

I find myself staring at those lips a beat too long before I spring into action. "Just let me get ready and we'll head out."

She smiles. "I'll just get Jeb fed and put away while you get ready." She leaves my room in a flash, closing the door behind her.

I move through the motions of getting ready, missing my sleep as I do. I was up late last night, working on a quick sleight of hand trick that I would love to test out on somebody soon. I wonder how Briar feels about magic.

After I throw on a baseball cap and get myself somewhat presentable, I head out to the living room. The moment I step into the space, I freeze.

What the hell happened here?

It's not a disaster, per se, but it's certainly... chaotic.

This bird, I think, shaking my head.

The entire room looks like it's been overtaken by a bird-themed carnival. There are feathers scattered everywhere, like confetti after a parade. Toys, bird perches, and what can only be described as a miniature jungle gym dominate the area. Tiny swings, mirrors, and ropes dangle from various furniture pieces, and even a makeshift bird ladder leans against the couch. This bird must have had one hell of a morning workout.

"Wow," I mutter, stepping cautiously around a brightly colored toy that looks suspiciously like a bird-sized seesaw. "What... happened in here?"

Briar's in the kitchen, laughing sheepishly as she looks through my pantry. "Oh, that. Yeah, Jeb likes to keep himself entertained."

"Entertained? It looks like he hosted a bird rave while I was asleep," I say, lifting a small rubber ball with a bell inside and giving it a shake. The bird, perched proudly on his stand, squawks in response, like he's proud of his handiwork.

Briar leans against the counter, a grin on her face. "He gets a little carried away sometimes. It's... his version of fun."

I raise an eyebrow, looking at the bird, who is now preening himself like the king of the castle. "I'm starting to think Jeb thinks he's running this place." *Not on my watch, buddy.*

Briar laughs. "Oh, he definitely thinks he does. But hey, it keeps him busy."

I glance around at the chaotic mess. "Busy is one word for it. This is like a bird version of an amusement park in here."

"Well," Briar says with a wink, "it's his world—we're just living in it."

I sigh, shaking my head. "Good to know I've got some stiff competition for attention around here."

"Don't worry," Briar teases with a blush. "I'm sure I can make room for one more." Her green eyes sparkle as I stare at her. Her tight little body is tucked nicely into a pair of jean shorts and a yellow babydoll tee with a bird on it holding up two claws like a peace sign. Underneath the bird are the words, *'Free bird.'* Her sexy legs go all the way up, and I nearly drool as I stare at her a bit longer.

"Let's get to the store," I say, grabbing my keys by the door.

"Let me get Jeb put away," she says, gathering a few of his toys and getting the bird into the cage in the living room.

"I thought he'd be staying in your room?" I ask her.

She shrugs. "He'd be more comfortable out here while we're away. So he can protect me."

"Jeb protect Briar," the bird squawks, and I roll my eyes once more as Briar laughs.

I follow her out of the house, checking our surroundings to make sure her ex isn't around. I know he's most likely not, but I'm always on high alert. Any other job, I'd send someone else to the store, but I know I can take her scumbag of an ex in a fight if it comes down to it, so I'm not too worried having her on this side of town. Saint Pierce is a big city, and we're nowhere near her apartment or the zoo.

Chances are, he's nowhere around.

"What does Jason normally do on his days off?" I ask Briar once we're in my SUV and heading to the store. I've read his file, knowing he works a nine-to-five job in some accounting firm. Boring type financial shit job, but he makes okay money. He works Monday through Friday, and since it's a Saturday afternoon, it makes me wonder where the fucker is.

She fiddles with the air conditioning controls. "He liked going to the races, making bets."

"Gambling?" Now that wasn't in his file.

"Yeah, but never anything too crazy."

I wonder if he owes money. It's definitely something to take a look into. "Let's be quick in and out at the store." Wonder if he's after Briar's parents' money. It's definitely an angle to explore. I'll have to text Dean to look into it.

She smiles, saluting me as she says, "Yes, sir."

I roll my eyes at her sarcasm. "I'm serious."

"I really can't believe this has all escalated to this degree."

"What do you mean?" I ask her as I turn into the parking lot of the closest grocery shopping store.

"I just never thought Jason could be capable of going to the extremes. Part of me wants to tell my mother to calm down and call off the watchdog."

I back into a spot. "Me being the watchdog?" I pull out my phone and shoot off a quick text letting Dean know about the gambling with Jason.

"I'm sorry. I just feel like some of this has been blown out of proportion. I think if Jason could just see how it's over, then he would move on."

"How many times have you told him it's over?"

She purses her lips. "Well, maybe ten times."

I place my hand over hers, her tiny hand small compared to my big one. "It's not your fault. Okay? This is all on him. And a man who won't take no for an answer is someone you should be careful of." It's one thing to fight for something you believe in. It's another to be told no over and over again, and not accepting that answer.

"Thank you." Briar's mesmerizing eyes gaze into mine and my heartbeat kicks up in tempo. We exit the vehicle, and she smiles at me as we walk toward the entrance.

"No funny business inside the store," I tell her, making sure we can get in and out undetected. "You stay by me. At all times." I'm already sizing everyone up, looking for the exits, and scanning the area. Always on guard.

"Sure thing, Mr. Bodyguard, sir." She salutes me, and sashays away as I shake my head with a grin.

She's so *fucking* cute.

Chapter 5

Briar

Can I admit something? I think Orion is a fucking rockstar. No, not like a real one, but just as cool as one. He's got this aura about him that makes him irresistible. I can't stop staring at him.

He's gigantic with more muscles than I've ever seen on any normal man before. Like he not only works out in the gym, but eats the gym for breakfast too.

And when his eyes lock with mine and they glaze over, I can only imagine he's having dirty thoughts about what he'd like to do with me.

Crazy, right? I know he's not *really* thinking that. But a girl can hope, right?

He's probably thinking I'm some crazy bird lady that gets on his nerves.

Ugh. I hope I'm not getting on his nerves.

I want to make sure we're in and out of this store, so I cross my arms over my chest and get into busy shopping girl mode, ready to attack each aisle with a plan.

Because if I don't have a plan, I might just gawk and stare at Orion, and that's not a good idea. I travel down the pet aisle first, looking to see if there's any new bird toys that Jeb might like. We don't stay away from home often, so I know he hates being off his routine. I want to make sure he's rewarded for being a good bird.

"I think he has enough toys," Orion grumbles beside me.

"A bird can never have enough toys." I pluck a toy off the shelf.

Orion scans the aisle, keeping me close to him since we've walked in the store. "Fine. What about you?"

I blink. "I don't need any toys." And then my mind goes somewhere naughty, thinking about the types of *toys* adults play with, and how I'd love Orion to use some of those *toys* on me.

Stop that. I can't have these thoughts. My cheeks burn with heat and I know I'm blushing.

Orion blinks at me, like he can read my every thought. "I meant food. What kind of food do you want?"

Without missing a beat, I list off my favorites, ticking them off on my fingers like it's a perfectly reasonable request. "Chocolate chip pancakes, of course. Also, grilled cheese. Macaroni and cheese. Pizza. Oh! And chicken nuggies."

He raises an eyebrow. "Nuggies?"

I stand up a little taller, jutting my chin out proudly. "Yes, chicken nuggets. They're a staple. Who doesn't love them?"

Orion's stoic as he studies me. "You eat like a five-year-old."

I flash him a playful smile, folding my arms over my chest. "I know. It's a weakness of mine. I love all the easy food. The good stuff."

He shakes his head. "All the unhealthy stuff, you mean."

"Hey!" I say, giving him a light shove, but the man is a rock the size of Gibraltar, and doesn't budge. "Don't knock it. It's comfort food. Pure nostalgia. And, let's face it, delicious."

Orion looks at me with an amused expression. "So, let me get this straight. If you had to choose between a fancy steak dinner and a plate of chicken nuggets, you'd pick the nuggets?"

"Every time," I say without hesitation, smiling brightly. "Why complicate life when nuggets exist?"

He chuckles, the sound warm and rich, like he's trying to wrap his mind around my questionable food choices. "You're something else, Briar. I've never met a woman who'd admit to loving 'nuggies' with so much pride."

I smile. "You'd be surprised, Orion. I'm not your average girl."

Orion shakes his head in disbelief. "Well, if you say so. But I'm still buying something green for you at some point. I've got to keep you alive somehow."

I dramatically roll my eyes. "Fine, you can sneak in a salad if it makes you feel better. But don't you dare touch my nuggies."

He holds up his hands in mock surrender, his eyes twinkling with amusement. "I wouldn't dream of it."

"Okay," I say, giving in with a playful sigh. "I'll compromise. We can do one of your meals tonight, and one of mine tomorrow. Then, at work, I'll eat whatever they've got." I hold out my hand, grinning as I tease, "Deal?"

Orion takes my hand in his, his grip firm yet warm. "Deal," he says, sealing the agreement like we've just negotiated a high-stakes business contract instead of arguing about chicken nuggets versus salad.

We continue shopping, wandering through the aisles, me grabbing my comfort foods and Orion sneaking in some vegetables and actual meal ingredients whenever he thinks I'm not looking. Twenty minutes later, we've got everything we need, and we head back to his place with full bags.

The moment I step inside his house, I hear the familiar squawk of Jeb belting out, "Welcome to the Jungle!" His rendition of the song is both chaotic and charming.

"He sings too?" Orion asks, eyes wide with disbelief as Jeb's warbling fills the house.

I chuckle, placing a bag of groceries on the kitchen counter. "Oh, Jeb does it all. He really should be performing at this point."

Orion raises an eyebrow as he helps me unpack the bags. "So, why isn't he? I mean, clearly, he's got the talent."

I shrug, laughing at the idea of Jeb headlining a show. "Stage fright. If you can believe it."

Orion pauses, turning to look at me. "Stage fright?" He glances over at Jeb, who's now making exaggerated parrot noises that sound suspiciously like laughter.

I nod, holding back my own laughter as I explain. "Yeah. He's a diva when it's just me around, but the moment there's an audience? He clams up."

Orion shakes his head as we continue unpacking. "So, your bird is an introverted rock star?"

"Exactly," I say, grinning at how absurd it sounds. "He's the real deal when no one's watching."

As we finish putting away the groceries, I catch Orion watching me with a soft smile on his face. "What?" I ask, feeling my cheeks warm under his gaze.

He shrugs, leaning against the counter. "You just… you're full of surprises, Briar. I never know what to expect next."

I laugh, rolling my eyes. "Stick around long enough, and I'll introduce you to all my quirks. But be warned, there's a lot."

Orion smirks, that playful glint returning to his eyes. "Good thing I'm not scared of a challenge."

I blink, and the air between us seems to shift, growing heavier, more charged. The playfulness fades, and suddenly we're standing a little too close, his arm brushing mine, his presence overwhelming in the best possible way. My heart starts thumping so loudly I swear he can hear it.

For a second, I forget how to breathe as his dark eyes lock on mine, their usual teasing glint replaced with something deeper, something that makes my stomach do a somersault. The space between us feels smaller, the room quieter, and for a wild, insane moment, I think he's going to kiss me.

But that would be silly, right? I mean, sure, we've been getting along well, and he's got that whole charming-bodyguard thing going on, but a kiss? Here, in his kitchen, with Jeb still muttering, "Welcome to the jungle" from across the room? No way.

Right?

But then he leans in ever so slightly, and my pulse spikes. I feel the warmth of his breath against my skin, and I wonder if he's feeling the same magnetic pull I am. It's like the whole world narrows down to just us, his hand resting on the counter, mine gripping a half-unpacked box of cereal like it's my lifeline.

"I—" I start, but my voice cracks, betraying the fact that I'm about five seconds away from totally melting into this moment.

His lips twitch into a small, knowing smile, and he reaches up, brushing a loose strand of hair behind my ear. The light touch sends a shiver down my spine, and I wonder if he can tell just how badly I'm unraveling inside.

"You okay?" he asks, his voice lower, softer now. The kind of voice that feels like a secret.

I clear my throat, forcing a laugh that sounds way more nervous than I intended. "Yeah, yeah. Totally. Why wouldn't I be?"

Orion's smile widens, and for a second, I swear he knows exactly what's running through my mind. It's like he's perfectly aware of how close I am to hoping, wishing, that he'll kiss me. But instead, he steps back, the intensity between us dissipating just as quickly as it had built.

"Good," he says, his tone back to that easy, teasing warmth. "Because I still have to teach you how to make a proper grilled cheese, and you look like you're about to pass out."

I laugh, my face burning as I snap out of whatever romantic daze I'd been in. "Grilled cheese it is," I say, relieved and disappointed all at once.

As we go back to the simple task of making lunch, I can't help but wonder—was I imagining things, or was there something real in that almost-kiss? Either way, one thing's for sure: this is going to be a lot more complicated than just chicken nuggets and macaroni.

"I'M SO SORRY," I say, darting after Jeb as he swoops into the living room like he owns the place, his wings flapping dramatically. He's stolen Orion's keys that were hanging by the front door, laughing in pure Jeb fashion as he bobs his head. I swear this bird is trying to give me a heart attack.

Orion watches Jeb with narrowed eyes, arms crossed, clearly less amused than I am. "How often is he out of the cage?" he asks, his voice laced with mild irritation.

I wince, feeling a bit guilty. "Not usually this much, but… I feel bad because he's off his routine." I glance over at Jeb, who's now perched triumphantly on the back of the couch, squawking something that sounds like '*Hotch!*' I blush. "He's a *Criminal Minds* fanatic, just like me."

Orion raises an eyebrow, clearly trying to piece together how a bird has a TV-watching routine. "What do you two normally do when you're at home?" His tone is half-curious, half-exasperated.

I shrug, offering him a sheepish smile. "We watch *Criminal Minds*. It's kind of our thing."

Orion stares at me for a beat, like he's trying to decide if I'm serious or messing with him. Finally, he sighs, shaking his head, but there's a hint of a smile there. "Seriously?"

He grabs the remote, walks over to the TV, and flips it on. Within seconds, he's scrolling through the streaming service, finds *Criminal Minds*, and presses play. The familiar intro music fills the room, and Jeb immediately perks up, bobbing his head like he's about to start reciting the script.

Orion turns to me with a mock flourish. "Ta-da. Ask and you shall receive."

"Jeb eat popcorn."

Orion stares at the bird like he's nuts. "Seriously?"

"It's a good snack. I'll just pop some in the microwave for him. You won't even notice we're here," I say, rushing into the kitchen to look for the popcorn I bought for Jeb.

Jeb squawks from the living room and I smile at Orion who's followed me into the kitchen.

"That bird's got you wrapped around his little claw," he says, and I blush.

"Yeah well…" I can't help but laugh, feeling a warm flutter in my chest. "Thank you for making us feel at home here," I say, meaning it. For all Orion's gruffness, he's going out of his way to make me—and my feathered drama queen—comfortable.

Orion stuffs his hands into his pockets, his earlier annoyance replaced with something more relaxed. "Sure, no problem." He gestures vaguely toward the hallway. "I'm going to get a little work done in my office down the hall. Let me know if you need anything."

I give him a playful salute—again, for reasons I still can't explain. It's like every time I'm around this man, I lose the ability to act normal. "Sure thing, boss."

He chuckles, shaking his head as he walks away, and I place the bag of popcorn into the microwave, my heart doing that stupid little flutter it's been doing ever since Orion came into my life. I glance at Jeb, who's still staring intently at the screen, like he's fully invested in catching the unsub.

"Don't get too comfortable, buddy," I mutter under my breath. But honestly, I'm not sure if I'm talking to Jeb or myself.

"*BRIAR,*" a voice calls, distant but familiar, pulling me from the depths of a nightmare. "Briar, are you awake?" It sounds like Jason. My heart pounds in my chest, the panic rising as I'm pulled into a tunnel of darkness. Everything feels heavy, like I'm trying to swim through thick tar.

I try to scream, but nothing comes out. My mouth opens, but the sound is trapped inside me. I run, but Jason's right behind me, getting closer with every step. My legs feel like lead, and I trip, falling again and again, the ground swallowing me whole.

"Briar, wake up!" The voice cuts through the chaos, but I can't reach it. I tumble deeper into the nightmare, Jason's footsteps pounding in my ears. Desperation builds until, finally, a scream erupts from deep within me. It's raw and loud, splitting the silence. My throat burns as I cry out again and again.

Suddenly, strong arms wrap around me, holding me steady. "Briar, you're safe. It's me, Orion. I've got you."

His voice is like a lifeline, pulling me back to reality. The falling stops, and my eyes snap open. I blink, disoriented, the room slowly coming into focus. I'm on Orion's couch, his arms still around me, the soft glow of the TV casting shadows across the room. Jeb is perched nearby, watching with a curious tilt of his head.

Breathless, I take in my surroundings, my heart still racing. "What... what time is it?" I ask, my voice shaky.

Saving What's Mine

Orion gently lets go, his eyes full of concern as he kneels beside me. "It's late, just past nine," he says softly. "You fell asleep during the show."

I glance at the TV, where Criminal Minds continues to play, the characters investigating some dark, twisted case. "I had a nightmare," I murmur, my voice still shaky. I wipe the sweat from my forehead, feeling the remnants of fear still lingering.

Orion doesn't move, his presence grounding me. "It's okay," he says, his voice low and soothing. "You're safe now."

I nod, trying to shake off the lingering dread. "Thanks... for waking me up. I felt like I was stuck."

He gives me a small, reassuring smile, brushing a strand of hair from my face. "I'll always wake you up if you need me to."

His words make my chest tighten, and for a moment, I can't find the right thing to say. I glance down at my hands, feeling the warmth of his touch still lingering.

Jeb squawks from his perch, breaking the tension. "Jeb is watching!"

Orion chuckles softly, standing up and giving me space to breathe. "Even Jeb's got your back," he jokes, trying to lighten the mood.

"Aww, you used his name." I smile weakly, grateful for the distraction, but as I settle back into the couch, I can't help but feel a sense of comfort in knowing that Orion's right here.

"Come on, I made you macaroni and cheese with chicken nuggets," Orion says, a teasing smile tugging at his lips. He holds out a plate like it's a prized offering, and honestly, it is.

I can't help but grin wide. "My favorite!"

He laughs, the sound rich and warm, filling the cozy kitchen. "You really do eat like a child, you know that?"

I grin even bigger, feeling like a kid on Christmas morning. "I love it," I say, plopping down into the chair at the little dinette set by the kitchen, the smell of cheesy goodness wafting up to meet me.

Orion shakes his head, amused, as he sits down across from me. "You're something else." He pauses for a moment, his smile fading just a little as his eyes soften. "What are your nightmares about?"

His question catches me off guard, and I glance down at my plate, my fork suddenly feeling heavy in my hand. The playful atmosphere shifts slightly, the air growing thick with unspoken tension. I try to shrug it off, though my chest tightens a little. "I don't really know," I lie, twirling the fork in the cheesy noodles, avoiding his gaze.

He doesn't buy it. I can tell by the way his eyes stay fixed on me, his expression turning more serious. "Did you have the nightmares before you started dating Jason?"

The question lands hard, and I feel my stomach twist, the comfort of the food in front of me suddenly distant. I shake my head, already knowing where he's going with this. He's right, and we both know it. "No," I admit quietly, my voice barely a whisper. "The nightmares started after I began dating Jason."

The words hang in the air between us, a heavy truth that neither of us wants to acknowledge but can't ignore. I keep my eyes on my plate, avoiding his gaze. It feels like admitting that out loud makes everything even more real, like my subconscious was trying to warn me long before I realized it myself.

Orion doesn't push, but I can feel the concern rolling off him. He leans back in his chair, watching me carefully, giving me space to breathe. "It makes sense, you know," he says after a beat, his voice gentle. "Going through what you did with him... it leaves a mark. In your mind. Even when you think you're past it."

I nod, my throat tight. "I guess," I manage to say, though the weight of it all feels like so much more than that. There's no easy way to explain the kind of fear Jason instilled in me—the way it lingers, even now, creeping into my dreams.

Orion reaches across the table, his hand hovering for a moment before gently touching mine. The warmth of his fingers calms the nerves racing beneath my skin, grounding me. "You're safe here, Briar," he says, his voice steady. "You don't have to go through this alone."

I glance up, meeting his eyes for the first time since we started this conversation. There's something in his gaze—something strong and unwavering that makes me believe him. It's not just empty words. He means it.

I manage a small, grateful smile, my heart swelling just a bit. "Thanks," I whisper, my fingers curling slightly around his, holding on to that tiny thread of reassurance he's offering. For now, it's enough.

Orion squeezes my hand before pulling away, giving me space again. "Now eat your nuggies before they get cold," he says, his teasing tone back in place, trying to lighten the mood.

I let out a small laugh, grateful for the shift. "Yes, sir," I reply, picking up a chicken nugget and taking a big bite. It's a silly moment, but I welcome it—anything to keep the darkness at bay for just a little longer.

Chapter 6

Orion

What's that old saying? If you can't handle the heat, get out of the kitchen? Yeah, well, I practically had to run from the kitchen, because if I stayed there one second longer, watching Briar nibble on her mac and cheese and chicken nuggets like they were the best things in the world, I'd lose it. I'd practically jumped her bones right there, and that's... not exactly professional.

It also breaks every fucking rule in my book.

However, she's stunning in this way that's almost too much to take. Not in the conventional sense of the word, but in that adorkable, completely irresistible way. The girl next door. There's something about the way her eyes light up over the simplest things—like comfort food, or how she talks to her bird like he's a person. It gets to me. More than I want to admit.

Saving What's Mine

I had to get out of there. Fast. The heat wasn't just in the kitchen, it was building in me, and I needed a break.

After she started eating, that damn bird let out his usual squawk for attention. "I'm hungry!" he screeched. I swear, that bird never stops. If I didn't know any better, I'd think he was trying to outcompete me for Briar's attention. The little bastard's always on her case, squawking this and that.

Briar didn't miss a beat, though. She hopped up, grabbing Jeb's food like it was second nature, as if she hadn't just settled down to enjoy her meal. The way she multitasks, feeding both herself and Jeb with this casual, natural ease... it's endearing. Like she's been doing it her whole life.

Meanwhile, I made my way to my office, grateful for the distance. I need a minute. Hell, I need more than a minute. Just one second alone with my thoughts, away from the pull she has on me.

I close the door behind me and sink into my chair, running a hand through my hair. I can still hear Briar in the other room, chatting softly to Jeb as she eats, and it makes me smile despite myself. The tension in my chest loosens just a little. She doesn't know what she does to me, how much self-control it takes to keep things professional.

But I need to keep it together. I'm here to protect her, not get caught up in whatever this is between us. I rub the back of my neck, trying to refocus. I came here to do a job, and I can't afford to get distracted. Not by her smile, not by her infectious laugh, and definitely not by the way she looks at me like I'm her hero.

I take a deep breath, glancing at the paperwork piled on my desk, trying to get my head back in the game. But even as I try to concentrate, my mind keeps drifting back to her—to the way she makes this feel less like a job and more like... *something else*.

Which is dangerous.

I grab my cell and pull up Dean's contact info, my finger hovering over his name for a second before I hit call. The phone barely rings once before he picks up, his voice coming through the line with that no-nonsense tone I've grown accustomed to.

"Talk to me," he says.

Straight to the point. Typical Dean.

"Were you able to get all the background info on Jason?" I ask, leaning back in my chair, the tension in my shoulders still lingering from earlier.

"Yes. I was just putting the file together and about to email it over," Dean replies. Efficient as ever.

"Good," I murmur, nodding even though he can't see me. "Thank you."

There's a pause on the other end, and I can hear the faint tapping of keys, probably as he finishes up the email. I rub a hand over my face, the weight of this whole situation pressing down on me. I trust Dean—his instincts are solid, and I need a second opinion to validate the gut feeling that's been gnawing at me since I took this case.

"What do you think of this whole case?" I ask, my voice quieter now, more serious.

Dean hesitates for just a second, which is unusual for him. Normally, he's quick to respond, but this time, it's like he's choosing his words carefully.

"Honestly?" he asks, the weight of the question lingering in the air.

I chuckle softly, trying to lighten the mood. "No, lie to me," I tease. "Yes, honestly."

He lets out a short laugh, but it's tinged with something heavier. "All right, then. Honestly? This guy Jason... he's trouble. But not the kind of trouble that's gonna throw hands or storm the place guns blazing. He's more... insidious. I've seen guys like him before, Orion. They're not physical right away—they wear you down, push just enough to get under your skin."

I frown, staring at the ceiling. "So, you think he's dangerous in a psychological way?"

"Exactly," Dean confirms. "He's manipulative. The kind of guy who'll make Briar second-guess her own sanity. That's the real danger here. He's already done it, hasn't he? Gotten inside her head."

I think about Briar, about the way her nightmares started once Jason entered the picture. She tries to play it off, but I can see the toll it's taking on her. And yeah, I've seen this before. Dean's right—Jason isn't just some typical jerk ex-boyfriend. He's playing a long game.

"He's already there," I admit, sighing heavily. "She's had nightmares. Ones where she's running from him. It's like he's still haunting her, even though he's physically not around."

Dean's voice softens, but there's an edge of steel in it. "That's what makes him dangerous. Guys like Jason? They don't need to be in the room to mess with your head. That's why we have to handle this carefully. I'll keep digging, but you need to watch her closely, Orion. She's vulnerable."

"I know," I say, running a hand through my hair, frustration building. "But how do we fight something like this? It's not like I can just knock the guy out and call it a day."

Dean chuckles, but there's no real humor in it. "No, this is gonna take finesse. Restraining orders, evidence, paper trails... It's all about building a case to pin him down legally. In the meantime, you keep doing what you're doing. Protect her, make sure she feels safe. That's half the battle."

"I think there's more."

Dean pauses, before asking, "Like what? The gambling?"

"Her parents are loaded. He gambles. It doesn't take a genius to know he's probably got a hefty gambling debt."

"I'm looking into that now," Dean says, tapping more keys on his keyboard in the background. "Just keep an eye on her until we can sort this all out."

I nod, staring at the phone, the weight of Dean's words sinking in. "Okay. Obviously I'll keep an eye on her. Thanks for the insight."

"No problem," he says, his voice firm. "We'll take this one step at a time. Keep me updated."

"Will do," I say before hanging up.

I hate that this is happening to her. I hate that this dumb fuck is trying to weasel his way back into her good graces. I wish I could just knock the fucker out and call it a day. It'd be better to get her back to her place, and for me to get off this job as quickly as possible because I haven't even known Briar for a full twenty-four hours and already I want to sink my fat cock deep inside her.

What the hell, Orion?

Absently, I grab the deck of cards lying on my desk, the smooth surface cool against my fingers. I begin shuffling them, the soft rustle of the cards offering a small comfort as I practice a few sleight-of-hand maneuvers. The repetitive motions are soothing, almost meditative, as I wait for Dean to send over the file. I focus on the cards, blocking out the nagging worry about Briar and the uncertainty of Jason's influence on her.

Just as I'm about to try a more complex trick, there's a soft knock at my office door.

"Come in," I call out, not bothering to look up from my cards.

The door creaks open, and Briar steps over the threshold, her presence lighting up the dim room. "I put Jeb to bed and cleaned up the kitchen. Are you hungry?" Her voice is soft, but it carries a genuine concern that warms something inside me.

I keep shuffling the cards, trying to maintain a casual demeanor. "I'm fine," I reply.

"What are you doing with the cards?" she asks, her curiosity piqued as she leans against the doorframe, arms crossed.

I give her a half-smile. "Magic," I say, letting the word hang in the air like an invitation.

Briar raises an eyebrow, clearly intrigued. "Magic, huh? Like, actual magic? Or just card tricks?"

"Both, depending on how you look at it," I respond, leaning back in my chair and fanning the cards out in front of me. "Want to see a trick?"

She steps further into the room, her skepticism giving way to enthusiasm. "Absolutely. Show me what you've got!"

As I demonstrate a simple card trick, her laughter fills the space, cutting through the tension that had settled in my chest. Watching her happy in something as trivial as a card trick makes me forget about Jason and the heaviness of the situation for just a moment. It's in these small, light-hearted exchanges that I realize how much I want to keep her safe and how deep my feelings for her really run.

The atmosphere in the room shifts, and for a brief second, I allow myself to imagine a world where her smile isn't tinged with fear. A world where we can just be.

Chapter 7

Briar

If you had told me that this big, bad alpha male—who spends his days protecting people and facing danger head-on—was also a magician, I'd have laughed at you and called you silly. I mean, it's just so absurd, isn't it? The image of Orion, all broad shoulders and piercing gaze, pulling rabbits out of hats or making cards vanish into thin air feels like a scene straight out of a comedy film.

As I watch him shuffle the cards with practiced ease, a mixture of awe and disbelief swirls within me. Here he is, this fierce protector who can take down threats without breaking a sweat, suddenly engaging in something as whimsical as magic tricks. The contrast is almost comical.

But then again, there's something endearing about it. Seeing this serious man—who carries the weight of the world on his shoulders—light up when he talks about magic brings a smile to my face. It's like catching a glimpse of a playful side of him that most people never get to see.

I can't help but chuckle to myself. This isn't the kind of thing I expect when I think about Orion. He's not just a fierce warrior; he has this delightful, quirky edge that's utterly unexpected. The way he concentrates, furrowing his brow as he tries to master a sleight-of-hand move, makes him look surprisingly approachable.

Approachable but deadly. And let's not forget the fact that he's stunningly gorgeous. Like he's so hot the chickens lay hard boiled eggs in his presence.

He sets the deck of cards down and smiles at me, the corners of his mouth curving up in a way that sends a flutter through my stomach. "It's late. You should probably try to get some rest."

I nod, perhaps a little too quickly, as I rush out, "Right. Sleep. Sure thing." My mind races, and just as I'm about to salute the man again, I stop in my tracks. A chill runs down my spine, and all I can think about is the nightmare that had gripped me earlier.

"Um," I whisper, feeling foolish for what I'm about to ask. My cheeks heat up, and I can't tell if it's embarrassment or something else.

"What is it?" he asks, rising from his chair with an ease that emphasizes his strength. There's a warmth in his gaze, and for a moment, the shadows of the day melt away, leaving just the two of us in this cozy space.

"I was wondering if you'd lay with me? Until I fall asleep," I rush out, my voice barely above a whisper. The words tumble out before I can overthink them, and suddenly I feel vulnerable, laying bare my fears in front of this formidable man.

The request hangs in the air between us, and my heart thunders in my chest, half hoping he'll say yes, half terrified of what that means. Would he think I'm childish for needing company? Or would he understand the comfort that comes from not being alone in the dark? I hold my breath, waiting for his response, feeling the weight of my own emotions pressing against me like a storm ready to break.

He nods. "Of course I will."

Together we move down the hallway, toward the back guest bedroom, and I peel back the covers. We're silent as Orion crawls into the bed beside me, wrapping an arm around me so I can rest my head in the crook of his shoulder.

"Thank you," I whisper, my voice barely audible in the stillness as Orion turns out the light. The room is bathed in soft shadows, and for a moment, I'm left with just the sound of his steady breath and the rhythmic beat of his heart, strong and reassuring. It's strange, but comforting, being this close to him. I've always felt so guarded, but right now, as I lay beneath the warmth of his presence, my defenses start to dissolve.

"Who's in bed?" Jeb squawks from his cage in the corner of the room.

"Oh, Christ," Orion says, and I quickly get up.

"Let me just put his blanket over the cage," I say, knowing he'll fall asleep as soon as I do. I say a quick goodnight to Jeb, who's obviously upset about Orion being in here. I snuggle back into bed with Orion, and everything slows down. It feels right here.

Sleep pulls me under slowly, like being wrapped in a cocoon of safety, and I let go. The world fades.

At some point, though, I stir. Something firm presses into my back, and for a second, I can't piece together where I am. My mind fumbles through the fog of sleep, but then the warmth and scent—fresh and woodsy—register. I blink, trying to refocus. Soft morning light filters through the window, casting a pale glow across the room, and that's when I feel it.

An arm. Not just any arm. Orion's heavy arm, draped over me.

My breath catches in my throat. He's behind me, his body close, the warmth radiating from him like a furnace. I can hear his soft, even breathing, and my heart does a somersault as I realize the situation I'm in. I'm in bed with him. Well, technically he's in bed with me, but *still*.

I freeze, my thoughts a jumbled mess. What do I *do*? Do I move? Do I stay here? My mind flits to the ridiculous idea that I should be analyzing what's pressing into my back.

Oh my god.

I realize the thing poking me in the back is him. Like *him* him.

I jolt upright, his arm falling off me. This action wakes him up and he groans. It's so sexy too. However, I try my best to pretend I didn't just wake up to Orion pressing his hard dick against me.

And from the weight of it. The size of it.

It's massive.

Like the Titanic of dicks. Probably even bigger than that.

I bound out of bed, trying to escape the awkwardness as quickly as humanly possible. *Smooth, Briar. Really smooth.*

My feet make a beeline for the bathroom down the hall, and as soon as I shut the door, I let out a slow, deep breath. I lean against the sink, staring at my reflection in the mirror, heart still pounding.

Did he actually wake up? I wonder, hoping against hope that he didn't notice me bolting like a startled deer.

I quickly do my business, splash some cold water on my face, and exit the bathroom. With ninja-like precision, I steer clear of the bedroom. No way am I risking another awkward moment there. Instead, I head for the kitchen, and like some kind of wizard, Orion is already there, standing at the counter, brewing a pot of coffee.

Great. Of course, he's up.

"How'd you sleep?" he asks, his back still turned to me as he fiddles with the coffee maker like some expert barista.

I freeze, my brain suddenly swarmed with one very specific, very inappropriate thought: I wonder if he's still hard.

*Nope. Nope. **Nope**. Abort mission, Briar. Focus on literally anything else.*

I plaster on a smile and answer way too quickly, "Great! Like a baby." Then, because I apparently have zero self-control, I keep talking. "Although I never get why they say that because babies don't actually sleep. My cousin's baby slept maybe an hour a night and cried the rest of the time. Honestly, it was more like sleeping next to a banshee."

I stop mid-ramble, realizing how far off the rails I've gone. I clamp my mouth shut, suddenly wishing for a time machine.

Orion turns just enough to raise an eyebrow, his expression mildly amused. "You talk a lot, don't you?" His voice is low and casual, like this is all perfectly normal while he masterfully works the coffee machine, barely glancing my way.

"Only when I'm nervous," I whisper, inwardly cringing.

Why did I just admit that?

He stops mid-coffee-pour, blinking at me as if I've said something far more interesting than intended. His eyes lock onto mine, amusement still dancing in them. "Are you nervous now?"

Cue internal freak-out. "No! I mean—*yes*. I mean—" I throw my hands up in surrender. "I woke up with you in my bed, okay? I'm a little… flustered."

He smirks. "You bolted pretty fast."

I shrug, playing it off like I'm totally cool and collected. "I have a strong bladder."

He chuckles, turning his attention back to the coffee. "You should work on your exit strategy. Maybe next time, don't run like I'm chasing you."

"Next time?" I raise an eyebrow, trying not to think too much about the implications of that statement.

"Who knows," he says, smirk still in place as he pours another cup. He slides one across the counter to me. "Stranger things have happened."

I take the mug, hoping the warmth of the coffee hides the flush creeping up my neck. "Yeah, like a big bad bodyguard who also dabbles in magic tricks."

He grins at that. "Hey, never underestimate the power of sleight of hand." He winks, and damn if my stomach doesn't do a little flip.

I take a sip, trying to distract myself. "Yeah, well, just don't pull any disappearing acts on me."

Chapter 8

Orion

Have I mentioned how cute Briar is? She's the kind of cute that sneaks up on you and stays lodged in your mind, like a catchy tune you can't stop humming. She has this effortless way of making you smile—her whole vibe is like sunshine wrapped in a messy bow, and before you know it, your heart is pounding like you've just run a marathon. I try to play it cool, but there's no denying the effect she has on me.

She tilts her head, eyes bright with curiosity as she leans against the counter, cradling her coffee mug like it's the most natural thing in the world to stand here in my kitchen. "What's on the agenda today?"

I shrug, trying to keep it casual, even though the thought of spending more time with her has me internally buzzing. I take a slow sip of my coffee, using it as an excuse to gather my thoughts. "Well, I need to get a bit of work done," I say, though honestly, I doubt I'll be able to focus much with her around. "But I thought maybe later we could take a stroll along the beach. That is, if *the bird* allows it."

I throw in the last part with a smirk, and her face lights up like I knew it would.

"Jeb's pretty easy-going," she says with a grin, taking a sip of her coffee. "He'll let us out of the house, but only if we promise him a starring role in the rest of our day."

I chuckle, shaking my head. "Sounds like we're at the mercy of a diva."

She laughs softly, and the sound is like a balm to my senses, soothing and addictive all at once. I could listen to that laugh on repeat and never get tired of it.

Briar sets her mug down and taps her fingers lightly on the counter. "I'd love to go to the beach. I mean, I haven't been in... forever. I could use some sun, sea air, and maybe a little bit of magic." She throws me a teasing glance, referencing the little magic trick I'd done the night before.

"Magic, huh?" I arch an eyebrow, leaning back against the counter, arms crossed. "I think I can manage that." I give her a slow, playful grin, and her cheeks flush just slightly.

She swats the air between us like she's trying to bat away the flirtation, but the glint in her eyes tells me she's enjoying it. "Well, don't expect me to pull a rabbit out of a hat. I can barely get through a deck of cards without dropping half of them on the floor."

"I've got the magic tricks covered," I say smoothly, "You just bring the charm."

Her eyes roll, but there's a smile tugging at her lips. "Oh, please, like I'm any match for Mr. Magic over here."

I laugh, and it's impossible not to feel lighter around her. "Trust me, Briar, you're the real magic in this equation."

What the fuck is wrong with me? I never flirt. Never like this. And *never* with a client.

Her smile falters for a split second, something soft and real flashing in her eyes before she quickly hides it behind her usual playful banter. "Careful, Orion," she says, mock-serious, "You might actually start sounding like a romantic."

"I've been known to have my moments," I say, giving her a wink, watching as her cheeks turn a shade pinker. And just like that, I know I'm in deeper than I ever intended to be.

And it's at this moment I know I should call Dean and get her reassigned. I shouldn't get in any deeper than I already am.

I'm attracted to her. And that's dangerous as fuck.

However, I can't stay away. The thought of any other man protecting her makes me want to throw something heavy into the ocean. The thought of her not being around makes me want to snap a tree trunk in two. Even the bird is growing on me, however, I'd never admit that to her.

So, that's why I have zero plans of calling Dean. I want to be the *only* man protecting Briar. No one else.

ONE THING I know for sure is that it's going to suck when this job ends. Hard. The thought of Briar returning to her own place, no longer sharing my space, no longer filling the quiet with her laugh, is already gnawing at me. She's embedded herself in my system. In two short fucking days the woman has already left a lasting impression.

Maybe it's because I haven't fucked a woman in ages. Maybe it's because I've never met a woman like Briar before. But there's something going on deep in my chest that's making me want to stake a claim here.

It makes me understand why Jason's not willing to let her go either. But let's be real—Jason's an asshole. A possessive one at that. Still, even assholes can have the sense to recognize what they'll be losing. He just doesn't deserve her.

I watch her as she leans back in her beach chair, toes buried in the sand, the salty ocean breeze whipping strands of her hair around her face. There's something about her here, under the sun, that makes everything feel more vivid. Like the world is brighter just because she's in it.

"Tell me," I say, breaking the comfortable silence that's settled between us. "How did you break things off with Jason?"

She looks over at me, her expression shifting from relaxed to a little guarded. I know it's a sensitive subject, but I need more details, for the case, yes, but also because I want to understand more of what she's been through.

She sighs softly, glancing out at the horizon where the waves crash against the shore in a rhythmic, calming pattern. "It wasn't easy," she starts, her voice quieter now. "I think part of me didn't want to believe I had to. I kept hoping he'd change, that things would go back to how they were at the beginning."

I nod, staying quiet so she'll keep going. I can tell this is a wound she's hesitant to reopen, but there's strength in her voice that wasn't there before. She's not the same woman who let Jason control her life.

"He became... different," she continues, her brow furrowing as she pulls her knees up to her chest. "At first, it was subtle, you know? Little comments here and there. A few controlling tendencies I brushed off. But then it escalated. He started isolating me from my friends, demanding to know where I was at all times." Her hands clench the armrests of her chair, like she's holding onto something invisible, something heavier than the beach chair beneath her.

I clench my jaw, feeling a rush of anger I didn't expect to feel. I'd seen this kind of behavior before, with other cases, but hearing it from her—it hits differently.

"He had this way of making me feel like it was my fault," she admits, shaking her head slightly, as if she's still trying to shake off the hold Jason had on her. "Like I was the one doing something wrong, like I was overreacting or imagining things."

I take a breath, trying to keep my voice steady. "And when you finally ended it?"

"It was messy," she says, hugging her legs tighter. "He didn't take it well. There were a lot of angry phone calls, text messages, showing up unannounced. He wouldn't take no for an answer." She pauses, biting her bottom lip as she looks down at the sand. "I was scared, Orion. Scared he'd never stop."

I reach over, gently placing my hand on hers. She looks up, surprised by the contact, but doesn't pull away. Her skin feels warm under mine, and for a moment, neither of us says anything. The only sound between us is the ocean's steady, relentless rhythm.

"I won't let him hurt you again," I say, my voice low but firm. There's more to those words than just a professional promise.

She offers me a small, grateful smile, though there's still a hint of sadness in her eyes. "I know. I believe you."

For a moment, I forget about the case, the job, and everything else. All I can think about is how much I want to protect her—not just from Jason, but from everything that's ever hurt her. It's a dangerous feeling, but one I can't shake.

I lean closer, an overwhelming need building inside me, pulling me toward her like a force I can't control. Her eyes lock with mine, wide and searching, filled with a mixture of vulnerability and something else. It's something that makes my pulse race even faster. Maybe this isn't the best moment, not right after she's just opened up about Jason and all the crap she went through. But damn it, I can't stop myself.

My heart pounds in my chest, drowning out every rational thought. The ocean breeze tangles her hair, framing her face like a painting that's too perfect to be real. For a split second, I hesitate and think maybe I should give her space, give her time. But then my gaze falls to her lips, soft and slightly parted, and that tiny flicker of doubt disappears.

Three seconds. That's all I give myself to contemplate before thinking, *fuck this shit*. My body moves on instinct, and I close the distance between us, leaning in until her warmth is right there, just inches away.

Then I capture her lips with mine.

The kiss is soft at first, tentative, like I'm testing the waters, waiting to see if she'll pull away. But she doesn't. Her breath hitches, and she responds, her lips melting against mine with a heat that catches me completely off guard.

I feel her hands, tentative at first, slide up to grip the front of my shirt, pulling me closer. It's like something snaps between us—this electric charge that's been building for days finally erupting, and I deepen the kiss, my hand sliding up to cradle the back of her neck.

Her taste is intoxicating, a mix of sweetness and something entirely her, and I can't get enough. Every brush of her lips against mine makes me want more, need more. The world fades away—the sound of the waves, the seagulls, the soft rustle of the wind in the palm trees—it all disappears, leaving just us in this moment.

I feel her breath catch again as the kiss intensifies, her body pressing into mine like she's anchoring herself to me, and I tighten my grip on her waist, pulling her into my lap, her legs straddling me. I can feel the rapid thrum of her heart against my chest, matching the wild rhythm of my own.

When we finally break apart, both of us breathless, I keep my forehead resting against hers, not wanting to move, not wanting to lose this moment. Her eyes flutter open, and I catch the dazed look in them, her lips still slightly parted as if she's just as shocked as I am by what just happened.

Neither of us says anything for a long beat, the tension still thick in the air. Her fingers are still fisted in my shirt, and I'm not ready to let her go.

Chapter 9

Briar

Did that really just happen?

I gasp, my mind spinning, trying to grasp what just unfolded. My lips are still tingling from his kiss, and my heart is pounding so hard I'm convinced he can hear it. This is foreign territory for me, uncharted waters, and I'm totally lost at sea.

This man. Orion.

He's not like anyone I've ever met before. I take a shaky breath, still clinging onto him, trying to make sense of it all. He's strong—like, really strong—physically, but also in this quiet, commanding way that makes you feel safe just being near him. But at the same time, there's this softness in him too. This side of him I've glimpsed in the little moments, like when he made me mac and cheese, or when he turned on *Criminal Minds* for me because he knows it makes me feel at home.

He's smart, funny, with this dry sense of humor that always catches me off guard. And he's kind. Kind in a way that surprises me every time, especially considering what he does for a living. You'd think someone who spends their life protecting others would be hardened, but not Orion. He's the opposite. He's gentle, careful, and understanding in a way that makes me melt.

It's almost too much, too perfect. Guys like this? They're the ones you read about in romance novels, not the ones who actually show up in your life. They're the complete package. And girls like me? Well, we don't end up with the complete package kind of guy. We end up with the Jasons of the world—the ones who seem perfect at first, but who slowly unravel, revealing their flaws one by one until you're left wondering how you didn't see it sooner.

But this is Orion. He's not Jason. He's not like any guy I've ever known.

His eyes lock onto mine, and I feel like he's seeing right through me. It's like he can read every thought swirling in my mind, every doubt, every insecurity. My breath catches in my throat, and I grip onto him tighter, because the truth is, I don't want to let him go.

I don't just want him. I need him. I need more of him, more of this—whatever this is between us. And the way he's looking at me right now, like he's trying to figure out how the hell we ended up here too, makes me feel like he needs this.

And that thought, that possibility, makes me feel like I'm flying.

"I'm sorry—"

"Don't," I cut him off, my voice barely steady, but firm. I will *literally* cry if he tries to backpedal right now. I can't let this moment slip away. Not after everything that's happened, not after the way my heart just flipped inside my chest. "Don't," I whisper again, my lips brushing against his, my breath mingling with his, as I pull him closer to me.

For a second, everything seems to stand still. The ocean, the world, the universe. It all fades away. There's nothing but him and me, locked in this moment.

His hesitation melts as I close the distance between us, and then his mouth opens over mine. The kiss deepens. His lips are warm, firm, but soft at the same time. It's not just a kiss—it's something more, something that feels like I've been waiting for it my entire life. His tongue slides into my mouth, tracing circles against mine, and I shiver under the sensation. A surge of warmth rushes through me, making my knees weak.

I cling to him like he's my anchor, the only thing keeping me grounded in the storm that's swirling inside me. Every stroke of his tongue sends sparks of electricity through my body, like we're communicating in a language only we understand.

I can feel his heartbeat through his chest, matching the frantic pace of mine. His hands find their way to my waist, pulling me even closer, as though he's afraid I might slip away. But there's no chance of that. Not now, not ever.

I lose myself in him, in the taste of him, in the feeling of his body pressed against mine. It's overwhelming and intoxicating, and I never want it to end. Every nerve in my body is alight, humming with a sensation I've never felt before. It's as if I've been searching for this kiss my whole life, and now that I've found it, I don't know how I'll ever live without it.

He rests his hands on my hip, and I grind against him. He growls against my ear, and my heartbeat picks up speed.

He's rock hard beneath me and I can feel every single inch of him, and boy, are there so many.

This thought spurs me on, and I grind against him again.

"You keep that up and I might just take you back inside and fuck you til the sun goes down."

I want to tell him to do just that, but this isn't right, right? I mean, he's my bodyguard.

Besides, does he do this with all the women he protects?

That thought right there has me climbing off his lap. The mood vanishes quickly between us. Oh god. I'm mortified. He probably sleeps with all the women he's assigned to.

"I'm sorry," I say, rushing back toward his house, my feet kicking up sand in my wake.

I don't bother to turn around to see if he's chasing after me. Hopefully he isn't.

I feel foolish, caught in a whirlwind of emotions as soon as I step back into Orion's place. With a quick motion, I let Jeb out of his cage, and the little bird flutters around the room before landing on my shoulder.

"Jeb hungry!" he squawks, his voice loud and demanding.

"I'm going to feed Jeb now," I reply, trying to match his enthusiasm as I navigate my way into the kitchen with him. Establishing a routine for Jeb has become my small act of normalcy in a life that feels anything but. I hate that I've uprooted him from his familiar surroundings, and the guilt gnaws at me. All because of Jason.

The kitchen is bright, sunlight pouring through the window, but it does little to warm the chill creeping into my heart. I can't shake the worry that when this is all over, when the dust settles and I'm back in my own life, Jason will still be lurking in the shadows. He's made it clear before—he once told me he'd always want me. Was that just a desperate attempt to hold onto something he knew he was losing? Will a restraining order actually keep him away, or will it only make him more determined?

As I busily prepare Jeb's lunch—chopping up fresh fruits and nuts—my thoughts spiral. I try to focus on the task at hand, but each slice of fruit feels heavy with the weight of my uncertainty. I can almost feel Jason's presence looming behind me. Jeb hops to the countertop, watching me with curious, beady eyes, and I find a bit of comfort in his innocent gaze.

"Hang tight, Jeb. You're going to love this," I say, forcing a smile as I mix together his favorite snacks.

The sliding back door opens, and Orion steps inside, the early afternoon light casting a warm glow around him.

"Hey," he whispers, stepping closer, his voice low and filled with concern. "Are you okay?"

I busy myself with Jeb, the little parrot perched on the kitchen counter, and force a smile, trying to mask the swirl of emotions inside. "I'm fine," I breathe out, but my heart races under his gaze.

"I'm sorry… about earlier. I didn't mean to…" His words trail off, and I feel a blush creeping up my cheeks, heat radiating from the memory of that kiss.

"It's fine. It was my fault. I've just never had…" Oh god, I can't tell him I've never had a man look at me the way he looked at me. Or touched me the way he did. Or kissed me, for that matter. The weight of my confession hangs in the air, heavy and unspoken.

"Never had what?" he asks, inching closer, curiosity etched on his handsome features.

I glance down at my bare feet, realizing I've tracked sand into his pristine kitchen, little grains sparkling on the white tile like tiny reminders of our day at the beach. "Oh my god. I'm so sorry. I've tracked sand inside," I stammer, feeling utterly mortified.

Orion lifts a hand, his fingers brushing lightly against my arm, and I feel a shiver run down my spine at his touch. "Forget about it," he says, his voice steady and warm. "You've never had what?" he prompts again, his eyes searching mine with genuine interest.

I stop fidgeting and take a deep breath, gazing into his eyes that seem to hold a thousand unspoken words. "It's nothing," I say, busily finishing up Jeb's snack.

Orion drops the subject, locking the slider as he pulls the blinds closed. "Next time don't run away from me. When we're out of this house, you stay with me at all times."

I glance at my feet once more. "I'm sorry. I just…" I don't want to tell him why I ran. I don't want to voice what I know to be true.

Orion sleeps with all the women he protects, and I'm just another notch on the bedpost for him. I feel ashamed.

Orion studies me for a moment and then wanders off down the hall, shutting himself into his office.

I feel so foolish I could scream, but I won't. Instead I feed Jeb, and then head off to the bathroom to take a long, hot shower, and try my hardest to forget about that kiss.

However, easier said than done.

I GRIP MY BROOM TIGHTLY, my heart drumming a frantic beat in my chest. Focus, Briar, I remind myself, sweeping up the stray feathers and bits of bird poop scattered across the walkway. The humid air in the aviary clings to my skin, and the chorus of parrots and cockatoos provides the usual soundtrack to my workday. Normally, the chatter is comforting. Today, it only heightens my nerves.

Orion stands a few paces behind me, his tall frame impossible to miss even if I weren't trying to ignore him. I can feel his presence like a static charge in the air, prickling the hairs on the back of my neck. We haven't spoken much since yesterday, when he kissed me on the beach. It was a kiss that turned my world upside down, and I'm doing everything I can to push it out of my mind while I'm on the clock. But how can I forget when he's right here, watching my every move?

I shove the broom across the concrete path a little more forcefully than necessary, trying to channel my racing thoughts into something productive. Usually, work is my escape. But now, the sense of security I normally find here has been overshadowed by the constant buzz of fear that Jason could appear at any moment. *Don't be ridiculous, Briar*, I scold myself for the hundredth time. He can't just waltz in here without a ticket or a plan.

Still, I catch myself checking every corner, every shadow. The flutter of feathers from the cockatiels makes my heart jump, and when a man with blond hair brushes past me, I freeze, thinking it's Jason for a split second. My mouth goes dry, and I have to swallow down a wave of panic before I realize it's just a stranger, a random guest. Not Jason.

From behind, I sense Orion shifting his stance. Is he about to come over? My heart skitters at the possibility. *Focus, Briar.*

Sweep. I force my attention back to my broom, inhaling through my nose as I bend to collect some stray feathers.

I catch sight of my coworker, Heath, approaching with a sympathetic smile. He's wearing the standard khaki uniform minus the Tweed jacket, and there's a half-eaten granola bar in his hand. "Everything okay?" he asks, concern etched in his brow. "You look kinda frazzled."

"I'm fine," I lie, pulling the broom close to my side, my knuckles turning white around the handle. I glance over my shoulder without thinking. Orion's dark eyes meet mine, and the intensity there makes my pulse spike all over again. I snap my gaze back to Heath. "Just a little jumpy, that's all."

Heath bites his lip, looking like he doesn't quite believe me. "You sure? You've been glancing around like you're expecting someone to jump out at you."

I force a shaky laugh. "Don't be silly. Probably just had too much coffee this morning." My attempt at a joke falls flat, and Heath's concerned expression deepens.

Suddenly, someone tall and imposing steps in from my left, and my nerves jolt again. But this time, it's Orion. He's practically towering over both of us, arms crossed, eyes flicking between Heath and me. "Briar," he says in a low voice, "you all right?"

My cheeks blaze. The way he says my name wraps me in warmth, even though I'm painfully aware of how transparent I must look. "I'm—"

"She was just telling me she's fine," Heath interjects, sounding doubtful.

Orion's gaze slides toward Heath, assessing him with a cool detachment I've come to recognize as his protective mode.

"Thanks," he says curtly, turning his attention back to me. "I'll take it from here."

Heath raises his hands in a gesture of surrender. "All right, no problem. I was just—"

"Thank you for checking in, Heath," I say, cutting off any friction before it starts. He nods and heads off, leaving me alone with Orion.

The air crackles with tension as Orion steps closer, his stance stiff, his expression unreadable. "You sure you're good?" He lowers his voice, leaning in slightly so only I can hear. "You keep looking around like you're expecting Jason to pop up."

"I'm just... paranoid, I guess," I admit, hugging the broom handle for dear life. "Every time I see someone with blond hair, I think it's him."

Orion's jaw tightens. I can see the muscle flex beneath his skin. "He's not going to get near you. Not while I'm here."

His alpha confidence sends a strange mixture of relief and butterflies through me. "I appreciate it," I whisper, glancing away. For a moment, I wonder if he's remembering that kiss the same way I am. My lips still tingle at the memory.

Orion shifts closer, and I catch a whiff of his aftershave. "If you see anything—anyone—suspicious, you tell me. Immediately."

I nod, my stomach churning with fear and something else I can't name. "Right."

His eyes flick over me, making sure I'm steady. "Now, why don't you finish your shift? I'll be right here if you need me."

I let out a slow breath and manage a small smile. "Thanks."

With that, he steps back, giving me space—but not too much. I can still sense him behind me, vigilant, ready to pounce if a threat arises. Part of me feels reassured, but another part feels unsettled by how much I like having him so close.

Trying to ignore the sudden warmth in my chest, I refocus on the scattered feathers on the ground. I push the broom forward, forcing myself to concentrate. But no matter how hard I try, I can't entirely shake the sensation of Orion's eyes on me, watching, keeping me safe... and making me think of that kiss I can't seem to forget.

Chapter 10

Orion

Here's the deal. Employees at zoos don't normally have a bodyguard following closely behind them. And for some reason, the more I try to blend in, the more I stand out.

However, I don't give a flying fuck if people notice me watching Briar. Maybe word will get back to her prick of an ex, and he'll finally get the hint.

Yet, life isn't that simple.

I stand near the perimeter of the aviary, arms crossed over my chest, scanning the area with practiced focus. Exotic birds flit overhead, their colors a blur of blues, greens, and yellows. Most people would find the spectacle captivating, but I'm only half paying attention. My priority is Briar.

She's a few yards away, talking with her boss—Marcie, if I recall correctly. The woman looks no-nonsense, dressed in khaki shorts and a crisp polo shirt with the zoo's logo. She's listening intently as Briar explains the situation: her mother hiring me as a bodyguard because her ex-boyfriend's become a problem. The second Briar mentions an "ex giving her trouble," Marcie's expression hardens.

I shift my stance, watching them. Briar's posture is tense—shoulders slightly hunched, gaze flicking my way every so often. I can see the worry etched in her eyes even from here. She wants this job, loves it, but she also knows she has to face the reality that danger might follow her anywhere. My instincts prick at the sight of her anxiety. I want to walk over, put a hand on her shoulder, let her know she's not dealing with this alone. But I hold back. She needs to handle this conversation on her own.

Marcie says something I can't quite make out. Briar nods, a flash of disappointment crossing her face. A moment later, Marcie reaches out and gives Briar's arm a quick squeeze. I see Briar's lips move, forming what looks like a "thank you." Then Marcie glances at me, her gaze sliding over my broad frame, weighing me up. I give her a small nod in acknowledgment. She returns it curtly, then heads off in the opposite direction, leaving Briar standing alone, shoulders visibly sagging.

I take a step toward her, letting my boots hit the ground with enough sound so I won't spook her. When she sees me approaching, she attempts a smile, but it doesn't quite reach her eyes.

"How'd it go?" I ask, keeping my voice low.

She tucks a stray strand of brown hair behind her ear and looks around, as if she's suddenly self-conscious. "Marcie said... well, she said I should probably take some time off work until everything's settled. With Jason, I mean."

I nod slowly, taking in the disappointment flickering across her features. She loves this place—anyone can see it. "That make sense to you?"

She shrugs, a shallow movement. "I guess. I mean, I hate to admit it, but maybe I do need some time away. Just… until this mess gets sorted out."

My protective instincts flare up. I want to tell her that yes, she absolutely needs time to stay safe, but I know her pride might bristle if I phrase it wrong. "It's not forever," I say gently. "You'll come back once things are under control."

She lifts her gaze to mine, and for a second, that spark of determination I've come to admire shines through. "Yeah. I will." Then her expression softens. "But it still sucks."

I reach out, brushing her elbow lightly with my fingertips. It's a small gesture, meant to steady her. "It's gonna be okay," I say, trying to keep my tone level, reassuring. "I'll be with you every step of the way. Let's go pack up your stuff."

She hesitates, glancing around the aviary as if memorizing every detail before she leaves. I wait, giving her the moment she needs. Finally, she releases a resigned sigh, nods, and leads the way toward the staff lockers.

It doesn't take long for her to gather her belongings—just a backpack and a small duffel. I stay a half-step behind, scanning for anything—or anyone—suspicious. My senses are on high alert, but the zoo remains a happy, chaotic swirl of tourists and staff, oblivious to the turmoil in Briar's life. Good. I want it that way.

We don't speak much as we head out to the parking lot. I help her into my SUV and lock her door.

The ride back to my place is quiet. Briar stares out the passenger window, lost in thought, while I keep my eyes on the road, one hand draped over the steering wheel. Part of me wants to fill the silence, ask if she's all right, if she wants to talk. But I can tell she's processing, and sometimes that requires stillness.

When we arrive, I help her out of the car, her bag slung over my shoulder. She's already fumbling for the door before I catch up, and I spot the tension in her shoulders again.

I open the door, and make a quick sweep of the place to ensure everything's the same as we left it.

However, I suspect Jeb would let us know if anyone had been in here. Briar moves to his cage, checking on him as I head into the kitchen.

"You hungry?" I ask her. "I can whip something up." I think about making her a steak, or a pasta salad, however I remember the food she likes instead.

"No, I'm just going to sulk on the couch."

I smile softly as I enter the living room through the archway. "It's not forever, Briar. We'll be able to deal with Jason once we know exactly what he wants."

Briar plucks at a pillow in her lap. "Well, it seems like what he wants is me."

I run a finger over my bottom lip, my mind briefly thinking about how I want the exact same thing, and then I push back my shoulders. "Yes and no."

She faces me, her eyes wide. "What does that mean?"

I sit down next to her. "I'm thinking Jason might want your parents' money. Maybe he has some gambling debt. Dean's running a few searches on Jason. We'll know more in a few days."

Briar's face appears confused, and then she blinks at me. "My parents' money? Wait, now that you mention that he was always talking about a man, I forget his name, but he was always checking in with him. Saying they needed the deal to go through. I always thought it had to do with work, but one time he mentioned that he would talk to the guy after he got out of work. So, it made me think this man and him didn't work together. I don't know."

"Hey, this is very helpful. Do you remember anything else?"

She shrugs. "No. I just know toward the end of our relationship he was starting to unravel. Always talking on the phone, always stressed."

I stare at Briar for a long moment as I try to process what she's saying. It pisses me off she was in a relationship with this asshole. "Was this man somebody he knew from the races?"

She shrugs again, and I briefly stare a little too long when her shirt slips off her slender shoulder. "I don't know. I could call him and ask. Maybe do a little recon mission."

My heart nearly explodes in my chest from anxiety at the thought of Briar ever speaking to that asshole again. "No," I clip out. "You'll never speak to him ever again." Not if I have anything to say about it.

"Okay," she whispers.

I want to comfort her in some small way, but I know if I touch her right now I'll be tempted to kiss her again, and that was a huge mistake. I can't let myself go there again. "You hungry?" I ask her, my voice gruff and threadbare.

She shakes her head. "Not really."

"I'll make you some soup."

She nods. "Orion," she says. "Thank you." She blinks up at me, her green eyes the same shade as the grass on a warm, sunny day.

Something about the way she says it makes my chest feel warm. I stand from the couch, deciding it's better not to linger on that feeling too long. "You're welcome."

She offers me another soft smile, and for the briefest moment, my pulse kicks up a notch. Then I clear my throat and step aside, giving her space to breathe.

I'm her bodyguard, after all. Protecting her is my job. But the longer I'm around her, the more it feels like something else—like a promise I'm determined to keep, no matter what.

I STIR the pot of soup with one hand, the steam rising up and enveloping me in a comforting warmth. The kitchen is quiet except for the gentle bubbling of broth. I glanced over at Briar not too long ago—she was curled up on the couch in the living room, flipping channels with Jeb perched on the backrest. A few minutes later, I heard the soft sound of her breathing deepen, and I figured she was drifting off.

My phone vibrates on the counter, drawing my attention, but I decide to let it wait. I give the soup another swirl, taste-testing with a spoon, and nod in satisfaction. I don't cook often, but for her, I'm willing to make the effort.

Suddenly, there's a muffled cry from the living room. My heart lurches. I turn off the burner and rush toward the sound. The moment I round the corner, I see Briar thrashing on the couch, her face contorted in fear.

"Briar?" I call softly at first, stepping closer. "Briar, wake up."

She doesn't respond. She lets out another whimper, and I can feel my protective instincts flare. Kneeling beside her, I place a gentle hand on her shoulder and give her a soft shake. Her breathing is ragged, shallow.

"Briar," I say, louder now, and she jolts, eyes snapping open. She looks at me in wild confusion, like she doesn't quite recognize where she is or who I am. Her chest heaves as she pulls in frantic gulps of air.

"It's okay," I whisper, sinking onto the cushion beside her. I carefully slide my arms around her, gathering her against my chest. She doesn't resist—if anything, she clings to me, trembling like a leaf in a storm. "It was just a bad dream," I soothe, brushing a strand of hair away from her damp forehead.

She closes her eyes, letting out a shuddering breath. "I… I'm sorry," she manages.

"Another dream about Jason?" I ask, though it's more an affirmation than a question. I already know the answer.

She swallows hard and nods, pressing her forehead against my collarbone. "Yes," she whispers, voice cracking on the single syllable.

My jaw tenses. I can feel anger prickling at the edges, not at her, but at Jason—for haunting her even now, for lingering in the corners of her mind where he has no right to be. I need to find out what this bastard wants so we can go back to normal. At least that's the plan, but if I'm being honest with myself, I'm starting to wonder if I actually want "normal." Because having Briar here, in my space, in my arms, feels… right in a way I can't easily explain.

I tighten my hold on her, letting her rest against me. "We'll figure this out," I say, my voice dipping low, meant only for her. "We'll find out what he wants, and we'll make him back off for good."

She nods against my chest, and I catch her scent—a mix of something floral with a hint of citrus. It's unexpectedly intoxicating. Her body trembles slightly, and I wonder if she's still caught in the grips of that nightmare, or if it's something else entirely.

"Thank you," she breathes, and then her eyes flutter open, searching mine. There's a vulnerable edge there, a plea to be believed, to be protected.

Without thinking, I bring a hand up to cradle her cheek. My thumb brushes against her soft skin, and electricity crackles down my spine. We're close now—so close that I can see the flecks of gold in her irises, the faint flush creeping up her neck.

She leans into my touch, and my heart kicks into high gear. God, I want to kiss her. I did once, but that felt like it was in the heat of a moment. Now, it's just us, the two of us, breathing in sync, tethered by a tension that's as charged as lightning in a summer sky.

I lower my head a fraction, my eyes locked on hers, silently asking permission. Her lips part slightly, and I feel her breath mingle with mine—warm, inviting. Her grip on my shirt tightens, her fingertips digging into the fabric like she can't bear to let go.

An urge surges inside me, hungry and insistent. I brush my mouth over hers, tentative, testing. The softest contact, yet it's like a flame igniting. She exhales a shaky sigh against my lips, and it's all the encouragement I need. My hand slides to the small of her back, pulling her closer until there's no space left between us.

The kiss deepens, slow and purposeful, a whispered promise between us. Her lips tremble for a heartbeat, then part in response, and my pulse roars in my ears. I taste her uncertainty, her relief, and beneath it all, a spark of want that matches my own.

For a few seconds, it's only that—her mouth on mine, the warmth of our bodies pressed together, the lingering fear from her nightmare melting under the heat of something far stronger.

Eventually, I force myself to pull back, just enough to see her face. Her eyes remain closed for a moment, her lips slightly swollen from the kiss, her breathing uneven. When she looks up, there's a question in her gaze, one I'm probably wearing in my own expression.

I press my forehead to hers, fighting the urge to claim her lips again. "You okay?" I whisper, my voice laced with all the desire and concern coursing through me.

She nods, her breath fanning my cheek. "Yes," she whispers, her voice unsteady. "Better now."

I wrap my arms around her once more, holding her tight as if I can shield her from the nightmares, from Jason, from everything. And for a moment, it feels like maybe I can. Because right now, in this moment, nothing and no one else exists but us.

Chapter 11

Briar

I sit up, still recovering from the searing kiss Orion just gave me. My heart hammers against my ribcage, and I can't seem to catch my breath. He's leaning over me, concern etched across his features. A thousand questions swirl in my mind, but the one that surfaces first is *Does he do this with all the women he protects?* The thought makes my stomach flip. I remind myself he's only here to keep me safe, that what just happened probably doesn't mean anything beyond a heated moment.

I clear my throat, desperate to dispel the thick tension hanging in the room. "I—um—would love some soup," I blurt, voice shaky but determined. My nightmares, this kiss, the adrenaline—everything's got me exhausted, and I realize I'm starving.

Orion blinks, clearly thrown by my abrupt change of subject, but he nods. "Right. Soup. Let's get you fed."

He stands, offering me a hand. The warmth of his skin sends a spark through me again, but I quickly tamp it down. I let him guide me into the kitchen. The comforting aroma of whatever he's cooking wraps around me like a soft blanket. I slip onto one of the chairs at the small table, pressing my hand against my still-thudding heart, willing it to calm down.

Orion ladles soup into a bowl and sets it in front of me, a slight frown tugging at his features. "I'm sorry about the kiss," he says quietly, grabbing a spoon and placing it next to the bowl. "I shouldn't have—"

"It's fine," I cut in, though my cheeks burn at the memory. More than fine, part of me wants to add, but I squash that thought. "I mean, it happened. Don't worry about it."

He stands across the table, arms crossed, watching me as I take a tentative sip. The soup is savory and soothing, warmth spreading through my chest. He's not as relaxed as he was before. I can feel the tension in the air. I swallow a spoonful and decide to address it head-on.

"So, what happens now?" I ask, trying to keep my voice steady. "How long do we have to stay holed up here while Jason is out there, doing God knows what? I hate not knowing. I want to go back to my normal life—go home. Pretend he was just a bad dream."

Orion's eyes flicker with something—anger, worry, maybe both. He exhales, resting his hands on the back of a chair. "I know it's frustrating. We can't say for sure how long this will take. It depends on the restraining order, the investigation, and whether we can actually pin something on him."

He hesitates, then his gaze drifts back to me, more intense now. "Briar... I need to know more about Jason. About what he's done. Did he ever—" He stops, jaw clenching like he's trying to force the words out. "Did he ever hurt you physically?"

My stomach twists as the question hangs in the air. I stare down at my soup, stirring it absently. Memories flash through my mind: Jason's accusations, his grip on my arm, the way he'd corner me. I press my lips together, feeling a swell of shame for letting it get that far—even though I know it wasn't my fault.

"He never left bruises," I say finally, voice quieter than I intend. "Not obvious ones, anyway. But there were times he… grabbed me, shoved me. It started small. I tried to convince myself I was overreacting, that he was just upset. Then it got worse. Words turned into harsher words, threats. Eventually, I realized he would never change."

I sneak a look at Orion. His knuckles are white, gripping the chair so hard I'm worried he'll snap the wood. A muscle twitches in his jaw, and his eyes burn with anger. The protective stance he's in radiates a kind of quiet fury—like he wants nothing more than to track Jason down and make him pay.

"Thank you for telling me," he says, his voice tight but controlled. "I'm sorry you had to go through that."

I swallow hard, trying to rein in the tears pricking at the corners of my eyes. "It's fine," I murmur. "I just want him to leave me alone. Let me live my life."

Orion rounds the table and crouches beside me, gently placing a hand on my knee. His touch calms the tremor in my chest. "He won't hurt you again," he says, determination lacing every syllable. "Not while I'm around."

I manage a wobbly smile, relief and warmth flooding me in equal measure. "Thanks," I whisper, returning my attention to the soup in front of me. My stomach is still twisted in knots, but I force myself to eat. For now, this is as normal as things get—warm soup, Orion's comforting presence, and a fragile hope that someday soon, Jason will just be a distant memory.

MY PHONE FEELS UNUSUALLY heavy in my hands as it lights up for the first time in what feels like an eternity. I haven't turned my phone on since the first day I was here, and I brace myself as the barrage of missed notifications begins to flood the screen. The constant buzzing feels like a relentless reminder of the world I've been hiding from. Jason's name pops up repeatedly among the missed calls and texts, sending a shiver down my spine. But it's the string of messages from Heidi, work, and particularly my mother that catches my attention and knots my stomach.

Heidi's texts are filled with increasing worry, her emojis ranging from concerned to downright panicked. I can almost hear her voice chattering through the messages, asking if I'm okay, if I need anything, why I'm not answering. There's a guilt that tugs at my heart for making her worry.

The messages from work are polite, a check-in to see if I'm managing okay, a subtle nudge to let me know they're there. It's comforting, yet another layer of normalcy I'm not quite ready to return to.

Then, there's my mother. Her texts escalate from concerned to demanding, each message more pointed than the last. She wants an update, details, reassurances. And, unsurprisingly, she wants to meet Orion—the man she's paying to protect her daughter. She's insistent on a dinner, an opportunity to size him up herself.

"Briar?" Orion's voice, steady and calm, pulls me from the cascade of messages.

I look up, tucking my phone under a pillow reflexively as if hiding it could shield me from the responsibilities it holds. "Yeah?" My voice is more tentative than I intend.

He steps into the doorway, his own phone in hand, a shadow of concern crossing his strong features. "Dean just texted me. Your mom wants to meet."

I nod, pulling the phone back out with a resigned sigh. "Yeah, she sent me a ton of texts. She's... thorough. Wants to make sure you're the right man to protect her daughter." I roll my eyes.

Orion's smile flickers, amused. "Guess I better be on my best behavior then."

"It's not just that," I continue, feeling the weight of everything starting to press in. "She's worried, and I guess, seeing you in person might help her feel like I'm in good hands."

Orion walks over and leans against the back of the couch, his presence comforting. "Makes sense. When's this dinner supposed to happen?"

I swipe through the messages, finding the one where she mentions her availability. "She's suggesting this weekend. Says it's non-negotiable." I can't help but smile at her assertiveness. It's so typically her—caring aggressively.

He nods, his gaze thoughtful. "This weekend works. We'll make it happen. I'll call Dean to iron out the details and ensure everything aligns with our... precautions."

My stomach knots slightly at the mention of precautions. It's a stark reminder of why Orion is watching over me in the first place. Jason's shadow looms over everything, even a simple dinner.

"So, we're really doing this?" I ask, needing to hear it out loud.

"We are," Orion confirms, his tone reassuring. "It'll be good, Briar. We'll manage it carefully, and maybe having your mom more involved will give her some peace of mind."

I let out a slow breath, the reality settling around me. Meeting my mom under these circumstances isn't ideal, but maybe it's necessary. "Thanks, Orion. For everything. I know this isn't exactly standard bodyguard duty."

Orion chuckles softly. "You'd be surprised. Besides, I'm here to keep you safe, Briar. Whatever that requires."

I manage a weak smile, my heart fluttering slightly at his words. There's comfort in his commitment, a strange warmth in knowing he's here, not just as a protector, but as someone who genuinely cares. However, I have to remind myself it's just his job. It's not real. He's paid to care about me.

The conversation shifts back to the present, to the need to prepare for the dinner. I think about what I'll wear, how I'll act, and what I'll say. The logistics feel overwhelming, but with Orion here, it feels just a bit more manageable.

As he steps out to make the call to Dean, I sit back on the couch, the phone still clutched in my hand. Turning it off again is tempting, but I know I can't keep the world at bay forever. Instead, I start typing out replies—to Heidi, to work, to my mother—reaffirming that I'm okay, that I'm safe.

As I type, I try my best not to open any of Jason's messages, however, I accidentally click on one.

> Jason: Answer me, you bitch.

I SNAP THE PHONE OFF, my nerves kicking into high gear. Orion watches me from across the room.

"You okay?" he asks me.

"Just Jason," I say, holding up my phone.

"Can I take a look at the messages?"

I swipe my phone back on and open up Jason's message thread. I hand it over, not looking at anything he's sent.

Orion slides next to me on the couch, reading the messages, and I can tell he's getting angry while reading.

"You okay?" I use his same question back on him.

"Yeah. I'm just going to screenshot some of these messages to myself."

I smile, for all the wrong reasons. I smile because now I'll have Orion's phone number, which is something I should not be smiling about. However it makes me happy, and a bit more secure knowing I can get a hold of him if needs be.

He makes quick work of my phone, and slides it into my hand. "Now you can reach me if you ever need me."

I suck in a breath, thinking about how badly I need him. I say a quick thank you, and close my eyes, wishing more than anything things could return to normal.

But I don't think anything will ever be the same again.

Chapter 12

Orion

I stand on the front step of the Green family's mansion, shoulders squared, my eyes scanning the lawn like I always do in a new place. Always be on guard. Always look for any threat. The late-afternoon sun casts a shine across the sprawling estate, highlighting every painstaking detail of the ornate columns and intricate ironwork. I can't deny it—I'm a little on edge. I didn't grow up with money, so this is all new to me. However, meeting your client's mother is one thing; meeting a client that you're highly attracted to's mother is another.

Briar stands by my side, her arm brushing mine briefly. The contact sends a small jolt of want through me. She offers a soft smile, like she can sense my need.

"You ready?" she asks, her voice low.

I take a breath, forcing a quick nod. "As I'll ever be."

Before she can respond, the massive double doors swing open. A tall, silver-haired man in a sharp navy suit appears, posture as impeccable as the foyer behind him. My gaze flicks over the entryway—high ceilings, a sweeping staircase with a lush red carpet, and a crystal chandelier dripping overhead. The place screams old money and refined taste.

"Hello, sweetheart," the man greets Briar, his lips curving into a wide smile. Then his eyes land on me, warm yet assessing. "You must be Orion."

I extend my hand, forcing a confident grin. "Yes, sir. Orion Locke. Pleasure to meet you."

His handshake is firm, but not confrontational. "Harold Green. Come in." He steps aside, gesturing for us to enter. My footsteps echo on the polished marble floor as we move into the grand foyer. It feels like stepping onto a movie set.

Before I can fully take in the beauty, Briar's mother appears from around the corner, gliding toward us in a sophisticated yet understated dress. Her hair is pinned back, revealing a face that's strikingly similar to Briar's. Warm green eyes crinkle at the corners when she smiles.

"You must be Orion," she says, extending a graceful hand. "I'm Minnie Green."

The moment I clasp her hand, she gives me a quick once-over, sizing me up. I try to keep my posture relaxed, remembering that I'm here to reassure this woman that her daughter is safe with me.

And she *is* fucking safe with me.

"Yes, ma'am. It's a pleasure," I say, offering my most polite tone.

Briar's mother waves off the formality. "Please, call me Mrs. Green or Minnie—whichever you prefer." She gestures for us to follow her deeper into the house. "Come along. Dinner's just about ready, but I'd love to chat in the sitting room first."

We pass through a large arched doorway into a lavish sitting room filled with antique furniture. Plush sofas in muted gold tones are arranged around a glass coffee table, and a massive fireplace occupies one wall. Oil paintings—landscapes, portraits—line the walls, each set in a gilded frame. The smell of fresh flowers mingles with the faint scent of something delicious cooking.

Briar and I take seats on one of the sofas, while Mr. and Mrs. Green settle opposite us. A maid discreetly appears, offering drinks on a silver tray. I politely decline anything alcoholic—best to keep my head clear—and Briar does the same.

"So," Mrs. Green begins, leaning forward with an air of poised curiosity. "I've been in close contact with Dean, but I'm eager to hear from you directly. How exactly are you handling this… Jason situation?"

Right to the point. I admire it.

I clear my throat softly and keep my tone calm. "As Briar's personal security, my role is to ensure she's not in harm's way. I've gone over all available information regarding her ex-boyfriend, Jason, and I'm coordinating with Dean to track any potential threats he poses. Legally, we're securing a restraining order and collecting any evidence that might help the authorities put a stop to his behavior."

Mrs. Green nods, her gaze flicking to Briar and then back to me. "And you have ways to… keep him from coming near her, if he tries?"

"Absolutely," I reply. "I run regular checks on her phone, her surroundings, and keep her in my line of sight whenever possible. We've also discussed safe house options if it comes to that. But I'm hoping we can resolve this with minimal upheaval."

Briar's father rubs his chin, studying me thoughtfully. "How serious do you believe this threat is?" His voice is quiet but resolute. I sense his protective instinct for his daughter, the same instinct I have toward her now.

"Serious enough that we're taking every precaution," I say, meeting his gaze directly, cutting the bullshit. "I don't believe Jason will stop harassing Briar on his own accord. He's proven persistent."

Mrs. Green presses her lips into a thin line. "Well, I'm just glad you're here to keep her safe. It's been a nightmare, worrying about her. She's never been very good at—" She pauses, catching Briar's eye, and corrects herself. "At reaching out for help."

Briar flushes, but I sense she appreciates her mother's concern more than she lets on. "I'm trying to be better about that, Mom," she says gently.

Mrs. Green softens. "I know, dear."

A warm tension settles over us, the weight of everything unsaid. After a moment, Mr. Green clears his throat and stands, gesturing toward another corridor. "Shall we move to the dining room? I believe dinner's ready."

We follow him down a hallway lined with more artwork and tall windows that overlook an immaculate garden. The dining room is just as grand, with a long mahogany table set with gleaming silverware and a centerpiece of fresh lilies.

Briar slips an arm through mine as we walk, casting me a sideways glance. I sense her gratitude in that small gesture. For all her bravado, I can tell she's relieved I'm here to shoulder some of the parental questioning.

We take our seats—Briar and I on one side, Mr. and Mrs. Green on the other—and a couple of staff members begin to serve a decadent meal: a creamy soup, followed by roasted vegetables, seared salmon, and fluffy rolls. Briar's eyes widen, and I can't help but smile at her reaction. She's definitely a mystery in all ways. How does a woman who has grown up with all of this wealth eat chicken nuggets for every meal?

As we start eating, the conversation meanders between safe topics—Briar's work at the zoo, the weather, casual mentions of the local sports teams—before inevitably drifting back to Jason. This time, though, Mrs. Green keeps the questions gentler, as if sensing that too much talk of him will only sour the meal.

At one point, Mr. Green addresses me directly. "You must be extremely busy, Orion. I imagine Briar's not your only case."

I pause, placing my fork down. "For the moment, she's my primary concern. Dean has assigned me to her until we can resolve this situation. I'm not taking on any additional clients for now."

Mrs. Green offers a tight smile. "And that's exactly why we hired your firm. We want someone dedicated to Briar."

"Yes, ma'am," I reply, glancing at Briar. Our gazes lock for a second. There's a flicker of warmth there—an understanding that we're both treading carefully through this new territory. Protecting her isn't just a job anymore, I think, but I can't say that aloud. Not yet.

By the time dessert arrives—an impressive chocolate mousse—the tension has eased. Laughter mingles with the soft chime of silverware against plates. Briar looks more relaxed, and I catch glimpses of the playful energy I've seen when she's with the birds at the zoo. Her mother and father both seem genuinely pleased, and if there was any initial skepticism about me, it appears to be fading.

When we finally stand to leave, Mr. Green shakes my hand with a reassuring nod. "You're doing good work, Orion. I appreciate it." His words are simple, but the sincerity is unmistakable.

Mrs. Green gives me another once-over, then leans in to press a light peck on Briar's cheek. "Take care of yourself," she says, and then, looking at me, adds, "Both of you. I trust you'll keep us in the loop?"

"Of course," I answer. "I'll keep Dean informed, and we'll update you as soon as we have more news."

She smiles, and there's relief in her eyes. "I feel better knowing you're on the case."

Briar and I exchange a look, a sense of shared accomplishment passing between us. We came, we dined, and we tackled the dreaded parental inquisition. As we step through the door, onto the front steps, I inhale deeply, the cool evening air wrapping around us.

Briar slips her arm through mine again, and we descend the steps together. My heart hammers in my chest, but for all the right reasons now. I can't help thinking that maybe we're one step closer to resolving all of this.

Chapter 13

Briar

I can't stop staring at Orion. When my mother and father were asking him about how he plans to keep me safe, all I could think about is how this alpha hero is never wavering in his protection of me. It's like I'm the most important thing in his orbit. I personally don't get it, but I feel like Orion would take a bullet for me if the situation were ever to arise.

Oh god, I hope that situation never arises.

Yet, here I am, the most important thing to Orion, and I have to keep reminding myself that I'm only a job to him. Right? This is what he's trained to do. Assess every danger. Keep me safe.

"You got any personal items of Jason's?" Orion asks me as we drive back to his place, interrupting my inner monologue.

"I have a few things back at my place. Old pictures, stuff like that."

He nods. "We're going to swing by there and get it. I want to know everything there is to know about this motherfucker."

The way he speaks makes my body shake with need. We're talking about nothing normal, and I should hate the subject, but the way his voice is low and all growly, turns me on. What would it be like to have this beast of a man pounding deep inside me?

I bet he likes control. I bet he'd be a little rough. With a gentleness too. I hate thinking about the fact that he's probably slept with hundreds of women before me. Maybe even more.

"What's going through your head over there?" he asks me as he navigates the streets to my place.

I cross my arms over my chest. "Dinner was nice, right?"

He glances at me briefly before returning his focus back on the road in front of him. "No."

"No?" I cut in.

"Let me finish," he smiles lightly, "I said, no, what were you thinking about?"

My cheeks flush. I can't tell him I was thinking about the way he'd fuck me if given the chance.

"Oh, nothing."

He pulls into the parking lot of my apartment building and parks the SUV. He turns toward me, resting his hand on my knee. "It wasn't nothing. Were you thinking about Jason?"

I laugh. "That was by far the furthest thing from my mind."

His eyes search mine, like he's searching for answers. He finally drops it, and removes his hand from my knee. "Let's get in and get out. I don't want to be here any longer than we need to."

I nod. "Right," I say, remembering why we're here.

Jason and I weren't together for very long, a few months, so it's not like I have tons of keepsakes of our time together. However, I have a few things that might be helpful.

I unlock the door to my apartment, the familiar click echoing through the dark, empty hallway. It hasn't even been that long since I've been here, but it feels like years since I last walked over this threshold. My stomach twists with a mixture of unease and nostalgia.

I glance up at Orion, who's standing behind me, quietly surveying the surroundings. He flicks on a nearby lamp, and a soft, amber glow illuminates the small living room. Everything looks exactly as I left it. Like time has stood still while I was away.

"It's weird being here. I'm sort of on edge," I say softly, my gaze traveling around the space. I can't shake the feeling that any moment, Jason might appear from behind a corner, or show up at the front door demanding answers. It's irrational, but that's my reality right now—constant fear.

"You're safe. I'm here and won't let anything happen to you," Orion replies, his voice low and reassuring. He closes the door behind us and flicks the deadbolt shut. I watch him pocket the key, his movements smooth and controlled. "We'll grab what we need and get out."

I nod, remembering why we're here. Dean and Orion both suggested I gather any old photos, notes, or gifts from Jason, in case we need evidence or a timeline. Part of me doesn't want to hold onto anything that reminds me of him, but another part knows this could help build a stronger case.

I lead Orion through the living room and down the short hallway to my bedroom. The overhead light sputters when I flip the switch, and the coziness of my bed, with its mismatched pillows and blankets, hits me in an unexpected wave of longing. This was my haven. But now, I can't ignore the tension seizing my gut as I recall how Jason used to barge in whenever he wanted, picking fights about me "ignoring" him or not being quick enough to respond to his messages. My safe space was never truly safe with him around.

"I think there's a photo in my nightstand," I say, crossing the room to rummage through the drawer. My fingertips graze against old receipts, random pens, and the occasional chapstick until they land on a small, slightly bent photograph. "Here," I add, pulling out a snapshot of Jason and me from a few months ago.

I stare at it for a moment before handing it to Orion. Jason's arm is slung around my shoulder; I'm smiling, but the grin doesn't reach my eyes. I remember that day. He'd been sweet earlier, buying me a little stuffed parrot from a gift shop, but that sweetness evaporated the moment he got jealous of a guy who asked me for directions. How many times did he switch from Jekyll to Hyde in the blink of an eye? I quickly shove the memory aside.

Orion takes the photo carefully, studying Jason's face like he's committing it to memory. I watch his brows knit together, that protective glint in his eyes intensifying. "Any more?" he asks, voice soft but firm.

I shrug, hugging myself. "I'm not sure. Maybe a couple in an old shoe box in the closet."

"Let's gather up everything, just in case," he suggests, then gently places the photo on my nightstand. It feels like such a small, innocent thing, yet it carries so much of my past—one I'm still trying to fully escape.

I sift through my closet next, pulling out boxes and rummaging through old notebooks, trinkets, and birthday cards from my mom. Orion stands near the door, arms folded, quietly observing. Every so often, I look his way, grateful for his presence and the subtle sense of safety he brings just by being here.

"You know," he says at one point, "I didn't realize how far your bird obsession actually goes. You've got all these bird plushies and pictures. Where'd that interest come from?"

I pause, a small smile tugging at my lips. "I've always loved animals, but there's something about birds—their freedom, their ability to fly anywhere they want. My dad used to take me to this aviary when I was a kid, and I'd just stand there for hours, transfixed by them. I guess it stuck."

He nods, stepping forward to help me lift a particularly heavy box, setting it on the floor with ease. "Well, it's a noble passion. You're doing good work with them."

I feel a flush of warmth at his words, surprising me with how much I crave his approval. "I don't know if it's noble. It's just… what I love to do," I murmur, brushing dust off the shoebox now perched on my knees.

"You love it enough to make it your career," he points out. "That's something."

There's genuine admiration in his tone that catches me off-guard. I swallow, focusing on flipping the lid open. "So, what about you?" I ask, trying to shift the spotlight away from my own vulnerabilities. "What got you started in… well, protecting people?"

A hint of a smile crosses his lips. "I was in law enforcement. I guess once you're used to watching your partners' backs, it's hard to get that out of your system. When I met Dean he offered me a job, and I wanted to use those skills in a way that felt meaningful—protecting people who need it."

I pause, looking up at him, my curiosity piqued. "What was it like being a cop?"

His gaze hardens for a split second, as though a shutter closes behind his eyes. "Dangerous," he answers simply. "But also eye-opening. You learn a lot about human nature, both the good and the bad." He shifts his weight, and I sense there's a lot he's not saying. "It taught me discipline, taught me to trust my instincts."

I pick up on the tension in his shoulders. "Did you… did you ever have to…?" I trail off, not sure how to finish.

"Kill people?" he says it for me, his jaw tightening. My breath catches. I hate that I'm so curious, but part of me needs to know.

"Yes." My voice is barely above a whisper.

He inhales a long, measured breath. "Yes," he says, meeting my gaze head-on. "It's something you never truly forget."

A chill snakes down my spine. I search his face, but he doesn't look away. "I'm sorry," I say, not sure what else to offer. It feels inadequate, like I'm apologizing for something that was forced upon him by circumstance.

"You don't need to be," he replies gently. "It was my job. I did what I had to do to keep people safe. Still… it changes you."

Our eyes lock for a moment, a shared understanding that life can be cruel, and choices aren't always easy. *Maybe that's why he's so protective now,* I think. He knows what real danger looks like.

I clear my throat, returning my attention to the shoebox. Inside, I find another small Polaroid—just Jason alone, leaning against a car. I pluck it out, grimacing at the memory of how that day ended in a shouting match because I took too long talking to a friend. He always found a reason to be angry. I hand it to Orion wordlessly.

He slips it into an envelope, and I turn to check if there's anything else worth taking. A second later, a faint noise pricks my ears—a crunch or a scrape from outside. My entire body goes rigid.

"Did you hear that?" I whisper, my eyes darting toward the window. It's dark out, the streetlamp casting long shadows across the pavement.

Orion immediately goes on alert. His posture straightens, and he sets the envelope down, placing a finger to his lips to signal for silence. My heart thuds painfully. I watch him cross to the light switch, flicking it off to keep us hidden from whoever might be outside. The sudden darkness in the room sends my senses into overdrive; every little sound seems amplified.

"Lock this door behind me," he whispers, nodding toward the bedroom door. "Stay put."

My voice trembles, but I manage to speak. "Be careful."

He offers a tight smile, then reaches behind his back. To my shock, he pulls a gun from under his jacket. The faint metallic gleam catches the dim light coming from the hallway. My stomach drops. Of course he's armed. He's my bodyguard, I remind myself, but seeing the weapon in his hands drives home the seriousness of the situation.

Orion edges into the hallway, moving silently. I peer around the doorway, heart hammering. "Lock the door," he repeats, motioning with his hand. Reluctantly, I close the door and twist the flimsy bedroom lock with a click. It feels woefully inadequate to keep out any real threat, but it's all I have.

Adrenaline surges through me as I listen for sounds of struggle or confrontation. My ears strain, picking up only the pounding of my own heart. I inch closer to the window, careful not to expose myself, and peek outside. The yard is dark, illuminated only by the glow of a distant streetlight. A silhouette flickers at the brink of my vision. I yank my head back, pulse skyrocketing. Is that Jason? My entire body trembles.

Seconds tick by like hours. I hear the distant sound of Orion's footsteps, a creak of the back door. A hush falls, broken only by a muffled rustling outside. My imagination runs wild. Could it be a raccoon? A neighbor out late? Or is it Jason, lurking, waiting for the chance to catch me alone?

The door to my bedroom rattles softly. I nearly jump out of my skin until I realize it's Orion. I scramble to unlock it. He steps inside, still holding the gun at his side. He's breathing a bit heavier, but he looks composed.

"I checked the perimeter," he says quietly, eyes flicking around the room to be sure we're still secure. "No sign of anyone. Might've been a stray cat or an animal rummaging around."

I let out a long, shaky exhale, relief washing over me in a dizzying wave. "God, I'm paranoid," I mutter, though a part of me isn't sure if it really was an animal or if he's just trying to spare me the worry.

Orion lifts a hand, gently resting it on my shoulder. "You're not paranoid. You've got every reason to be uneasy. But I'm here, and I'm not going to let anything happen to you."

I look up, my gaze snagging on the gun in his hand. Swallowing hard, I nod. "Thank you."

He slips the weapon back into its holster, hidden beneath his jacket. His presence calms me in a way I can't quite explain, like an anchor in a storm. Finally, he looks around the room, exhaling slowly. "Let's finish up here. The sooner we're out, the better."

I agree. We gather the last few items—letters, random scribblings Jason once left in my mailbox. Each piece feels like a fragment of a nightmare I desperately want to forget, but I remind myself it's important to have this evidence. The legal system thrives on proof, after all.

When we're done, Orion carefully packs the items into a small envelope. I linger by the bedroom window, still peering through the narrow gap in the curtains. The parking lot remains empty, the shadows still. My heart rate finally starts to settle, though an unsettling residue of fear clings to me like a stubborn stain.

"Let's go," Orion says, his tone gentle but firm. "We've got what we need."

I nod and follow him out, switching off the lights as we move through the apartment. Each step away from this place feels like a step away from the ghosts of my past, from the suffocating grip Jason once held on my life.

We pause at the front door. Orion checks the lock, then double-checks it. I appreciate the thoroughness, the way he leaves no detail to chance. As we step into the cool night air, I chance a glance back at the apartment. The windows stare back at me like vacant eyes, revealing nothing but darkness inside. I can almost picture Jason's face in them, but I push the image away.

Orion nudges me softly, offering a reassuring smile. "You okay?"

I inhale, then exhale slowly. "Yeah," I say, surprising myself with how steady I sound. "I'm okay."

He presses a hand to my lower back, guiding me toward the SUV. We climb inside, and as he starts the engine, I find myself whispering a silent goodbye to the life I had here. Maybe I'm running away, or maybe I'm finally moving on. Either way, it's progress, and with Orion at my side, I feel like I might just make it out of this mess in one piece.

Chapter 14

Orion

As I lead Briar to the SUV in the lot, I spot something on her car in the lot. I put her into the SUV. "Lock the door," I tell her.

"What? Where are you going?"

I place a reassuring hand on her shoulder as she sits in the SUV. "I just want to check a few things," I tell her, hoping she doesn't see the obvious note on her car too.

She nods, and I shut the door. She stares at me, and I tap on the window.

"Lock up," I tell her once again.

She locks the doors, and I head off in the direction of her vehicle in the lot. I pull the wiper back and clutch the small scrap of paper. I stare at the note, and in sloppy handwriting is scrawled:

• • •

You think he can save you?

THERE'S NO SIGNATURE, but we don't need one. Everything about this screams Jason. The clipped, threatening tone, the sense of being watched. He knows I'm here, and he wants Briar to know it.

Motherfucker. Part of me wants to hurl a curse into the darkness. Instead, I clamp my jaw shut and breathe. I need to tell Briar about the note.

Not now, I decide, slipping the note into my jacket pocket. Later, when she's calmer. She's in enough distress as it is. We have time to strategize. Let her rest for now.

By the time I climb into the SUV, Briar turns to face me. "Everything all right?" she asks, voice low, eyes darting to me.

I force a reassuring smile. "Just needed to double-check a few things. Thought I saw something but it was probably my imagination. Let's get out of here."

She studies me, uncertainty lining her features. But after a moment, she nods, and we drive off, the streetlights flashing over us in a rhythmic pattern. All the while, my mind hums with the note in my pocket. *You think he can save you?*

We reach my place without incident. The tension in my chest starts to loosen once we're inside. I flick on the living room light, illuminating the space. Briar sets her purse on the coffee table, her shoulders slumping from exhaustion. She looks so worn down. I want to wrap my arms around her, shield her from all of this. But that's not exactly in the standard job description, is it?

Yet this is more than a job now. I can't keep lying to myself about it. Ever since the first time I saw her, something has twisted inside me—a fierce need to protect, yes, but also the recognition that I like her, a lot more than I should.

"Jeb put to bed," Jeb screeches from his cage. "Jeb *neeeeeds* sleep."

Briar, ever so patiently, heads off toward the bird's cage to deal with him. She takes him out of the cage for a few minutes and then takes him back to her room to put him to sleep.

"How about some tea?" I offer once she's back, trying to ease her into a calmer headspace.

She nods absently, following me into the kitchen. "Yeah. Tea. That'd be nice."

As I fill the kettle, she leans against the counter, arms crossed. "What did you see out there, really?" She doesn't even look at me, just at the floor. "You keep getting that look. The one that says you're worried."

I hesitate, feeling the weight of the note in my pocket. I should tell her. But her voice is already trembling with the question, and she's had enough fear for one night. "Probably just a trick of the light," I say carefully, turning to meet her gaze. "But I checked it out anyway. We're safe here, Briar."

Her lips part, and for a moment, she looks like she wants to argue. Then she exhales, dropping her gaze. "Okay," she says softly, though her eyes remain clouded with doubt.

I power through the moment, busying myself with the kettle. The stove's blue flame flickers, casting faint shadows on the walls. Briar hovers by the fridge, hand resting lightly on the handle. She doesn't open it, though, just stands there, lost in thought. The silence weighs heavy. So much has happened in the span of just a couple hours—fear, memories, that note I haven't shown her. And the adrenaline from it all swirls inside me, mixing with something else. Something that stirs whenever I look at her.

I shut the stove off once the kettle whistles and pour steaming water into two mugs, dropping in tea bags. When I turn, she's watching me with an expression that's equal parts confusion and longing. My heart speeds up as I cross the few steps between us. "Here," I say, handing her a mug.

"Thanks," she whispers, the ceramic warm in her hands. She takes a tentative sip, her eyes drifting shut at the heat. "I'm sorry for being so jumpy. I know this is your job, and I keep—"

"Hey," I interject, setting my own mug aside. My free hand lifts to brush a stray hair from her forehead. "You don't need to apologize for being scared. You've been through a lot."

She glances up at me. For a moment, I see the vulnerability in her eyes, that raw place where Jason's caused so much pain. The protective part of me roars to the surface, wanting to fix it all. But there's also an undeniable attraction pulling me in, a gravitational force I can't deny. And judging by the way she's looking at me, she feels it too.

I can't help myself. I lean in, letting my forehead touch hers lightly. Her breath hitches, and I feel the warmth of it against my lips. "We'll figure this out," I murmur. "One step at a time."

Her mug trembles slightly in her grasp. She sets it on the counter with a soft clink of ceramic against stone. "I know," she manages, voice low. Then she closes the distance between us, standing on her tiptoes. Her lips brush mine, gentle at first—like she's testing the waters.

Heat flares in my chest. Cupping the back of her neck, I let the kiss deepen, the taste of mint tea mingling with a sweetness that is entirely Briar. She sighs into my mouth, and I feel her body relax against me, like she's letting go of the tension that's been piling up for days, maybe weeks.

I press her back against the counter, my hand braced on the surface beside her. She grips the fabric of my shirt, pulling me closer, and a jolt of electricity courses through me. There's something raw and urgent in the way she clings to me, as if needing this contact to prove she's alive and safe.

Her fingers slide up to my shoulders, then curl around the back of my neck, drawing me down. A low sound escapes my throat—a mix of hunger and relief. With every brush of our lips, every shift of our bodies, the tension between us swells, and I'm finding it harder and harder to hold back. Her breathy little gasps spur me on, and I move my hand to her waist, anchoring her against me.

Time blurs. The worries of the night—the suspicious figure, that damned note—fade to the outer limit. Right now, the only thing that exists is her warmth, her scent, the flutter of her pulse beneath my fingertips. She arches into me, and I thread my fingers into her hair, reveling in the softness.

"Orion," she murmurs, my name catching in her throat. It's a plea and a question all at once.

I break the kiss, just enough to catch my breath. My forehead dips to hers, my own breathing ragged. In the silence, I can hear the steady tick of the kitchen clock, the hum of the fridge. "Is this okay?" I ask, my voice thick, my thumb gently stroking the curve of her jaw.

Her eyes flick open, darkened with emotion I can't quite name. Fear is still there, but so is need, and something that feels a lot like trust. She nods, swallowing hard. "Yes," she whispers. "I want this."

A surge of relief and desire courses through me, and I capture her lips again, this time more insistent. She responds with equal fervor, her hands sliding under my jacket, pressing against my shoulder blades. I feel the steady pound of her heart through the thin layers of clothing between us.

I lift her onto the counter, and she lets out a little gasp, her legs instinctively wrapping around my waist. The position sends a flare of heat right to my core, and I tighten my grip on her hips. She clings to me, her mouth parting, inviting me in deeper.

It's a rush—an intoxicating blend of passion and the unspoken promise of safety. Each soft moan from her lips, each little whisper of my name, urges me forward, and I'm consumed by the need to protect her, to shelter her from everything that threatens her. But I also want to claim this moment, to indulge in the spark that's been growing between us from the start.

Her fingers twine in my hair, drawing a low groan from my chest. My own hands roam her sides, feeling the warmth of her body through her dress. Every point of contact feels supercharged, and we lose ourselves in the press of lips and the glide of hands.

Eventually, we pull apart, panting. Our foreheads rest against each other again, and I can't help the grin that tugs at my lips. She mirrors it, though her cheeks are flushed. The tension in her eyes is gone, replaced by something softer, something hopeful.

"Wow," she whispers, laughing a little at how breathless she sounds.

I slide a hand up to gently cup her cheek, brushing my thumb across her flushed skin. "You okay?" I ask. It's become my standard question these days, but in this moment, it carries a deeper meaning.

She nods, leaning into my touch. "Better than okay."

For a few heartbeats, we stay like that, just breathing each other in, letting the kitchen's quiet hold us. A pang of reality creeps back in. Jason. The note. But I swallow it down, not wanting to ruin this fragile moment of peace.

I cradle her face with both hands, my voice gentle. "We'll deal with everything else tomorrow, all right?"

She tilts her head, her eyes drifting to my lips before returning to meet my gaze. "Yeah. Tomorrow." A flicker of shadows crosses her features, as if she senses I'm keeping something from her. But instead of pushing, she lets it go, and I silently thank her for that mercy.

I lower her from the counter, holding her steady until she's on her feet. The air between us is still charged, every nerve ending in my body vibrating with the memory of her touch.

"Stay here," I tell her, removing the gun from its holster so I can lock it away. I remove my jacket before returning to Briar in the kitchen.

I scoop her into my arms, carrying her to my bedroom at the end of the hallway. Tomorrow we can worry about everything. But for tonight... *she's all mine.*

The way Briar's staring at me should be illegal. It's pure sin and frustration. I don't even think about it as I scoop her into my arms.

A roar erupts from my throat. "I can't stop thinking about being inside you," I groan out.

I set her down, her feet landing firmly on the hardwood.

She blinks up at me. "Wait."

I halt, my eyes meeting hers. "What's wrong?" My heart's pounding inside my chest, hoping she doesn't put a stop to this whole damn thing.

"Do you do this often?"

"Do what? Sex?"

She nibbles on her bottom lip. "Yes, with all the women you protect. Is this what you do?"

I step back, my eyes locking with hers as I tell her, "No. I never cross this line. You ask me if I have sex often, and the simple answer is yes… a lot. But I haven't in a while, because no woman's held my interest in a long time, but you… I'm so damn interested. And I've never crossed this line. Fuck, I shouldn't even be crossing this line now, but I can't not kiss you again." I lean in, capturing her lips with mine. Our kiss is explosive at first, and my hands trace over the soft skin of her face. I inch closer, her eager body pushing against mine.

A soft moan escapes her lips, and I swallow it down, claiming it. *Claiming her.*

My body grows needy, wanting more of this soft woman and her feminine curves. She drives me insane. Makes me go primal with one flick of her eyes at me.

"More," she whispers against my skin and I roam my hands over her hips, tugging her body closer to mine. The feel of her against me makes me see stars.

I want this woman in the worst way.

Together we move in tandem to the bed, falling together, our limbs tangling together as I deepen the kiss.

I press my hard dick into her center, upset that we're still wearing way too many damn clothes. "Off," I tell her, tugging at the hem of her dress.

She lifts a little and I help her get the dress off, flinging it onto the other side of the room. I toss off my shirt as well, adding it to the pile.

"Wow," she whispers as her eyes take me in. "I've never seen so many muscles up close. And your tattoos." She traces her fingers over the intricate tribal design on my left pec. She pushes up further, her mouth connecting to the skin and I suck in a deep breath of air.

"Your lips on me feel so damn good," I hiss out.

She blinks up at me. "You're so gorgeous," she whispers, and I plunge my hand into her hair, fixing her gaze up to meet mine.

"No, you're gorgeous. You're fucking beautiful. Fuck, you look so good in my bed. Like you belong here." I tug her hair slightly, pulling her closer toward me so I can kiss her again.

My heart ramps up as I push my tongue past her lips and into her mouth. This woman is everything.

She's ripe for me, and I lay her back, her legs opening for me as I do.

I settle above her, in between her legs as she closes her eyes. "No ma'am. Open your eyes. Watch me eat this perfect pussy." I hook my thumbs into the sides of her panties and drag them down her legs.

"Oh, Orion," she moans out as I run my tongue over the silky skin of her inner thigh.

With her pussy wet, her nipples incredibly hard, and her breathing labored, I gaze at her. Studying her. Memorizing every single rise and fall of her chest.

"You're so fucking pretty," I tell her. "Now spread these legs for me." I push her thighs apart further, getting my fill of her pussy on display for only me. I swipe my tongue through her wetness, her taste turning parts of me primal with need. "Fuck," I whisper across her heated skin.

She leans her head back, her fingers flying through my hair. "I've never…"

I pop my head up, stopping everything. "Never what? Are you a virgin?" I hold my breath for her answer.

"No, I'm not a virgin, but…" Her gaze meets mine, her green eyes shining bright. "I've never had anyone do *this* before."

Pride fills my chest at being the first man to eat this pussy out. "You've never had anyone lick your pussy before?"

She turns her head from side to side, slowly. "No, I've never had this done before. It's… really nice."

I chuckle, my chest rumbling with the sound. "Nice?"

She nods, her eyes searching mine. "Yeah."

"Nice?" I question again, my hands poised on either side of her inner thighs. "Honey, I can tell you one thing…when I'm through with you you'll be using all kinds of adjectives to describe the fucking I'm about to give you… and nice won't be one of them. Nice is a grandmother baking you cookies after school. Nice is a stroll in the park. This won't be a stroll in the park." My chest catches fire with desire as I gaze into her eyes.

"Oh," her mouth falls open, "you're turning me on."

"Woman, you ain't seen nothing yet." I push her thighs further apart and drag my tongue along the length of her pussy. I settle on the bundle of nerves, sucking her clit between my teeth as she nearly bucks off the bed.

I try to remember my fucking name as I continue eating her pussy, my mind hyperfocused on her every single move. Her every *fucking* breath.

I increase the pressure, my tongue lapping at her wetness. With her taste on my tongue, I issue a command.

"Watch me eat this pussy out. Eyes on me, sweetheart."

The noises she's making feed my hunger, driving me even more insane as I drag a finger through her sweet cunt. I push the finger deeper, her pussy tightening around me as her body shakes uncontrollably. I close my eyes, savoring her.

My heartbeat drums in my ears, a riot of passion explodes in my chest as I continue pumping my finger in and out of her cunt. I push another finger inside her, and she tightens her grip on my hair.

"Oh, Orion. Oh my god," she calls out, and I suck her clit into my mouth, flicking the nub with my tongue.

"Fuck, Briar, the way you're looking at me has me all kinds of fucked up." And it's true. *I'm fucked.*

I know I'm fucked.

This woman owns me, and I haven't even gotten my dick wet yet. And already she *fucking* owns me.

She shifts her hips and *Christ*, her pussy clamps down around my fingers.

My dick's as hard as steel as I think about fucking her. How I've thought about fucking her since I first saw her. There's a fire in her eyes as she watches me finger fuck her tight little cunt.

"You like this, huh?" I push a third finger into her, merely getting her ready for the size of my dick. It's not me being cocky. I know it's big. I know women usually shy away from the mere girth of it, but I want Briar to enjoy herself.

I want her ready.

And her pussy's fucking tight. Too tight.

She tenses slightly when I push in the third finger, and I spread her legs further apart.

"This is nothing," I tell her, glancing down at her sweet body. "Just wait until you've got my thick cock filling you up."

"Ah, Orion." Her hot little body rides my fingers, her breathing nearly out of control. "I'm so close."

Her sounds are like music to my ears as I watch her take what she wants. I use the pad of my tongue against her clit, letting her ride my face as her body unravels. She spasms. She goes wild. My fingers keep fucking, and my chest is on fire with need.

I need to fuck her.

Briar's grip on my hair tightens as the first wave of her orgasm washes over her. "Oh, Orion," she calls out. "Wow, Orion."

When the last of her orgasm tremors through her body, I lift up, unbuttoning my jeans. I kick my jeans and boxer-briefs off my body, fisting my dick in my hands.

"The taste of your cunt has me rock-*fucking*-hard."

She glances down at my dick in my hand and sucks in an audible breath. The look on her face has me smiling, pulling me in deeper.

LOGAN CHANCE

Fuck this woman is gonna be the death of me.

Chapter 15

Briar

Oh, wow. Like double wow. Like I don't know what else to say, or think but...wow.

The man's dick needs its own zip code. "There's no way that thing is going to fit inside me," I tell him, completely serious.

He smiles, and the sight of him smiling nearly takes my breath away.

He's gorgeous. He's beyond that. Like a lethal combination of sex and sin all rolled into this unbelievably muscle-packed package.

My whole body tingles with need as he strokes his dick with one hand. The head of it looks angry, all purple and veiny, and monstrous. Completely monstrous.

"It'll definitely fit." He moves closer, his eyes completely on fire as he stares at me.

I feel completely self conscious as his eyes rake over me. I try to cover my breasts, but he stops me by grabbing my wrists.

"Don't you fucking dare cover up. I want to see every part of you." He strokes his dick once more, moving closer. "Let me grab a condom for this thing, and then I want your legs wrapped around me all night long." He reaches for the drawer in the night table by the bed. He slides it open, and sits back up in a rush once he's grabbed a condom out. He rips it open with his teeth, depositing the wrapper along the floor.

I watch with eager eyes as he masterfully slides the condom down the length of him. I can't believe it even fits. "Orion," I whisper as he positions himself between my legs.

His gaze meets mine. "Yeah?"

"You'll go slow at first?"

He moves to where he's lying flat on his back, his dick ready and waiting. "Hop on and you can control how fast you want to ride me."

I rake my bottom lip between my teeth as I straddle him, placing my palms flat on his chest as I sink down over his dick, my heartbeat out of control.

"Oh fuck, that's it."

I slowly glide down over him, letting him fill me up completely. "Wow," I whisper, because obviously I don't know any other words.

He's bigger than anyone I've ever been with. Much bigger than Jason. Jason never cared if I liked sex or not. It was all about him, however, gazing into Orion's eyes right now... I can tell he cares.

His hands roam over my body, making my breath hitch with every touch. "Fuck, your pussy's so perfect."

I feel like telling him no part of my body is perfect, but he appears so earnest in his words. Like he's not just saying it to hear himself speak. It's like he believes what he's saying.

As if he senses my disbelief.

He sits up, cupping my cheeks with both hands, resting his forehead against mine, making his dick push in even deeper. "Did I say something wrong?"

I shake my head slightly, as much as I can with his hold on me. "No, I just…" I don't know how to form my thought into words. "I just wouldn't use the word perfect to describe anything about me."

He grips onto me tighter. "I wish you could see yourself the way I see you. For one fucking second I wish you could feel what I'm feeling when I look at you." I suck in a breath. "Because if you could, you'd know you fit my fucking cock like a glove, and that shit's perfect." He thrusts his hips upward, his dick hitting deep inside me. "You're fucking perfect, and I've never said that shit to another woman ever."

I gaze into his eyes as he wraps a hand around my throat, his finger on my pulse point. He licks his lips as I grind against him. "Never?"

"No. Never. And… I've never given a woman control in the bedroom. Normally I take control. Normally I'd fuck you so hard you'd be screaming, clawing, and begging for more."

I push off him. His face drops, like he's unsure of what I'm doing. His vulnerability is a complete turn on, but you know what turns me on more… "Show me," I say.

"You serious?" His eyebrows shoot up. He's so good-looking it should be illegal.

"Dead serious." Maybe I don't know what I'm asking for, but the way he's staring at me makes my body ignite with a need so raw. So overwhelming. So out of this world.

"I'm going to make you come like you never have before."

"I believe you." I do believe him. And what's even crazier is I trust this man. I don't know if it's because he's my bodyguard, tasked with keeping me safe, but everything about this bear of a man has me trusting him completely.

He plunges his hands into my hair, his eyes locking on mine before he leans in, kissing me. His tongue strokes hard into my mouth and my body spasms. "I'm not going to be gentle with you, Briar. Last chance to stop me."

"I don't want to stop you." I feel brave. I want this man everywhere. "I want you to ravage me."

"I'm about to do a lot more than that." He attacks my mouth once more, his tongue plunging into my mouth as his grip on my hair tightens.

This man.

Shaking, vibrating, I call out his name as he lowers me beneath him. His hands roam my body, his fingers digging into my flesh. My back bows as he continues licking a path across my heated skin.

He braces himself on one hand resting next to my head, as he pushes his way between my legs, his strong hand fisting his dick. "You want this, huh?"

I nod, and he plunges into me, his dick claiming me all at once. He snakes an arm under my back, lifting me off the bed so he can push me further up near the headboard. He gets a better angle, and pulls his dick nearly all the way out and then slams back into me.

My legs wrap around his waist as he's up again, tossing me once more as his tongue drags along my shoulder. His teeth nibble a path across my collarbone as he slams into me harder, my back bowing off the bed, my head dizzy.

His grip is tight, his force is hard. He's completely dominating me, his hands roaming all over me. His mouth closes over my breast, his tongue flicking my nipple. I hold him close, my legs squeezing together to keep him in place. It's raw. It's possessive the way he works me like he's got all the passwords to my pleasure.

He's so gorgeous as he keeps fucking me, his body pressed against mine completely. The pure weight of him could practically crush me beneath him, but I love it. I love the weight of him. I love the feel of him.

He picks me up again, changing our position to where I'm sitting on his lap again. He's sitting too, his hands gripping my ass as he fucks me endlessly. Our mouths are mere centimeters apart and we breathe each other's air.

I'm grasping at him, so needy for more.

He's overpowering. He's massive. I feel him… *everywhere*. His hands are all over me. His mouth following closely behind. My throat's on fire from screaming so dang much, and this man is completely owning me. Every part of me.

"Orion," I call out as something I've never felt before takes over my body. "What's happening?" I ask him, my body vibrating and shaking uncontrollably.

"What's happening is that you're coming completely undone for me, beautiful woman." He doesn't slow, only speeds up. His finger pushes against my clit. The air sizzles between us, and he moves his finger down, pushing it inside me.

My eyes widen, chest pounding. "What are you doing?"

"I want you spread thin," he says, pushing his dick and finger deeper into me. His thumb presses against my clit harder, and my body detonates.

I squeeze my eyes shut, my mouth falling open as I call out, "Oh, god, I'm coming."

His finger curls inside me, hitting my G-spot as his thumb keeps playing with my clit. "That's it. Give me that orgasm. I want it all over my hand. All over my cock." He keeps pushing with everything he's got. "Fuck me. Ride this cock."

My orgasm is relentless as wave after wave crashes over me. "Oh, Orion," I scream, my voice throaty and hoarse.

"Had enough?" he asks as my body calms slightly. His smirk is the last thing I see before he pulls out of me, flipping me over to where I'm flat on my stomach on the bed.

I couldn't even push up on my arms if I wanted to. My arms are weak. My whole body is spent. But that doesn't stop Orion from propping up my hips with a pillow, and slamming back into me.

"I like having you at my complete mercy."

And boy, does he have me there.

Chapter 16

Orion

I can't get enough of this woman. She's sexy, smart, and oh so fucking hot. The pure trifecta of a woman.

I don't do this. I wasn't lying when I told her I never give control over to a woman. I also wasn't lying when I told her she's perfect. However, she thinks I was only calling her pussy perfect, but let's be real here. *She's fucking perfect.*

And I've never felt that way about a woman… ever.

It's almost scary, but I don't want to think about things happening that have never happened to me before.

Not when I'm balls deep in this beautiful vixen and she's taking my cock nice and deep inside her beautiful pussy.

I dig my fingers into the hot flesh of her hips as I pound away inside her. "You handle me so well," I tell her. "*So fucking good.*"

I plunge my hand into her brown hair, tugging and scraping along her scalp as I pull her back so I can kiss her.

I kiss the fuck out of her, my tongue exploring every inch of her mouth. I keep pumping my cock into her sweet pussy as I wrap one hand around to fondle her tits. She's got great tits, and I love the way I can get a handful. I squeeze and play with each one, while my dick dives deeper.

This woman's pussy is heaven. Pure fucking heaven.

"Briar," I grit out, my cock so close to exploding it's insane. "Next time I fuck you there'll be no condom. Please put me out of my misery and tell me you're on the fucking pill."

"I'm on the pill," she calls out breathlessly. "I'm on birth control."

Halle-fucking-lujah.

I pull out of her quickly, removing the condom from my dick, and enter her wet cunt in a punishing stroke.

"Fuck," I groan out. "That's another thing I never do…"

"What?"

"I've never fucked bareback before."

She peeks at me from over her shoulder, her eyes burning into mine. "Really?"

I pull her back once again by her hair, my mouth so close to hers. I breathe against her. "Yes, why is it so hard to believe that this is different?" It's all so different with her. Every sensation feels different with her.

I don't know what's happening to me, but it's not something I've ever felt before.

And then she says the magic words, words I've never heard uttered from another woman before. "Come inside me."

"Yes." I close my eyes as I sloppily kiss her, our mouths not staying connected from the brutal pace of our fucking. "Yes," I groan out once more, my balls tightening with my need. *I'm so fucking close.*

I'm so fucking hungry for her.

I move my hand from her tits to her clit, and her pussy squeezes my cock tighter. I bet I could get her off once more before I shoot my load deep inside her.

Her taste on my lips, I leave her mouth, sinking my teeth into the side of her neck and gently bite her. I want to mark this woman up. I want the world to know she's *mine*.

My heart's nearly beating out of my chest, my mind focused on getting her off, I rub her clit like the fucker owes me money.

"Oh my god, Orion. Fuck, what are you doing to me?" She's coming. I can tell by the way her pussy grips my cock. It feels fucking out of this world, and I drag my tongue down her back.

"Same thing you're doing to me, Briar." My body goes off like a ticking time bomb, my orgasm shaking me to the core. It takes me a full minute to recover.

She flips over, her eyes on me as I get off the bed. "That was…" her words fail her, and I smile.

"I know, it was that for me as well." I head into the en suite bathroom to grab a washcloth to clean her up.

I've never knotted before. I've never had anything like that ever happen to me before, but then again, I've never fucked a woman like Briar before.

I SIT AT MY DESK, the clutter of papers spread out in front of me a reminder of just how tangled this whole situation has become. My phone is wedged between my ear and shoulder as I rifle through the documents we collected from Briar's apartment. There are receipts, notes with half-scribbled phone numbers, a couple of old photographs—but nothing that screams, I'm working with accomplices to ruin Briar's life.

"Tell me something, Orion," Dean's voice crackles in my ear. "Any chance Jason's part of a bigger scheme? Because he's not the type to be working alone. I mean, if he's hitting you guys with these threats and taunts, you'd expect a pattern, maybe an enforcer or some muscle behind him, but I can't find a damn thing that indicates he's got partners."

I shift a stack of papers aside. My office is nothing special—bare walls, a metal filing cabinet in the corner, and a single desk lamp offering a dull glow. Normally it's my sanctuary, but right now, it feels claustrophobic. "I've been combing through every shred of evidence," I say, resting my forearm on the desk. "Nothing suggests he's working with a team. I get that you think he might be, but so far, he's just a lone creep with a grudge."

Dean sighs, a heavy sound that buzzes through the speaker. "But why, Orion? Why go to these lengths? The guy's not an idiot—he knows if he keeps pushing, we'll eventually find a way to bury him. So there's got to be a motive beyond just wanting Briar back."

I flip open a manila folder. "Could it be he's after her parents' money? That's the only angle that keeps coming to mind."

"Likely," Dean agrees, "but according to our checks, he's not drowning in gambling debts or anything that would suggest an immediate need for cash."

I slump in my chair, pinching the bridge of my nose. "So if it's not gambling or a big con, what is it? Revenge? Obsession? I wish I had answers."

"Me too." There's a pause on Dean's end, and I can practically see him running a hand over his stubbled jaw. "I'll keep digging. You hang tight and keep an eye on Briar. The moment we find anything concrete, we'll move."

"Understood," I murmur, eyes lingering on a photo of Jason and Briar before I quickly set it aside. "Thanks, Dean."

We exchange quick goodbyes, and I tap the phone's screen to end the call. The hum of my desk lamp suddenly feels loud in the quiet. For a moment, I just sit here, letting the tension bleed out of my shoulders. This case is a damn riddle. Jason's crossed every boundary, but we have no proof he's got anyone else helping him. No clue what his endgame is, aside from terrorizing Briar.

Pushing back from the desk, I gather the scattered papers into a neat stack. That's all I can do for now, short of pacing a hole in the floor.

When I step out of my makeshift office, I hear Briar's voice drifting from the living room, light and coaxing. "That's it, Jeb. Good boy!" There's a chirpy squeak in response, and a soft flutter of feathers. I follow the sound, rounding the corner to find Briar crouched on the floor, a small dish of treats beside her. Jeb sits perched on a portable stand, bobbing his head.

"Good job, Jeb," she says, voice brimming with excitement. "Now, can you wave?"

Jeb cocks his head, as if in thought, then lifts one foot in a tiny wave. Briar laughs and hands him a treat, and I can't help but grin at the scene. It's a far cry from the tension we've been living under.

"Looks like you two are in the middle of some serious training," I say, stepping closer. Jeb turns his head to eye me, his red tail feathers twitching.

Briar glances up, a smile tugging at her lips. "Yeah, I figured it would be good to help him settle in. He's been off his routine, poor thing."

I nod, watching as Jeb takes another treat from her hand. "He's got a real knack for these tricks. Too bad he's not a performer. Like that other bird at the zoo. The famous one."

She chuckles, standing up and dusting off her knees. "Chester? Yeah Chester's in a league of his own—most famous bird in the world. Over twelve million followers on social media. A total superstar."

"Yeah, I bet Jeb could be more famous than him," I say, crossing my arms over my chest.

She barks out a laugh. "Oh, Jeb's definitely funnier and better in every way, but the stage fright. He'll do a bunch of tricks when it's just me, but bring an audience, and he clams up." Her face softens as she scratches Jeb's head. "Not everyone's cut out for the spotlight."

I watch the bird preen under her attention. "Well, he seems content to be your little buddy. Don't think he's too broken up about not being Internet famous."

Briar gives a playful shrug. "Probably not. But I can dream, right?"

I crack a smile. "Sure. I can see you and Jeb taking the world by storm—who needs Chester?"

She laughs, nudging me with her elbow as she steps past me. "Exactly. Who needs Chester?"

"Who needs Chester?" Jeb squawks out. "Who needs Chester?"

The moment feels light, unburdened by the weight of our troubles. But it doesn't last. My mind can't help drifting back to the lingering questions about Jason—and the note hidden in my jacket pocket. I haven't found the right time to show it to Briar yet. She's calm right now, and I don't want to yank her back into fear mode. Tomorrow, I decide, once we've formulated a better plan. Or maybe I should show her now…?

Sensing my hesitation, Briar tilts her head, eyeing me. "Hey, everything okay?"

I clear my throat, forcing a half-smile. "Just thinking about the conversation I had with Dean. We're all stumped about Jason's next move."

She nods, sighing. "Great. That's just what I need to hear—nobody knows what he's up to." Her voice wavers slightly, but she musters a brave face. "Well, I guess that's our cue to stay here."

"Exactly," I say, stepping forward to rest a reassuring hand on her shoulder. Her body relaxes under my touch, and I note the soft flush creeping across her cheeks. The memory of last night comes flooding back. Just looking at her has my dick growing in my jeans.

Jeb squawks, flapping his wings and turning his back on us, as if annoyed we're no longer paying attention to him. Briar laughs, stepping back to check on him. "Sorry, bud," she coos, offering him another treat, "didn't mean to ignore you."

I watch them for a moment. Briar's gentle, nurturing spirit is in full display, and it stirs something deep inside me. Despite everything, she refuses to let Jason's threats define her life. She finds these pockets of happiness—like training Jeb—to keep herself anchored. I admire that more than I can say.

"Well," I say, dropping my arms to my sides, "I'm going to step out for a minute, take a look around the property, make sure everything's secure."

She gives a quick nod. "Okay. I'll just finish up with Jeb, then maybe we can figure out dinner."

I pause at the threshold, glancing over my shoulder. "We can do that. Let's see… we might have some leftover ingredients for macaroni and cheese," I tease, recalling her fondness for "kid food."

She scoffs, a playful glint in her eye. "Listen, mac and cheese is a delicacy. Don't knock it."

I grin, stepping into the hallway. "I'd never dare."

Before I go, I catch one last look at her—face alight with a smile that hasn't been easy to come by lately. It warms something in my chest, a reminder of why I'm doing all this, why I'm so determined to keep her safe from any threat Jason or the world can throw at us.

I linger long enough to see Jeb wave again, Briar praising him like a proud parent. Then I slip outside to check the perimeter, hoping there's nothing lurking in the shadows. Because if Jason is planning something, I need to be one step ahead. For Briar's sake, and maybe for my own.

Chapter 17

Briar

I cradle my phone between my shoulder and my ear, trying to keep my voice low so I don't disturb Orion, who's somewhere on the other side of the house. Heidi's voice crackles a bit on the line, but it's enough to make me smile. It's been too long since we've had one of our marathon chats, and the familiar warmth of her voice calms the butterflies in my stomach.

"How's work?" I ask, kicking my feet up on the sofa. Jeb squawks from his perch, and I give him a reassuring pat.

Heidi lets out a dramatic sigh. "Oh, you know, we've got new drama every other day. Marcie's been on a warpath since you've been gone. She's bossy on a normal day, but this past week? Girl, she's unstoppable."

"Yikes," I murmur, imagining Marcie stomping around the aviary in her khaki uniform, giving everyone a piece of her mind. "Guess she's worried about how everything will run without me," I joke, though there's a note of sadness in my voice. I miss being there with the birds.

"I'm sure she is," Heidi continues. "Between Chester's rising celebrity, the VIP parties, and the new hire, she's got a full plate. Speaking of the new guy… how do you feel about Heath taking that bird trainer spot you wanted?"

My stomach sinks at the reminder. "I mean, I'm happy for him, I guess. But it's irritating, you know? I've worked my butt off, and I was so close to finally snagging that position. Then suddenly, here comes Heath, in all his shining Tweed glory, swooping in and impressing Marcie with his fancy degree." I can't quite keep the bitterness out of my voice.

Heidi snorts. "Fancy degree my foot. I heard he doesn't even have one. Jenny says he's not that bird smart. He's a decent guy but nowhere near as experienced with birds as you are. Everyone knows that."

She's just saying what I'm thinking, but it still gives me a little boost of confidence. "Well, once this whole Jason thing is sorted, I'm heading back and making my case for that position. I don't care if Heath was hired already. I'm not giving up."

"Damn straight," Heidi says, her smile audible even through the phone. "I miss you, you know. We all do. The place isn't the same without you around cleaning cages and giving unauthorized bird facts to tourists."

I laugh, a genuine, light laugh that feels good after so many days of tension. "I miss it too. And you. Though maybe I don't miss the cleaning cages part as much."

"Yeah, yeah," she teases. "So, any idea when you'll be back? Please say soon. I can't handle Marcie breathing down my neck 24/7. I need my partner in crime."

My chest tightens at the thought of returning to work while Jason is still out there, lurking. "I'm not sure. Orion—my bodyguard—wants me to hold off until we have more leads on Jason. But believe me, I want to get back to normal."

Heidi falls silent for a moment, then drops her voice. "Speaking of Jason… he was at work yesterday."

A chill slides down my spine, the phone growing clammy in my hand. "What?" I whisper, my heart pounding. "Why was he there?"

"He showed up near the aviary, asking about you. Tried to sweet-talk the new guy, Heath, into giving him info. Heath said he didn't know you, that he was new, but, you know, Jason's pushy."

My stomach churns. "Was Marcie around? Did anyone call security?"

Heidi sighs. "We were about to, but he slipped out before we could. Marcie heard about it, though, and she's on high alert. Honestly, the whole place is tense. It's weird seeing him, all… I don't know, calm, but clearly out for something."

I rub my forehead, fighting off the swirl of dread and anger. "He's desperate," I say finally. "To find me, to… who knows what. But it's not going to work. I'm safe where I am, and Orion has my back."

"Orion, huh?" Heidi drawls, an obvious grin creeping into her tone. "So… that's the mysterious man protecting you?"

I feel my cheeks heat up. "He's not mysterious," I protest, which is a lie—he totally is. "He's just doing his job."

"Mmhmm," she hums, knowingly. "Briar, I can practically hear the blush in your voice. C'mon, is he at least hot?"

My blush deepens. "He's... yeah. He's good-looking. And kind. More muscles than I've ever seen before. Strong. Professional." My voice cracks on the last word, because we've already blurred that line. But I'm not quite ready to lay all my cards out for Heidi.

She cackles. "Oh, you so like him. It's obvious."

"I never said I liked him!" I exclaim, but I can't keep the flustered note from leaking out. Jeb squawks behind me, as if voicing his opinion on the matter.

"Babe, you didn't have to," Heidi says, smug. "I know that tone. I'm your best friend, remember?"

I let out a defeated sigh, half-laughing. "Fine, maybe there's something there. But it's complicated. He's literally my bodyguard, and I'm literally being stalked by my psycho ex. Not exactly the ideal scenario for romance."

Heidi clicks her tongue. "True, but life's messy sometimes. Just... keep your eyes open, okay? You deserve a little happiness. Don't let Jason's crap sabotage that."

Her words strike a chord in me. I glance around the living room—Orion's living room—where a stack of my clothes lies folded on a chair, Jeb's makeshift perch stands in a corner, and my phone charger drapes over the sofa. I realize I've been here for days now, and it's starting to feel more like home than I ever expected. Orion's presence has a way of making me feel... safe in a deeper sense than just physically protected.

"Thanks, Heidi," I manage, my voice softer. "For everything. I'll keep you posted."

"You better," she warns, then rattles off details about her own life: she's got a date with Perry tomorrow night, and she's giddy like a schoolgirl, but also nervous. We share a moment of normalcy, gossiping about men and outfits. She tells me she's going to wear that sparkly top she got last month, and I squeal in excitement for her.

Finally, we say our goodbyes, promising to update each other soon. When I hang up, I catch Jeb staring at me. He cocks his head and lets out a squawk that sounds suspiciously like laughter.

"Don't judge me," I mutter, setting my phone down. But I can't wipe the small smile off my face. Despite the fear, despite Jason's lurking, there's a glimmer of hope. And maybe it has something to do with a certain alpha protector who's turned my life upside down in the best possible way.

WE'RE HALFWAY THROUGH DINNER—SIMPLE chicken, vegetables, and rice—but it tastes better than any gourmet meal thanks to Orion's company. He sits across from me, eyes warm and focused, his fork clinking softly against the plate. It's peaceful, and for the first time in what feels like forever, I can almost pretend the world isn't spinning out of control.

But that illusion shatters the moment I mention Heidi's call. I set my fork down and fold my arms on the table. "Heidi saw Jason at work yesterday," I say, voice low and steady. My chest tightens just speaking the words out loud.

Orion's brow knits together. "At your zoo? That doesn't sound right." He leans back, reaching into the front pocket of his jeans. He pulls out a small piece of paper, unfolding it carefully. "Because I've been meaning to show you this," he says, sliding the note across the table toward me.

My pulse kicks. I recognize Jason's sloppy handwriting immediately. *You think he can save you?* The menacing scrawl sends a chill skating over my skin, like ice water down my spine.

"Where did you——?" My voice trembles, and I dart my gaze to Orion, shock and fear battling in my chest.

He exhales, rubbing the back of his neck. "Found it under your windshield wiper at the apartment. I saw someone lurking around, but by the time I got there, they were gone. My guess is, Jason wanted to scare us. He obviously knows you're not working right now and that I'm around. So why would he be at your workplace if he knows you're here with me?"

My mind whirls, and my stomach twists. "I have no idea," I whisper. All appetite for dinner flees as I stare at the note, heart pounding. "But if he thinks scaring me will work, he's not getting the reaction he wants."

Orion's expression darkens, his jaw tight. "We're going to figure this out," he says, sliding his hand over mine and giving it a firm squeeze. The contact steadies me, just enough to manage a shaky nod.

"Yeah," I say, my voice steadier than I feel. "We'll figure it out."

However, I don't feel so confident right now. In fact, I squeeze Orion's hand, wanting more contact with him.

Chapter 18

Orion

I hate the look on Briar's face. It's a mixture of fear and worry. I hate this fucker... Jason. Fucking asshole. I hate that he's making her feel this way.

I hate even more that I can't do a damn thing about stopping him. At least, not the way I want to. I'd love to come face to face with the prick and end his life once and for all.

Briar's hand rests atop mine, and I stand.

"Come here," I say, reaching my hand out so she takes it.

She slips her tiny hand in mine and stands from her seat.

"Hey," I murmur, sliding an arm around her waist. She looks up, eyes brimming with fear and uncertainty. "He won't touch you. I promise."

Her lower lip quivers. "What if—?"

"No," I cut in, more harshly than I intend, but I can't bear seeing her so scared. "I'm here. He's not getting near you." My voice gentles as I cup her cheek, my thumb brushing away the faint streak of tears. "Trust me."

She sinks into my hold, as if all the fight has slipped from her limbs, letting out a shaky exhale. My heart thuds hard in my chest when she rests her forehead against mine. I can smell the faint hint of her shampoo, feel the warmth radiating off her. Slowly, I curl my arms fully around her, pressing her closer to me.

"Come on," I whisper, guiding her away from the window. I lead her down the hallway, past pictures on the wall and the faint glow of a small lamp, until we reach my master bedroom. The overhead light is off, leaving the room bathed in soft moonlight, pouring in through the curtains. I shut the door behind us, an unspoken barrier between her and the world outside.

Briar stands there, looking small and lost in the low light, hugging herself. I step forward, my hand sliding around her waist again, pulling her flush against me. My heart pounds. I can't stop thinking about how I could possibly lose her—how Jason's threats are still lingering in the shadows. I refuse to let that happen.

"Let me keep you safe," I breathe, voice low, urgency thrumming beneath each word.

She nods, eyes glistening. "Yes," she says, as if it's the only word she can manage.

My mouth finds hers in a rush of need and relief. Her lips part in a soft gasp, and I deepen the kiss, every nerve ending igniting at once. My pulse roars in my ears, drowning out everything except the sensation of her in my arms. She responds in kind, fingers curling into my shirt, clinging to me like I'm her lifeline.

Her quiet moan fans the flames burning in my chest. I tilt her head gently, angling to explore her mouth. Her warmth, her taste—it's overwhelming. A single thought loops through my mind: *She's here, she's mine, and I'll protect her no matter what.*

When we finally break apart, our breaths ragged, I press my forehead to hers. The echoes of the kiss still tingle on my lips. I want to promise her the world, to tell her Jason's threat means nothing because I'll tear it down. But words don't feel like enough.

Instead, I ease onto the edge of the bed, tugging her with me. She settles at my side, and I stroke a hand over her hair, calming my own heartbeat as well as hers. She leans into me, turning her face toward my shoulder. We stay like that for a moment, caught in a quiet, heated bubble of comfort and desire.

"No one's taking you from me," I say at last, voice gravelly. "No one."

She buries her face in my neck, her breath warm on my skin. "I believe you," she whispers, holding on like she never intends to let go.

In the hush of the bedroom, with Briar's heart thudding against mine, I vow silently: *I won't rest until every last danger is gone.* I lean her back, until we're lying side by side on the bed, facing one another. "I'll never let anyone hurt you." I kiss her lips, letting her know exactly how I feel.

We move closer to one another, like two magnets being pushed together. My hand wraps around her, and I bring her underneath me. I keep kissing, exploring her. I start with her jawline, planting soft kisses over her skin, moving to the column of her throat and ending at her collarbone.

She feels so good beneath me. Like she belongs here. And I'd be lying if I said I'm not thinking about a future with her. That I'm not thinking about having her here always.

My cock hardens at the thought, and I press into her body, upset that we're both still fully clothed. "I need you naked and ready for me," I tell her.

She blinks up at me. "I need that too."

It's like she knows exactly what to say. Slowly, with every ounce of self control I barely have, I remove her clothing. "You're a needy little thing, aren't you?"

She moans a yes, and I remove my own clothing until I'm rested on top of her, my cock heavy and full with need. I push inside her, my heartbeat ramping up in my chest. It feels like sliding into home. Because that's what she is... *my home.*

I keep pushing inside her, letting my thick cock fill her up. She's wrapped around me, her arms squeezing tightly around my neck. Her legs are wrapped around my back, and she's moaning as I keep slamming into her.

She handles my dick like she was made for me. Like she was born to fit my body perfectly.

"Oh Orion," she calls out, and I keep fucking her. Feeling her. Needing every bit of her.

"You handle this dick like a good fucking girl. Are you my good girl?"

I press a tender kiss to her temple, feeling the softness of her skin yield beneath my lips, before letting them drift down to capture the bottom of her earlobe. I suck gently, savoring the small gasp that escapes her as she arches ever so slightly beneath me. Even in that brief sound, I can hear how her breath quivers with need, how her heart races in a way that matches my own.

"And you're going to stay my good girl, right?" I ask quietly, releasing her earlobe and leaning back just enough to see her face. Her hair is tousled across the pillows, strands brushing against her flushed cheeks. It frames those green eyes that seem to glow in the soft light filtering into the room. The gentle illumination highlights the curve of her jaw, the rise and fall of her chest against mine, and that undeniable spark dancing in her gaze.

She nods, her lips parting slightly, inviting me to drink in her warm breath. Her legs tighten around my waist, guiding me closer, guiding me deeper. My entire body hums with the sensation of her warmth and the closeness of our connection. It's like a current, an electric pulse that radiates through every nerve in my body.

"Yeah," she whispers, the word trembling on her lips as it leaves them. "Always."

The weight of that promise envelops me. I feel something shift inside my chest, a wave of warmth I've never experienced before. It spreads, circling my heart, winding around my ribs, and filling me from head to toe with a heat that is both comforting and dizzying at the same time. The sensation is so intense, so new. It has to be love—what else could make me feel like this, so fiercely, so suddenly?

I've never been one to believe in fairy tales or stories of love at first sight. But now, as I gaze into her glimmering eyes, remembering the first moment I saw her, there's a gentle conviction that tells me those old legends exist for a reason. There's something in the way her hand rests on my shoulder, how her fingertips press into my skin with a reassuring firmness, and the way she draws me closer with each heartbeat.

I don't know if I can name the exact moment it happened—maybe it was the first time our eyes locked, or the first tentative touch of her hand in mine—but I recognize that I've been falling for her since that instant. Every time she smiles, laughs, whispers my name, or touches me with a mix of tenderness and longing, my heart swells a little more.

She reaches up, running her fingers through my hair, and tilts her chin to whisper my name. The sound is sweet and intimate, like a secret only meant for us. Our movements synchronize, and the rhythm we share cements my growing realization: I want this—her, this closeness, this undeniable warmth—in every way possible. Her promise to be my good girl, and my silent promise to cherish her in return, creates a bond more powerful than I ever thought I would feel.

I lean in and brush my lips over hers in a slow, deliberate kiss, trying to convey everything I can't put into words yet. Every breath I take is filled with her scent, every thought in my mind is of her. It's overwhelming and thrilling, a beautiful kind of chaos spinning through me. A complete riot in my chest as I thrust my hips, sinking in deeper, owning her.

As her arms cling tighter and her eyes flutter shut, I hold onto her, letting the moment last. For now, I surrender to the possibility that this is, indeed, love—fast, sudden, and overwhelming. And in the swirling rush of my emotions, I realize I'm not afraid.

Her sweet pussy grips my dick as I keep pounding, pumping, away inside her. I can't get enough of her. I won't ever be able to. I move my hand between our bodies and press a finger to her clit, and she moans.

"Orion, I love when you do that." She arches her back, and sinks her teeth into my shoulder. "I'm so close," she whispers out.

I love hearing those words fall from her lips. "Are you going to come for me?"

She sinks her teeth in even deeper as she nods.

"There's nothing prettier than you coming undone for me, sweetheart." I press my fingers to her clit as I continue pumping my cock in and out of her. I glance down to where our two bodies join, mesmerized by it. "You fit. You fucking fit my cock perfectly."

She tightens her hold on me, everywhere, her arms, fingers, legs, until her body spasms around me. "I'm coming," she calls out. "Oh, I'm coming," she says again like she can't believe it.

It's a fucking sight to see. Her unraveling. Her complete and chaotic orgasm wracking her body. I watch in fascination, completely gripped by her.

"That's it, sweetheart. Come on me. Milk my cock 'cause I'm so damn close." I keep pushing, filling her up completely as my body grows closer toward the inevitable. "Oh, fuck," I groan out as I move inside her, in and out, my orgasm crashing through me, hijacking my body completely.

As I gaze into Briar's soft green eyes, I know I'm royally fucked. But only in the best way possible.

MY PHONE BUZZES on the kitchen counter, and I glance at it, heart already thudding in my chest. Dean. It's gotta be important, or he'd wait until morning.

Fuck.

"Orion," he says the moment I answer. "Good news, bad news situation. We've got the restraining order in place—just came through. But Jason's gone dark. No sightings for twenty-four hours. BRAVO Team's tracking him, but so far, nothing."

I pinch the bridge of my nose, tension tightening my shoulders. "All right. Keep me posted." I suck in a breath. "Hey, let me ask you something."

"What's up?"

I probably shouldn't be asking this, but I no longer give a fuck about decorum. Dean met his wife, Sophia on a job. "How did you know Sophia was the one?"

Dean doesn't answer right away, and I'm about to backpedal before he sighs. "I think I knew the moment I first laid eyes on her, but when I knew a hundred percent was when she had a knife to my throat, telling me she was going to kill me."

"Wow," I breathe out. "How about for her?"

"Same time. She tells me when she had that knife to my throat, telling me she wanted to end my life and I tugged her closer and told her to *do it*, she just knew."

They'd been through some shit, but in the end it had all worked out. They went undercover to take down a crime boss, and honestly, I never thought Dean was the type to fall in love. But here we are. He's married.

"Thanks," I say, ready to get off the phone before he questions me about asking.

However, I'm not quick enough. "You got it bad?"

I hang my head low, cursing myself for breaking protocol, but I'd never tell Dean that. "Just keep me updated about Jason."

"Will do."

I end the call and toss my phone onto the counter with a soft clatter. Damn it. No sign of Jason could mean he's lying low, plotting his next move. And that's worse than him skulking around, at least from where I stand.

Briar's in the other room, having just put Jeb to sleep. I find her curled up on the sofa, knees drawn to her chest, staring out the window at the dark yard beyond. She glances up as I walk in, expression weary. My chest squeezes at the sight of her like this—worn and worried, carrying a burden she never asked for.

"You okay?" I ask, settling beside her.

She exhales, hugging her knees closer. "I'm not sure. I'm tired of being stuck in this... limbo." Her voice trembles just enough that I notice.

I rest a reassuring hand on her arm. "Dean called. The restraining order's official." When she looks at me with a flicker of hope, I continue, "But Jason's vanished—hasn't been spotted for a full day. Dean's got our BRAVO Team looking for him."

She bites her lip, eyes searching my face. "So... he's still out there," she whispers, voice tight with apprehension.

I shift closer, draping an arm around her shoulders. "Briar, we're on high alert. If he tries anything, we'll know. But I need to ask—does he have anywhere else he'd go? A hiding spot, family, or friends who might help him lie low?"

She hesitates, pressing her lips together. Then a frown creases her brow. "He has a brother in Magnolia Ridge. I remember Jason mentioning him once, said he owed him a favor or something." She lowers her gaze. "I never met him, though."

I nod, tucking that information away. "Magnolia Ridge. Got it." I fish out my phone again and tap off a quick text to

Dean, relaying the new lead. As I type, Briar shifts, leaning into my side. Her warmth is a jolt of comfort in the otherwise tense atmosphere.

My thumb hovers over the screen for a second before I hit send. The message zips away to Dean, and I set the phone aside, sliding my arm more firmly around Briar. She turns her face into my shoulder, eyes squeezed shut, and I can feel the slow, uneven rise and fall of her breath.

I let my hand rest lightly against her arm, rubbing in soft circles. "Hey," I say gently, "we'll find him. And until we do, you're safe here with me."

She nods, the movement barely there. "I know. It's just... part of me wonders if I'll ever go back to normal. My job, my friends... everything's on hold because of him."

My fingers curl around hers, giving a gentle squeeze. "You will. That's a promise." The words feel heavy in my mouth, but I mean them. "We'll get him off your back one way or another."

She lifts her head, our eyes meeting. In that moment, the worry swirling in her expression tugs at something deep inside me. This isn't just a job anymore—hasn't been for a while. Protecting Briar feels personal. Too personal, maybe, but I can't help it. I care about her, more than I probably should.

I catch my breath, drawing her closer. She settles against my chest, and I wrap both arms around her, letting her rest her head under my chin. She breathes out, a slow, shaky sigh that resonates in my own chest. For a while, we just sit there like that—her heart beating a staccato rhythm against my rib cage, the hush of the night enveloping us.

My phone buzzes again, and we both tense. She leans back enough for me to reach it. Dean's text reads: Got it. Sending BRAVO to Magnolia Ridge. Keep her calm. We'll find him.

I show it to Briar, and she nods. "Thank you," she murmurs, glancing up. "For… everything."

For a beat, neither of us speaks. My gaze drifts to her lips, and I remember the taste of her kiss. It'd be so easy to get lost in that again, to shut out the rest of the world. And maybe, for a moment, that's exactly what we need—to find a little solace in each other.

I brush a hand over her hair, clearing a stray strand from her cheek. "You don't have to thank me," I whisper. "Just let me protect you."

Her eyes, luminous and filled with vulnerability, meet mine. She nods once, a simple acceptance. And with her in my arms, I'm more determined than ever to ensure Jason never gets close enough to hurt her again.

I tug her closer, so she's straddling my lap as I kiss her lips. Her mouth is soft, fuckable, and more than anything I don't ever want to stop kissing her.

This is so wrong on so many levels, but I no longer care. What's right, anyway? All I know is the feelings I have for this woman are unlike anything I've ever felt in my life. Is it love? Quite possibly, but all I know is that when this is over… *she's staying with me.*

Chapter 19

Briar

Orion's eyes are impossibly intense as they lock onto mine, as though he's silently vowing to protect me from every danger the world might throw our way. In his gaze, I catch a glimpse of an unspoken promise—something warm, steady, and maybe everlasting. The thought of what that could mean stirs a flutter in my chest. *Forever,* the word whispers in my mind. *Wouldn't that be something?* To stand with him always, to have this remarkable, infuriating, and wonderful man as my partner in every sense.

For a heartbeat, I let myself imagine what it would be like—me in a white dress, the two of us hand in hand, proclaiming our devotion in front of people we love. The flutter in my chest becomes a rush of warmth. But the moment I allow that daydream to bloom, a wave of nerves and self-doubt follows right behind, making my stomach twist. *Am I ready for that? Are we?*

My cheeks heat, and I shake my head, trying to banish the thoughts before they take root too deeply. Orion notices, of course. He always notices. He's perceptive in a way that both comforts and unnerves me. His hand, broad and strong, slips to my hip.

"What's wrong?" he whispers, voice low and a breath away from my ear. The warmth of it draws a shiver from me, even though the room is far from cold.

"Nothing," I manage, looking down at my bare toes curling against the rug. My heart's pounding so loudly I half-expect him to hear it.

He presses in closer, gently nudging me to lift my gaze back to him. "Don't lie," he murmurs, and the timbre of his voice thrums with concern. "It's like you were thinking of something that made you smile... and then it didn't. Tell me."

I try to shrug off the question, but the intensity in his eyes doesn't waver. He's unrelenting in that quiet, protective way. Suddenly, I'm overwhelmed by how much I want to tell him everything—my thoughts about marriage, about love, about forging a future where we wake up side by side every morning and go to bed in each other's arms every night.

But I'm not sure I'm ready to voice it, to lay it out there when I'm still navigating the scars of my past ordeals. My words catch in my throat, and instead of the flood of confessions that rattle inside me, I give him a small smile, hoping he won't push. "Kiss me," I whisper, voice trembling with both desire and relief. "Please?"

A flicker of emotion flashes across his face—something between longing and a silent, *always*. He answers without words, leaning in to capture my mouth in a kiss that steals the breath straight from my lungs. My eyes slide shut under the heat of it, the world narrowing to the press of his lips, the gentle scrape of his stubble, the measured weight of his hand at my waist.

He kisses me like he's on a mission, one he's been training for his entire life. There's purpose in it, the same devotion he brings to every detail of my safety, but now directed at something far more intimate—this raw need to show me I'm cherished. And I feel it in the way he angles his head, deepening the kiss, a low sound rumbling in his throat.

My hands come up of their own accord, sliding across the firm planes of his chest, curling into the fabric of his shirt. For a moment, I'm dizzy, forgetting how to breathe. The warmth of him, the steady beat of his heart, the faint scent of his cologne that lingers after a day's wear—it all merges, threading into a tapestry of desire and comfort.

When he finally eases back, just a fraction, my lips are tingling, my thoughts a muddle of *more, please*. I open my eyes to find his gaze still pinned on me, dark and full of everything we're not saying out loud. My pulse trips again.

I manage a shaky laugh, leaning my forehead against his. "You sure you weren't trained in the art of seduction somewhere along the line?"

He cracks the faintest grin, but his voice is serious when he responds. "I was trained to protect. And I will always keep you safe."

I brush my fingers along his jaw, memorizing the shape of it, the rasp of faint stubble beneath my touch. He leans into my palm, eyes drifting shut for a moment like he's savoring it.

My mind flits back to that fleeting thought of a wedding, a future, a forever. The idea of belonging to each other in every way sparks a surge of warmth, but the flutter of uncertainty returns too. I can't help but wonder if he sees the same possibilities, if he imagines a ring on my finger and a vow that ends with "I do." I'm not sure how to ask, how to make words for something so simultaneously thrilling and terrifying.

He seems to sense my internal shift because he angles his head, searching my face. "If you ever need to talk, I'm here." He strokes the back of my neck gently. "And if you just need me to kiss you breathless, I can do that too."

A shaky exhale escapes me. "I might hold you to that."

He tilts his head, trailing his mouth across my jaw in slow, feather-light passes, until I'm trembling from head to toe. *Damn, how is he so good at this?* My heart's going off like a drumline, every cell in me singing *yes, this.*

His hand shifts to splay at the small of my back, tugging me closer as I straddle his lap. "I *fucking* need you," he whispers against my lips.

I need him too. Like my life depends on it. *How does one become so needy for another person?* I've never felt this urge to let anyone consume me ever before.

And consumes me he does. His hands are everywhere, pulling, tugging, removing my clothing as his tongue surges into my mouth. We fall and rise together, our bodies melding together to become one.

At one point we're both naked, lying together on the couch as he slowly enters me. His dick is large and pushes deep, filling me up completely. It's a sensation I welcome now. I have so many emotions bursting through me. He keeps pumping his dick inside me.

"Such a good girl," he whispers close to my ear, his hand smoothing over my hair. "Such a good girl."

His words cause a warmth to spread through me. I'm his *good girl*, and he's my *naughty hero*. His fingers dig into the flesh of my ass as he continues screwing me into the cushion of the sofa.

Stars line my vision as my body builds toward the orgasm looming just out of reach. Orion presses the heel of his palm against my clit, and it causes me to go off like a rocketship, shooting straight into the sky. "Oh god," I call out as he grips tighter onto me.

"That's it. Come all over me, Briar." He keeps pumping, pushing, thrusting into me as his body tenses slightly before he's coming right along with me. He groans as he pushes one last time deep inside me. "Fuck, you're everything," he whispers before we both collapse together.

I'M IN LOVE. It's official. I love Orion, and there's not a dang thing I can do to make the feeling go away. Believe me, I've tried. Okay, maybe I haven't tried all too hard, but trust me… I know this is wrong.

I know Orion feels something for me, but I can see the war he's having with himself about sleeping with one of his clients.

We lay in bed together, the night fading into sunlight.

I'm wrapped in his strong arms as I lay my head on his chest. "Will you get fired?" I ask him.

His fingers stop drawing lazy circles on my skin. "What?"

"Fired? For sleeping with me?"

He continues tracing my skin with his fingertips. "No, I won't get fired, but this *does* complicate things."

I feel horrible. "I don't mean to complicate anything."

He holds me firmer in his grip. "You haven't complicated anything. It's my fault, but when this job is over I'm going to march into Dean's office and tell him how I feel about you."

My chest floods with warmth. "And how do you feel about me?" I whisper-ask, not really sure if I'm ready for his answer. *What if he says it's just a fling, nothing more than a few nights of bliss?* I hold my breath while waiting for him to answer.

He sits up, repositioning me so he can gaze into my eyes. "I care about you, Briar. You've completely taken over every part of my life, and I can't imagine you not being in it day in and day out."

"I can't imagine you not in my life either." I snuggle in closer as he runs his fingers up and down my back.

I'm thinking about everything that's changed in my life over the past few days. Since I met Orion. How I never want to go back to 'normal' ever again.

Chapter 20

Orion

I fan the deck of cards between my fingers, concentrating on the fluid sweep of each card as I shuffle. The repetitive motion steadies me, gives me a moment to breathe. Sometimes I find myself doing these tricks without even thinking, like second nature. I still remember the first time I mastered a double lift —I was fourteen, holed up in my room for hours, obsessed with getting it perfect. That same thrill still zings through me now, years later.

Just as I'm about to practice a new flourish, I notice Briar stepping into the living room, her hair loosely pinned back and a curious smile on her face. I pause, cards poised in mid-shuffle.

"Oh, don't stop on my account," she says, settling on the sofa. Her eyes sparkle with interest. "I'm just here for the show."

I grin, straightening. "You want a show, huh?" With an exaggerated bow, I start running through a few quick moves—riffles and cuts, the deck dancing from one hand to the other. Her laughter encourages me, and I feel my chest warm at the sight of her so relaxed. We both need a bit of levity, I remind myself. All this fear and tension can't be the only thing between us.

"Let's see a real trick," she challenges, folding her legs beneath her. "Not just fancy shuffling."

"Okay, okay," I reply, feigning a dramatic sigh. "Pick a card, any card." I fan the deck out in front of her.

"Jeb pick a card," Jeb says, swooping in out of nowhere. He flies at my hands, snatching a few cards with his beak. "Jeb's card."

"Jeb, give that back," I say, holding my hand out.

"Jeb's card."

"Can you make him give the card back?"

Briar laughs, like this is the funniest thing in the world. "Jeb, why don't you give Orion back his cards."

"No, Jeb's cards."

Briar smiles at me, shrugging her shoulder. "Well, there you have it."

I glare at the bird. "What are you going to do with that card?"

"Jeb magic."

I shake my head, shuffling the rest of the deck I still have in my hand. "Briar, and only Briar," I say, looking right at Jeb, "pick a card."

Briar laughs, plucking one from somewhere in the middle, eyes flicking to it before pressing it tight against her chest so I can't see. "All right, what now?" she asks, a playful grin tugging at her lips.

I shuffle the remaining cards with a flourish. "Just slide it back in the deck," I instruct, holding the fan open again. She does, and I lose the card in the shuffle, or so it appears. In truth, I have a control on it—years of practice with a break at a certain point in the deck.

She leans forward, watching intently as I cut and riffle, sending the cards flying in a neat arc. One final snap and I spread them on the coffee table, face down. With a showman's flair, I flip the exact card she chose.

"No way!" she gasps, eyes lighting up. "How'd you do that?"

"A magician never tells," I say, biting back a grin as I gather the deck.

I shuffle the cards once more, looking over at the bird. "Do you want to choose another card?"

Jeb bobs his head. "Jeb's card." He chooses another from my hand, and Briar helps him.

I shuffle the cards again, letting the two of them place it back in the pile. I shuffle, and then show the card to the pair of them.

She laughs, shaking her head. "I can't believe you also do this in addition to, you know, shooting bad guys and punching things."

I raise an eyebrow. "I don't just shoot bad guys and punch things," I say, feigning offense. "Sometimes I tackle them, too."

She snorts, then tilts her head, curiosity dancing in her expression. "Have you ever wanted to be a full-time magician? I mean, it seems like something you love."

My hands go still around the deck. It's a question I've asked myself plenty of times. "I do love it," I admit. "There's a rush in performing, in watching people's faces light up with wonder. Being a bodyguard is… important, though. It feels good to protect people, keep them safe. But if I had to pick? I guess… magic," I say, shrugging.

Just as the words leave my mouth, a flutter of feathers interrupts. Jeb swoops in, landing on the coffee table with a triumphant squawk. Before I can react, the little thief snatches a few cards in his beak and hops off, flapping around as though showing off his prize.

"Hey!" I exclaim, lurching forward to reclaim my deck. But Jeb squawks louder, flapping his wings out of my reach.

Briar bursts into laughter, practically doubling over. "Jeb, you scoundrel!" she manages through her giggles. "Give those back!"

"Jeb can talk," the bird insists, muffled by the cards he's holding.

I glare at him, half amused, half exasperated. "Sure, you can talk. Can you listen?"

Jeb hops onto the armrest of the sofa, dropping one card in his haste. I scramble for it, then try to lure him in with a gentle motion. "Come on, buddy. You can't just steal a magician's tools."

Briar's laughter ramps up another notch as Jeb cocks his head. "Steal a magician's tools!" he mimics, voice surprisingly clear. Then he sputters some incomprehensible squawks, like his own form of laughter, and flutters down to the coffee table again.

"Should I grab some crackers as a bribe?" Briar suggests, wiping tears from the corners of her eyes.

"Anything to get my cards back," I grumble, though I can't help but smile at the absurdity of the moment. Compared to the danger circling us outside these walls, this silly scenario feels like a gift.

Briar heads to the kitchen and returns with a little dish of seeds and nuts, holding it out for Jeb. He eyes the offering, bright curiosity in his gaze. Dropping the cards, he bobbles over for a snack, giving me just enough time to snatch them up.

I breathe a sigh of relief, checking them for damage—only a few bent corners, nothing permanent. "Troublemaker," I mutter under my breath, but there's no real heat in it.

Briar sets the dish down on the table, then looks at me with a grin that sends warmth straight to my chest. "Hey, at least he's entertaining. Maybe you could incorporate him into your act?"

I arch an eyebrow, imagining the chaos Jeb would unleash mid-performance. "I'm not sure the world is ready for that."

She smiles, her features softening. "It's nice to see you unwind, Orion. You're... different when you're doing magic. Like you're truly yourself."

My heart does a small flip at her observation. "Maybe that's the secret. Show a guy a deck of cards, and he forgets about the weight of the world for a second."

She nods thoughtfully, her gaze lingering on me just a moment longer than expected. "Well," she says quietly, "I like this side of you."

I swallow the sudden lump in my throat. For a beat, the air crackles with something unspoken, and I realize I like this side of us. Card tricks, mischievous birds, and a moment of simple joy in a life that's grown too complicated.

"Thank you," I murmur, softly gathering up the deck. "I like it too."

I'VE ALWAYS TOLD myself I wouldn't get attached—wouldn't let my personal life bleed into my work. It's a mantra I've lived by for years. Keep it professional, keep it detached. Never thought I'd meet someone like Briar who'd make me question all of that. But here I am, leaning against the kitchen counter, spinning my phone in my hand, catching my reflection in the dark screen and realizing that, for the first time, I'm thinking about changing my whole life for a woman.

What the hell am I doing? I ask myself, but the answer comes easily. Whatever it takes. Because with every day that passes, with every kiss and heated glance, Briar's found her way under my skin in a way no one else ever has.

My phone buzzes—Briar's mother. *Minnie Green.* She wants an update on Jason, of course, and I can't blame her. She's paying for my services, after all, and her daughter's safety is on the line. I let out a long breath, steadied by the realization that I don't have many answers to give her right now.

I open my contacts and tap Dean's name. The call connects on the second ring.

"Any news?" I ask, skipping the small talk.

Dean exhales on the other end. "Some, but you're not gonna like it. We haven't found Jason, but we've intercepted chatter about a possible hit on the zoo."

A spike of alarm races through me. "A hit on the zoo? That's… that's bizarre. Are you sure it's connected to Jason?"

"We're not certain," Dean admits, his tone grim. "But we have reason to believe it's tied to the Bratva, led by a guy named Yuri Chekov. Heard of him?"

"Only in passing." My free hand clenches around the edge of my desk. Yuri Chekov is no small-time threat—he's the type who'd orchestrate something big, something brutal. "But why the zoo? That doesn't make sense unless Jason's working with them, or they're using him as a pawn."

Dean's quiet for a second, then a soft click tells me he's flipping through files or emails. "We don't have a clear motive. Could be they're after city officials, donors, or something else entirely. But we can't ignore the coincidence of Jason searching for Briar at that very same place. If there's some deeper angle here, the Bratva might be pulling the strings."

My gut twists at the thought of Briar—already terrified of her stalker—now caught up in the crosshairs of a Russian mafia syndicate. "We'll tighten security," I say, forcing my voice to remain calm. "Send me any intel you have."

"Already on it," Dean replies. "Hang in there, Orion. We'll get to the bottom of this." He pauses. "How are things going there?"

I blink. "What do you mean?"

He doesn't sugarcoat shit, and I appreciate that about him. "I can tell you're serious about this one. You're not letting your feelings get in the way of the job, are you?"

"Briar is nothing more than a job to me. I don't have feelings for shit." I lie. I can't tell Dean how I'm quickly falling in love with her.

When I hang up, I realize my heart's pounding, and it's not just from the news about the Bratva. It's the reality that Briar's life has become entwined with something a hell of a lot bigger than a jealous ex-boyfriend. A part of me whispers that I should step away, let the professionals handle it. But that's not happening. Not with how deep I'm in—emotionally as well as professionally.

I read Minnie Green's text again, fingers hovering over the keys. *I'll protect your daughter, Mrs. Green*, I think. *Even if it means changing everything I thought I knew about myself.* Because Briar's worth it. And God help anyone who stands in my way.

Chapter 21

Briar

I swear my entire body goes numb. My ears ring, my throat tightens, and tears prick at the backs of my eyes. He doesn't have feelings for me? The same man who held me at night and kissed me like I was the only person in the world? Who looked at me with such intensity that I thought my heart might burst? The man who swore he'd protect me, who wrapped his arms around me and told me everything would be okay?

I step back, nearly tripping over myself. My mind replays everything that's happened between us—the stolen looks, the gentle touches, the heated moments that left me breathless. Had all of that been... fake? Just for fun?

My cheeks burn with humiliation. God, Briar, how could you be so naive? All those times I felt safe with him, letting my guard slip because I actually believed he cared. The tears I've been holding back start to blur my vision, and I turn away from the door, forcing myself not to run as I hurry down the hall. I clamp a hand over my mouth to stifle the sob that tries to escape.

Once I reach the guest room that's become my temporary haven, I throw myself onto the bed, burying my face in the pillows. Tears flow freely now, hot and furious. My chest tightens, making it hard to breathe. I feel a whirlwind of betrayal, hurt, and anger roiling inside me.

How could he do this—tell me he really liked me, then turn around and lie about it?

I force myself to sit up, wiping my face on the back of my sleeve. The swirl of thoughts in my head feels suffocating, like I'm drowning in them.

"It's okay, Jeb," I tell the only person I *can* trust.

Jeb doesn't say anything, just watches me. He knows I'm upset.

I spot the cardboard box on the nightstand—my box of mementos from my old life. I grab it, pulling it onto my lap as if searching for some sort of solace.

The box is stuffed with random keepsakes: birthday cards from my mom, ticket stubs from movies I saw with Heidi, an old keychain that used to hang from my backpack, and pictures... so many pictures. My hand lands on one of Jason, and my chest constricts with a different kind of pain.

The photo is crumpled at the edges from being shoved into a drawer for so long. In it, Jason's arm is hooked around my shoulders, and I'm smiling. Why was I smiling so big? The memory of that day stings. I can't remember if I was actually happy, or if I was just pretending for the camera.

Then I spot another photo, one of just Jason. I don't think I've ever seen this one before. I look closer, wondering when it was. He looks different here, like maybe before he ever met me.

I'm about to toss the photo aside when something in the background catches my attention. Is that the zoo parking lot behind him? I lean in, studying the details—the row of cars, the sign just out of focus. My pulse kicks up a notch. The sign looks suspiciously like the staff entrance sign for the zoo. My gaze locks on Jason's smug grin. It's at that moment I notice something else.

My mind flits back to the conversation I overhead just now. Orion was also talking about something going on at the zoo. Fear and confusion twist inside me. Jason's been so fixated on me, on forcing me to come out of hiding. Could he be planning something at the zoo? A chill crawls down my spine, remembering Heidi's warning that Jason had shown up there a few days ago. I clutch the photo tighter, a surge of anger fueling me.

In a blur, I'm on my feet, the box of mementos abandoned on the bed. If Jason is messing with my workplace—the place I love more than anything—then I need to find out. And if Orion has no real feelings for me, then what am I doing just hiding here in his house, letting him dictate my every move?

"Jeb, I have to go. You'll be safe here with Orion."

"Safe," he repeats the word back to me.

"Yes, Jeb's safe. You can't tell him where I'm going. Okay?" I stare at his little black eyes. I love this bird, and I trust him to keep my secret. "I'll be back soon."

Tear tracks still streak my face, but my anger and heartbreak propel me forward. I grab my jacket, wincing at the pang in my chest. How could Orion lie to me? The thought stabs me again, and I feel another hot wave of tears behind my eyes. But I blink them away. I don't have time to wallow in that pain. Not if Jason is planning something serious.

Without a second thought, I sling my purse over my shoulder and tiptoe toward the back door. The house is eerily quiet, and my stomach clenches at the idea that Orion might be in his office, still on the phone, telling whoever's on the other end how he's just "protecting" me. No feelings, no attachments.

It's humiliating, and it stings more than I want to admit.

Careful not to make a sound, I slip out into the night. My heart thrums with a blend of fear and determination. A part of me knows this is reckless—Jason could be waiting around any corner. But I can't stay here in this bubble, not when Orion's apparently been stringing me along with lies, and not when the zoo might be in danger.

"I'll do this on my own," I whisper to the empty driveway, scanning the shadows in case Jason's lurking. But there's nothing. The air is cold, biting my cheeks as I jog to the curb, hailing a rideshare with shaky fingers.

As I wait, my mind is a jumble of scenes: Jason's furious expression the last time I saw him, Orion's arms holding me when I was at my lowest, Heidi's voice telling me about Jason lurking at the aviary. And woven through all of it is that one searing sentence: *No, I don't have feelings for shit.*

That's what hurts the most. Because for a fleeting moment, I thought I'd found something real with Orion. Something that made me feel safe and cherished. But I was just a job to him. And if I'm just a job, then I don't owe him any explanations.

A distant set of headlights glows down the street, and a dark car pulls up to the curb. My phone buzzes in my pocket, and I don't even have to look to guess it's Orion, probably realizing I'm gone. I let it ring. Let him wonder.

I slide into the back seat of the rideshare, my fingers still clutching my phone so tightly. "Where to?" the driver asks.

I swallow, heart pounding. "Take me to the Saint Pierce Zoo," I say, voice trembling with a resolve I can barely hold onto. I'm terrified, my chest throbbing from Orion's betrayal, but I can't stay idle any longer. Not when every sign points to something big brewing at the place I love—and no matter how hurt I am, I refuse to let Jason or anyone else ruin it.

The driver spins around and I see a face I'm all too familiar with. "You," I say. I reach for the door, but it locks with what appears to be a child lock. "Let me out," I scream.

The driver turns in his seat, and the passenger door opens and Jason slides into the front seat.

Jason spins around. "You won't be needing that," he says, yanking my phone from my hands. He breaks it as the driver accelerates down the road. Jason rolls the window down, tossing my phone out and laughs as he does.

"I hate you both," I tell them, wishing there was a way I could get out of this car.

Chapter 22

Orion

It's late when I finally head down the hallway to check on Briar. She's been holed up in her bedroom for ages, and I'm convinced she's asleep by now—especially since I spent the last hour making her favorite dinner, chicken nuggets and macaroni and cheese, something I hoped would cheer her up. The comforting aroma still lingers on my clothes as I push open the door to her room.

"Briar?" I call softly, stepping inside. The bedside lamp is off, and moonlight filters through a crack in the curtains. I pause, letting my eyes adjust to the dimness. There's a weird sense of unease nibbling at the back of my mind, but I brush it off and move closer to the bed.

It's empty. The sheets are rumpled, but there's no sign of her. My heart thumps with a sudden spike of adrenaline.

"She's not here," a voice says, startling me. In the far corner, Jeb sits perched in his cage, feathers ruffled.

I swallow hard, turning to face the bird. "What do you mean she's not here? Where'd she go, Jeb?"

"Briar left," Jeb repeats, bobbing his head. "Briar cries."

A fissure of dread cracks open in my gut. "Cries? She was crying?" I cross the room in a few strides, stopping in front of the cage. "What do you mean, Jeb? What was she crying about?"

Jeb bobs again, shuffling on his perch. Then, as clear as day, he squawks, "I don't have feelings for shit."

His words send a cold jolt through my veins. Shit. That's what I said on the phone with Dean, to cover my ass, to keep things professional. She must have overheard. I take a shaky breath, cursing myself for the lie. I never wanted Briar to hear that. I hadn't meant it—not even close.

"Jeb, buddy, where did she go?" My hand's already fishing my phone from my pocket. I punch in Dean's number, my pulse hammering as each ring sounds through the speaker.

The call connects, and Dean's casual "Hello?" grates on my nerves.

"Briar's gone," I bite out. "I need her location. Now."

"Gone?" Dean echoes, but I hear the quick clack of a keyboard in the background. He's doing exactly what I asked—tracking her phone. "Any idea where she might've gone?"

I pace the bedroom, my head spinning. "None. I just found out she left from—" I glance at Jeb, who's still muttering under his breath, "—her damn bird. She must've overheard something she wasn't supposed to."

Dean exhales a near-laugh. "If this wasn't so serious, I'd laugh."

"If you laugh right now, I'm going to reach through this phone and strangle you," I snap, my patience fraying with each second Briar is gone.

More keyboard clicks. Dean's tone grows grave. "I'm getting nothing on her phone. It's either off, or destroyed."

My stomach twists. I do a quick sweep of the bedside table. Nothing. On her dresser, just a few stray papers and a brush. "It's not here," I mutter into the phone. "She must've taken it with her."

"Then there's no way to track her right now."

I drag a hand through my hair, turning back to Jeb. He's pacing inside the cage, mumbling about cries and feelings. "Okay, thanks, Dean. I'll figure something out. Keep trying. Maybe she'll power it on eventually."

Dean gives a curt acknowledgment, then hangs up, leaving me in a tense silence, save for Jeb's agitated squawks.

I tuck my phone away, returning my attention to the bird. "Jeb, talk to me. You said Briar left. Did she say anything else?" My voice shakes with urgency. *Damn it, Briar, where'd you go?*

Jeb tilts his head, repeating softly, "Briar cries… I don't have feelings for—"

I grit my teeth against the wave of guilt that surges up. She heard me say it. I slam a fist against the bedpost, frustration roiling inside me. The last thing I wanted was to hurt her, but in trying to keep things strictly professional with Dean, I ended up lying in the worst way possible.

"Jeb," I say again, forcing calm into my voice. "If you know anything else, any word she said, you gotta tell me. Please."

But the bird just shakes out his feathers, turning away. I exhale, pressing the heel of my hand against my forehead. Briar could be anywhere, and if she thinks I don't care about her… who knows what kind of danger she's running straight into?

I do another quick sweep of her room, and notice a photo lying on the floor. I quickly snatch it up, and glance at a smiling Jason looking into the camera.

Asshole.

"Where is she?" I whisper to the photo.

"I'm safe," Jeb squawks out. "Jeb safe. Briar's not."

I glance at the bird, and then study the photo once more, noticing the location. It's the zoo, but that's not odd. Jason dated a zoo worker, so she probably took this photo.

I wish I could reach into this photograph and strangle Jason's neck right here and now. She has to be at the zoo. It's the only thing I can think of.

I take one last look at the photo in my hand, my gaze snagging on something I almost missed. There, in the far corner, is a stray arm draped in… tweed? A strange, old-fashioned sort of jacket—definitely not Jason's style. My brows knit together.

"Who wears tweed these days?" I murmur to no one in particular, squinting at the grainy image.

A sudden flutter of wings makes me glance over to where Jeb stands perched in his cage. The bird cocks his head and repeats, in Briar's voice of all things, "*Here comes Heath, in all his shining tweed glory, swooping in and impressing Marcie with his fancy degree!*"

My heart stutters. *Heath Hone—He's the new trainer at the zoo.*

"Say that again?" I demand, stepping closer to Jeb, my pulse kicking into overdrive.

Jeb tilts his head, repeating word for word: "*Here comes Heath, in all his shining tweed glory…*" I don't wait for him to finish. I'm already bolting for the door, keys clenched in my fist, the photograph crumpled in my other hand.

I'm in my SUV and firing up the engine within seconds, my brain spinning. *Heath Hone. The new bird trainer. A tweed jacket. Possibly connected to Jason.* The pieces snap together, conjuring images of Jason at the zoo, Jason's weird photo, and now this detail about Heath. It has to be more than coincidence.

Once I'm on the road, I punch in Dean's number, bringing the call up through the bluetooth. My tires squeal as I swing onto the main street, adrenaline coursing through my veins.

Dean picks up on the first ring. "Orion?"

"I'm guessing she went to the zoo." My voice is tight, anxiety tugging at my chest. The last thing I want is for Briar to confront Jason—or his accomplice—alone.

"Are you heading there now?" Dean asks, the sound of rapid typing in the background.

"Yeah, can you scramble a team? I know the zoo's running some kind of bird night show on Friday nights. I've got a hunch it's Heath Hone—the new trainer. I think Jason and him know each other. I have no clue what they're planning, but it's definitely happening at the zoo."

"Shit," Dean mutters. There's a flurry of keystrokes on his end. "How the hell did we miss that?"

I shake my head, teeth clenched, even though I know he can't see me. "No idea. But if Briar's gone, I'm guessing she's heading there now. She probably figured out Heath was in on this. Or at least suspects him."

Dean curses softly. "Right. I'm getting a team ready. We'll meet you there. Orion… be careful."

"Yeah," I reply, voice strained. My heart thumps as I blow through a yellow light, pressing the accelerator. "I'm not letting anything happen to her."

I hang up, gripping the steering wheel tighter. *Hold on, Briar.* I push the gas pedal harder, weaving through late-night traffic. The photograph rests on the console next to me, the torn edges a glaring reminder of how close I came to missing that crucial hint. If Briar's at the zoo, facing down a man she suspects of being in league with Jason, she's in more danger than ever. And I won't let her face it alone.

Chapter 23

Briar

I'm crammed into the back seat, my wrists aching from the rough cords biting into my skin. Moments after they abducted me, they'd pulled over to bind my wrists together. Every bump in the road makes me lurch sideways, shoulders bashing into the door. I'd give anything for one sliver of comfort, but there's none here. Just me, a swirl of dread in my stomach, and the two men in the front seats who won't answer a single one of my questions.

Heath is driving. Heath, the new bird trainer who showed up at the zoo not long ago, wearing that ridiculous tweed jacket. *Does he even know a thing about birds?* I can just see the back of his head, slightly turned so he can keep an eye on me in the rearview. Next to him, in the passenger seat, is Jason—my ex-boyfriend turned nightmare, the man I tried so hard to escape. It's strange seeing them together, an unholy alliance I never saw coming.

My heart pounds so hard my ribs feel bruised. The engine hums underneath us, and the headlights cast fleeting shapes across the deserted highway, but it's pitch-black out here, wherever *here* is. I can't see any signs, no exit ramps, no gas stations—nothing.

"Where are we going?" My voice sounds surprisingly steady, considering my pulse is a frantic drumroll in my ears. Neither Heath nor Jason responds. They just keep whispering to each other, the low murmur of their voices drowned out by the car's rumble. I struggle against my bindings, hissing at the sting. "Hello?" I shout, louder this time. "Heath! Jason! Where are you taking me?"

Heath throws me a glance in the mirror, but he remains silent. Jason turns around in his seat, and for half a second, the moonlight glowing in through the windshield catches the cruel twist of his smile. Then he faces front again, ignoring me. I bite my lip, frustration and fear mingling in my chest.

Why did I leave? The thought replays like a broken record in my head. I picture Orion's place—safe, warm, with Jeb dozing in his cage. And Orion himself, determined and protective, a man who would have moved mountains to keep me from danger. But *he lied to me*, the bitter voice inside me reminds. *He said he didn't have feelings for me.* Only now, trapped in this car, do I realize how foolish I was to let that overshadow the real threat. Now I'm paying the price.

The car jostles as Heath maneuvers onto a gravel road. I jolt upright, my wrists chafing painfully, and blink to clear my vision. The headlights sweep across a vast emptiness: weeds, broken fences, the outline of dilapidated buildings. My stomach churns. This place looks like it's been abandoned for decades.

After what feels like hours of creeping through the darkness, the car finally comes to a stop in front of a large, decaying structure. The headlights reveal warped metal siding, graffiti scrawled across the entrance. An abandoned warehouse, from the look of it. A chill seeps through my veins as Heath cuts the engine, plunging us into a suffocating quiet.

"Out," Jason orders, turning to me with a sneer. Heath steps out first, slamming the driver's door, while Jason swings open the back door on my side. I recoil, pressing myself against the opposite seat, but there's nowhere to run. His hand snaps forward, grabbing my arm so hard I yelp in pain.

"Let me go!" I twist, thrashing, but it's no use. My arms are bound, my legs are free but useless without a clear path. He yanks me from the car with a force that almost wrenches my shoulder. My feet hit the gravel, and I struggle to regain balance, wincing at the biting chill of the night air.

Heath stands off to the side, arms crossed, a smirk tugging at his mouth. This version of him is so different from the polite, poised trainer I met at the zoo. *He was always too smooth*, I think, remembering how Marcie lapped up his credentials without questioning. Now, he radiates smug confidence, like a cat that's caught a mouse.

Jason slams the car door and keeps a grip on my arm, guiding me—no, dragging me—toward a gaping entrance at the side of the warehouse. My breath forms puffs of fog in the cold air, and my heart hammers like it might burst from my chest.

The interior of the warehouse is even darker than outside, but as we move in, I see a faint glow from a distant overhead fixture. It illuminates piles of broken pallets, scraps of metal, and dust dancing in the stale air. The smell is an acrid mix of rust, mold, and something chemical that turns my stomach.

Suddenly, more figures emerge from the shadows. My pulse spikes as I register two men speaking in hushed Russian. They're big, broad-shouldered, wearing dark coats. One of them lifts a cigarette to his lips, his eyes flicking over me with casual interest, like I'm nothing more than another piece of cargo.

And then I hear the unmistakable squawk of a parrot. My heart lodges in my throat as I spot a cage in the corner, illuminated by the flickering overhead light. Inside the cage, perched on a branch, is a yellow-naped Amazon parrot—bright green with a splash of brilliant yellow on the back of its neck. My jaw drops in shock. "Chester?" I whisper, recognizing him instantly. Chester, the star of the zoo's bird show, the one with millions of social media followers.

"What the fuck? Who the fuck is she?" one of the Russian men mutters in heavily accented English, giving a nod toward me. His cold gaze sends a shiver down my spine.

Jason steps forward, tightening his grip on my arm. "We brought her to work," he says, directing his words at the Russians. "She's the bird expert. She can take care of Chester."

"What are you planning to do with him?" I snap, fear and anger warring in my chest.

The second Russian man waves a dismissive hand, as though my question is pointless. "You will do what you're told," he says flatly. "Chester is valuable. Your job is to keep him healthy and… content. Or else."

A wave of revulsion washes over me. They've kidnapped Chester, the zoo's most famous bird, for some sinister reason. And apparently, they need someone to care for him—and I'm the perfect candidate. I shoot Heath a glare, realization dawning. *He must know nothing about birds.*

Heath's smirk deepens, and he steps closer, tapping the cage with his knuckles. Chester flutters, letting out a sharp squawk and ruffling his feathers. My heart breaks for the poor thing. He doesn't deserve this. Neither of us does.

"What do you want with the bird?" I demand, trying to keep my voice steady. My heart's pounding so loudly I can scarcely think. "You realize the whole world knows Chester? He can't just disappear."

"That's none of your concern," Jason snaps, leaning in so close I can smell the stale coffee on his breath. "All you need to worry about is keeping him happy. And yourself alive."

I swallow, tasting bile. Orion warned me about the dangers lurking around Jason, around the zoo. Guilt roars in my gut. *I should have listened. I shouldn't have let my hurt feelings cloud my judgment.* Now I'm trapped in a grimy warehouse surrounded by men who clearly have no qualms about using violence to get what they want.

One of the Russians nods toward a rickety folding chair. "Sit." The command is cold, absolute. Jason and Heath maneuver me over, forcing me to sit. My arms are still bound, and my shoulders ache from the strain.

Heath crouches in front of me, that smug expression never leaving his face. "You're going to cooperate, aren't you, Briar?" he says, voice mocking. "Because if you don't, Chester won't be the only one in a cage." He glances at Jason. "I don't know what your obsession is with this bitch. We could have easily kept the bird safe on our own. I say we just kill her."

Jason steps forward, anger radiating off him. "Shut the fuck up." He steps closer. "We need her."

Heath rolls his eyes, and the Russians laugh.

My stomach turns. I glance over at Chester, who's now eyeing me with what looks like equal parts curiosity and fear. Parrots are perceptive creatures; he must sense the tension. I take a shaky breath, trying to gather whatever courage I have left.

"If you hurt him, I'll—"

"You'll what?" Heath cuts in, chuckling darkly. "Let's be real, Briar. You're in no position to negotiate."

I can't deny that. I'm bound, outnumbered, with no idea where we even are. The harsh truth sinks in: I need to bide my time, look for any opportunity to escape or call for help. And Orion… My chest squeezes at the thought of him. Does he know I'm gone? He must. But is he even looking for me? He lied to me. The memory stings. Yet a tiny flicker of hope remains—he might still try to find me, even if his feelings weren't what I believed.

One of the Russians nods at Heath and Jason. "Find her a place to sleep. She'll stay here until we're done."

My heart lurches at the finality in his tone. *Until we're done?* That could mean days, weeks—even longer. I glance at Chester, who shifts on his perch, letting out a low, uneasy whistle.

Jason wrenches me to my feet, dragging me away from the men and into a side corridor. It's dark, the flickering overhead light barely illuminating the chipped walls and broken pipes. I trip on a loose piece of concrete, wincing as I crash into Jason's side. He doesn't even slow, just continues yanking me along.

Behind us, I hear Chester squawking again, the sound echoing through the cavernous warehouse. The Russians' laughter bounces off the walls. My heart feels like it's in a vise.

Stay calm, I remind myself, forcing each ragged breath in and out. If I'm going to survive this, I have to keep my wits about me.

"You'll stay here," Jason says, shoving me into a room with a single cot in the corner. His eyes are on fire as he stares at me. "You let that bodyguard fuck you?" He pushes forward as I slink away to the other side of the room.

"It's none of your business."

Jason keeps stalking closer. "Did he stick his cock deep inside you? Do I need to fuck him out of you?"

Tears spring behind my eyelids. "Leave me alone." I try to stand my ground, but I know I'm losing control. I'm regretting my decision to leave the safety of Orion's home.

Jason reaches out his hand to touch my face, and I jerk away. "He's not coming for you." He laughs, loud and boisterous and it sends a chill skating through my system. "Even if he does, this is the *bratva*... he'll never find you." Jason steps so close to me, I flinch.

He laughs as I do, and then *finally* backs away.

He leaves the area. A few minutes later they place Chester's cage in my room, and I smile at the parrot.

"Looks like it's me and you. We need to get out of here."

Chester nods his little green head, like he understands everything I'm saying. And I'm pretty sure he does.

Chapter 24

Orion

I stand at the head of the conference table in Dean's high-tech security office, my hands planted on the polished surface. Monitors line the walls around us, showing a flurry of social media feeds, news broadcasts, and closed-circuit cameras—each display hammering home one brutal fact: Chester is missing, and so is Briar. Three days. Three agonizingly long days since she vanished.

The silence in the room is nothing compared to the chaos online. The disappearance of the zoo's star parrot has set the internet ablaze, and theories are spinning out of control: some say Chester was stolen by animal traffickers, others blame an underground black market for exotic birds. Only a few fringe whisperings mention the Bratva, but even that's enough to make me want to punch a hole through the nearest wall.

Dean stands at my right, arms folded across his chest. A heavy frown creases his brow. Around the table are Riggs, Gunner, and Maverick—three members of our elite BRAVO team. They're all similarly grim-faced. Each man radiates the same frustration I feel, but I can tell by the glances they shoot me that they're worried. Worried that I'm inches away from coming unhinged.

"How the hell did it get to this?" I mutter, slamming my palm against the table. The wood groans in protest. "We've got the entire city's security network at our fingertips, we're scouring everything for leads, and still... nothing."

Riggs, a broad man with thick arms folded on his chest, shifts his weight. He's a sniper for the Marines, and is on a short leave. Of course he'd be here helping instead of anywhere else. Like the rest of us, this is a family. These men are like brothers. "We've got eyes on all major airports, train stations, and we're scanning the roads in and out of the city. If she was moved, there must be a paper trail or camera footage somewhere."

Dean runs a hand through his hair, frustration etched into every line on his face. "We asked our informants—everyone who's ever sniffed around the Russian Bratva. Nothing. Yuri Chekov's name keeps popping up, but no one can pin him down. We can't even confirm if he's in the country."

"And the Russians themselves?" I press, trying to keep my voice steady. Inside, I'm a live wire of tension. "None of the guys who talk for us know a damn thing?"

Gunner, seated on the far side of the table, grimaces. "They're all spooked. The Bratva isn't known for open deals. If Chekov's involved, he's keeping a tight lid on it."

I clench my fists so hard my knuckles crack. Every time I close my eyes, I see Briar's face—pale with fear, or worse, imagining what they might be doing to her right now. Then there's Chester, a damn bird who got swept into this nightmare.

"We've got to find her," I growl, pointing a finger at Dean. "We have to. I don't care what it takes."

Dean exhales slowly, stepping forward. "Orion, you know I'm doing everything I can. But we can't step outside the lines too far without proof. The authorities are on this too, but they're focusing on Chester's disappearance as a high-profile theft. They don't realize it's more than that."

Maverick, a burly man with sharp eyes, speaks up. He's ex-military and as savage as they come. There's even been talk that he's taken on a few mercenary jobs in the past. Although nobody'd be dumb enough to ever ask him. "I called in a few favors from old contacts in the K9 units, trying to see if they can run any new angles. Dead end so far."

Dead end. *Everything's a dead end*. The phrase echoes in my mind like a death sentence. I press my fingertips to my temples, trying to keep the pounding headache at bay. *Three days*. Three days she's been gone, three days I've been replaying every moment in my head—her last known location, the zoo, the note, the hunch that she'd found out about Heath. All of it swirling, fracturing into a thousand cursed puzzle pieces.

The overhead fluorescent buzz fills the silence for a moment. Then Dean's phone vibrates on the table. He checks it, grimaces, and sets it aside. "Just more social media chatter about Chester. Nothing useful."

Riggs looks at me, sympathy in his eyes. "It's not your fault, man."

I fix him with a glare that probably looks murderous. "The hell it isn't. I'm the one who said I—" My throat tightens, and I can't bring myself to say it out loud. *That I didn't have feelings for her. That she was just a job.* She heard those words, and it drove her straight into the lion's den.

I spin away, pacing toward the monitors, the tension coiled in my muscles begging for release. "I should never have lied. If I'd just told the truth… maybe she would've stayed safe."

Gunner stands, his chair scraping the floor. "None of us thought this would escalate so fast. That zoo infiltration by Heath, the note—everyone assumed we had time to maneuver."

"Yeah, well, we assumed wrong," I snap, raking a hand over my face. A rush of guilt floods me. It's not their fault, I think, forcing my voice to calm. "Sorry, Gunner. I'm just—"

He holds up a hand. "I get it, man. We all do."

My phone buzzes in my jacket pocket. Quickly, I fish it out, hoping for a miracle. The screen reads *Ranger*. My chest loosens slightly at the sight of his name. Ranger's part of the team, and always a good guy to have at your back in a crisis. I nod at Dean and walk a few steps away, pressing the phone to my ear. The men's eyes follow me.

"Ranger?" I greet in a low voice.

"Hey, buddy," he says, his tone cautious. "I got your message. You're sure you want me to handle Jeb? I don't know anything about birds except how to eat 'em."

A ghost of a smile crosses my face. "He'll be fine. Just don't let him out of your sight. He might try to snatch your playing cards or something." For a moment, I remember Jeb's antics, how Briar used to laugh whenever he showed off. My chest constricts. "I'm heading out of town, Ranger. We got a few leads from the Russian informants—nothing solid, but I can't just sit around. I'll be gone a few days, maybe more. I need someone I trust to look after Jeb until I get back. Your job just wrapped, right?"

"Yeah, Tory's safe. So, I'm back to work and ready to help," Ranger says, sincerity in his voice. "Anything you need."

"Thanks, man. I'll drop him off soon. I appreciate it."

We hang up, and I slide the phone back into my pocket. When I turn, Dean is standing there, arms still folded. He nods at me to rejoin the group. I take a measured breath, crossing back to the table.

"You heading out?" Dean asks.

I nod. "I can't sit here and wait for the Russians to slip up. We've got a few leads suggesting a possible safehouse outside the city, near the Magnolia Ridge area. Or maybe deeper into the industrial district near the port. Either way, I'm going."

Riggs frowns. "You sure you don't want backup?"

The corners of my mouth tighten. "Don't worry, I'll have a team if I need it. For now, it's just recon. I need to keep a low profile—less chance of spooking them if I'm alone."

Maverick taps a pen against the table. "Couldn't you let the local authorities handle that?"

I send him a sharp look. "You know as well as I do that local cops can't handle Bratva. By the time they get the green light, Jason and Heath might move Briar again. Or worse."

Silence falls, each of us wrestling with the grim possibilities. Dean breaks it by clearing his throat. "All right. I'll coordinate from here. I'll keep the rest of the BRAVO team on standby in case you need backup."

Gunner's expression is solemn. "Be careful, man."

My heart pounds as I give them a terse nod. "Don't worry, I'm not going in guns blazing." *Yet*, I add silently. If I find even the faintest trace of Briar, I'm not letting anything stop me from getting her back.

Dean steps forward, catching my arm. "Orion," he says, voice low. "I know you're feeling guilty, but your head has to be clear. If you rush in half-cocked—"

"I won't," I lie. The truth is, my head's a mess, and the only thing driving me forward is the image of Briar's face, her laughter, the smell of her hair when she fell asleep against my chest. It's all I can focus on. "I'll keep you posted. If something turns up here, you call me."

Dean's gaze flicks over me, reading the turmoil I can't hide. He nods. "Deal."

I head for the door, the tension in my chest coiled so tight I can barely breathe. *Three days.* The phrase echoes in my mind, a reminder of how quickly life can change, how easily everything can slip away.

As I stride down the long hallway toward the exit, the overhead lights buzz with artificial life. The hush of the building around me is unnatural, considering the storm raging in my mind. Pushing through the front doors, I step into the crisp evening air, cold enough to sting my lungs. I inhale deeply, letting the chill sharpen my focus.

Sliding behind the wheel of my SUV, I close my eyes for a moment, imagining Briar's voice, her smile. Anger simmers beneath the surface. *I won't lose you*, I vow silently, gripping the steering wheel until my knuckles ache.

Firing up the engine, I pull out of Dean's security headquarters, my headlights slicing through the darkness. First stop: my place, to pick up Jeb and hand him off to Ranger. Then... I'm on the road, chasing any faint clue that might lead me to Briar. It's not much, but it's something, and if there's even the smallest chance I can bring her back, I'll travel to the ends of the earth.

The city's skyline looms, dotted with neon signs and flickering windows. Street lamps blur by as I accelerate, my heart pounding to the same beat: *Find her, find her, find her.* If it takes everything I have, if I have to confront Yuri Chekov himself, or tear down every last warehouse in this damned state—I'll do it.

Because three days is already too long. And I swear to God, if Briar endures one more minute of terror, I'll never forgive myself.

Chapter 25

Orion

"You think Yuri Chekov could be behind this?" Ranger asks, his gaze locked on Jeb like the bird's some kind of two-headed Pegasus.

"All I know is Dean mentioned the Bratva, and Yuri's the one in charge of their presence here in Saint Pierce," I reply, lifting Jeb's cage higher so it doesn't bang against the wall.

Ranger nods, leading me further inside his place. "By the way, this is Tory," he adds, gesturing toward the beautiful, blonde-haired woman sitting on the couch. She offers me a small, shy smile, and I give her a brief nod in return.

I glance at Ranger, arching an eyebrow. "I thought your job was finished?"

He tugs at the back of his neck, his cheeks coloring in a way I've never seen before. Ranger, blushing? That's new. "Yeah…

about that. Let's just say I broke the cardinal rule about protecting an asset."

A short laugh escapes me. "Really?"

He looks at Tory with a softness in his eyes I've never witnessed. "What can I say? When you know, you know."

I nod, understanding more than I care to admit. Because right now, if there's one thing carved into my bones, it's that I can't lose Briar. She's... *everything*.

After I run through Jeb's basic routine for feeding and care, Ranger pulls me aside near the front door.

"If you really think the Russians are involved," he says, voice pitched low, "I've got a friend over at Club Greed who's connected to Yuri."

My pulse ticks up. "Yeah? Who?"

"Name's Devereaux Huxley. He owns the club."

I rub my jaw, considering. "I've heard the name. Think he has any idea where Yuri's holed up?"

Ranger shrugs. "Could be. Worth a shot."

I give him a firm pat on the shoulder, grateful for the lead. "Thanks, man." Then I shoot Tory a quick wave and head for the door.

"I'll text you Devereaux's info," Ranger calls after me.

I nod and raise a hand in acknowledgment before stepping outside, already scrolling through my phone to call Dean. *We just might be onto something.*

Saving What's Mine

I STAND OUTSIDE CLUB THROWDOWN, the brisk night air cutting through my jacket as neon lights bathe the sidewalk in violent shades of red and purple. The building itself is made of dark brick and neon signs, its entrance guarded by two bouncers who eye me warily every time I shift my weight. This is the place Devereaux Huxley mentioned, a friend of Ranger's who claims he has leads on Yuri Chekov. Apparently, Yuri's in town running his latest venture, which is half bar, half underground boxing club.

I press a hand to my side, checking to ensure my concealed holster is still secure. Dean insisted I wait before going in, demanded I get backup. *Stand down, Orion*, he said over the phone, *Don't do this alone*. Usually, I'd resist that kind of order, but after everything that's happened with Briar, I'm trying not to let my temper lead me astray. So I wait.

Asher strides up to meet me, pushing through a small group of rowdy patrons out front. He's newer to the team, but his reputation precedes him: capable, calm under pressure, and just the right amount of cautious. Dean sent him as soon as Asher's mission wrapped up early, which is good, because every hour that passes is an hour Briar remains in danger.

"Orion," Asher says, nodding in greeting. He's a bit shorter than me, but his shoulders are broad, and there's a quiet confidence in how he carries himself. "Heard you needed a partner."

"Damn right I do," I mutter, offering him a quick handshake. "Glad Dean got you here fast. Let's do this."

He glances at the neon sign overhead—Club Throwdown, flickering in a broken pattern—then he flicks his eyes back to me. "This Yuri Chekov guy. Sure he's in there?"

"That's what Huxley says," I reply, keeping my voice low. "He's got an ear to the ground. Said Yuri's in town, overseeing some new 'business interests.' If this is anything like his usual, it's illegal underground fighting."

We exchange a quick look of understanding. Then we head for the door, the bass line of pounding music already rattling the pavement. The bouncers size us up, but once I drop Yuri's name and wave a nondescript ID from Dean's security firm, they step aside. Clearly, Yuri anticipates visitors and has prepped his crew to let certain people through.

Inside, the corridor is lit by dim blue bulbs that make everything feel claustrophobic. The air reeks of stale beer, sweat, and something metallic—blood, maybe. Asher's jaw tightens, and I can see he's on high alert. I mirror his tension, scanning every face, every alcove, for trouble. But no one stops us. They just stare, some in challenge, some in fear.

We pass a makeshift boxing ring surrounded by a rowdy crowd. Two fighters slug it out in the center, bare-fisted, blood dripping onto the stained mat. Yuri's brand of entertainment is as brutal as I'd imagined. People are cheering, placing bets, ignoring the fact that one punch could knock a man unconscious.

Eventually, we push through the throng into a back hallway. A couple of Yuri's men—big, broad-shouldered guys in black suits—stand like statues outside a door. I hold up my hands, palms out. "We're here to see Yuri," I say. "He's expecting us."

They exchange a look, then one nods, opening the door. Asher and I step inside.

It's a cramped office, walls lined with file cabinets and half-filled liquor bottles. The light is mercifully brighter here, revealing a large desk strewn with papers. Behind that desk sits Yuri Chekov. He's a hulking brute; big, messy, with slicked-back hair and an air of refined arrogance. When he glances up, his eyes spark with curiosity.

"Orion Locke, I assume?" he says, accent thick but words precise. He looks at Asher, tilting his head slightly. "And friend?"

"Asher," my partner supplies, keeping his posture relaxed yet ready.

"Dean says hi," I add, stepping forward. No point beating around the bush. "I heard you're in town."

Yuri reclines in his chair, steepling his fingers. "I move where business takes me. So what can I do for you, Locke?"

I grit my teeth, reminding myself to keep it civil. "I'm looking for someone—someone who might be connected to your operation."

His face remains impassive. "I see."

"Chester, a Yellow-naped Amazon parrot, was taken from a zoo. And a woman, Briar. She was also taken." My voice trembles slightly when I say her name, and I hate that. "I've got reason to believe the Bratva is involved."

Yuri's mouth curls into a smirk. "The Bratva is a very large, very powerful network. You expect me to know about every small theft or kidnapping that happens?"

Asher steps in, crossing his arms. "We heard you might have orchestrated it. Or at least, your associates might have."

Yuri exhales slowly, as though weary. "If you're implying I had something to do with stealing a bird, I can assure you—I have better things to do. I run many clubs, many legitimate and less-legitimate businesses. But petty theft? Kidnapping a woman or… a bird? That's not my style."

"Then whose style is it?" I ask, voice low.

Yuri waves a hand dismissively. "My sons, perhaps. Vlad and Dimitri. They've always been screw-ups. I banished them from my sphere months ago. They don't know how to keep their heads down, always cooking up stupid plans. If they're involved, I wouldn't be surprised. They're desperate to prove themselves, even if it means going rogue."

My adrenaline spikes. "Where are they?"

"Wouldn't I like to know," Yuri counters, tapping a pen against the desk. He sounds genuinely exasperated. "Last I heard, they were dabbling in the black market. Anyway, they're dead to me." His dark gaze flicks between Asher and me. "You want them, be my guest. I wash my hands of them."

Asher narrows his eyes. "So you have no loyalty to your own sons?"

A rueful laugh escapes Yuri. "Loyalty is earned. They have done nothing but shame the family name. Always needing bailouts. I've grown tired of bailing them out."

I clench my fists at my sides, resisting the urge to launch across the desk. "If they have Briar, they'll kill her once they're done with whatever plan they have for Chester. Especially if it goes bad."

Yuri's brow arches. "Hmm. Sounds like something Vlad and Dimitri would do. They lack… subtlety."

Asher shoots me a sidelong glance, alarm mixing with anger in his eyes. "We need an address."

Yuri leans back, expression bored. "I might have an old location they used. An abandoned property near Magnolia Ridge, on the outskirts. They were using it for storage. If they're still following their usual patterns, maybe they're holed up there."

He scribbles something on a slip of paper, then slides it across the desk to me. "Take it. If they're there, good luck. I want no part of this."

I snatch up the paper, adrenaline surging. An address. Something tangible. *Finally.* "Don't be surprised if we find proof they're under your orders," I warn, though some part of me believes he really has given up on them.

"If you find such proof, do let me know," Yuri remarks, leaning forward, lips curling into a razor-sharp smile. "I'd love to break their necks myself for tarnishing my reputation further."

I force myself to breathe, to focus. Briar could be at that location. I have to move now. "You're not calling them, warning them we're coming?"

Yuri's smile grows cold. "I told you—I wash my hands of them. If you want to arrest them or kill them, do what you must. But leave me out of it." He swats the air dismissively.

Asher and I exchange a brief look of mutual disgust. This is what we're up against—a father who'd abandon his own sons when they become inconvenient, criminals who see people as disposable. We've stepped into a cesspool, and Briar's trapped in the middle.

"Let's go," I say, nodding to Asher. Before we leave, I take one last glance at Yuri. "You'd better hope your sons haven't hurt Briar."

He snorts, returning his attention to a stack of papers on his desk. "Like I said, they're not my problem anymore. Good night, gentlemen."

We head back down the hallway, passing the boxing ring. The fighters have changed, but the scene remains the same: blood, cheers, and the stench of desperation. My stomach churns. In another life, maybe I'd bust this whole operation wide open. But right now, I have one goal—find Briar.

Outside, the cold air hits me like a slap, and Asher exhales a tense breath. "So, Magnolia Ridge?" he asks, tugging at the collar of his jacket.

I nod, unfolding the slip of paper Yuri gave me. The address is scrawled in a hasty script, barely legible. "It's not much, but it's something."

Asher slips his hands into his pockets, scanning the dark street. "We should let Dean know."

I'm already dialing, pressing the phone to my ear. My SUV sits at the curb, engine cooled by the night. The phone rings twice before Dean picks up. "Dean, we got an address," I say, voice tight with urgency. "Yuri's sons, Vlad and Dimitri, might be holding Briar and Chester near Magnolia Ridge."

"Good work," Dean replies. I can hear the relief in his tone. "Send the location. I'll get a team ready. Keep eyes on the property, but don't go in alone."

I bristle at the reminder—my instincts scream for me to charge in there now, to save Briar this instant. But I've screwed up once by being reckless. This time, I'll at least try to bring backup. "Fine," I say, cutting the call short.

Turning to Asher, I tuck the phone away. "You up for a drive?"

He smirks, albeit grimly. "Damn right I am. Let's find this place."

We climb into my SUV, the address burning a hole in my pocket, the memory of Yuri's smug grin lingering in my mind. My heart thuds with renewed determination. If Vlad and Dimitri are half as incompetent as Yuri claims, maybe I've got

Saving What's Mine

a chance to get Briar out alive. I crank the ignition, headlights piercing the darkness.

"Hang on, Briar," I whisper under my breath, gripping the wheel until my knuckles whiten. "I'm coming." Then I hit the gas, and Asher and I tear off into the night, bound for Magnolia Ridge and whatever hell Vlad and Dimitri Chekov have prepared there.

Chapter 26

Briar

I'm curled up on a makeshift bed in this dusty cage, muscles aching, stomach growling, and head throbbing. It's been days —*days*—since I was dragged here, though it feels more like a lifetime. My sense of time blurs. There's no sun, no clock, just flickering overhead lights that sometimes stay on through the night, sometimes shut off without warning. I'm never certain how many hours pass between the rattling echoes of voices and footsteps.

Chester's cage sits a few yards away, near the only lamp that still works consistently. The glow reveals his vibrant green feathers looking duller than usual, his posture listless. He hardly squawks anymore. It breaks my heart. The first few times I was forced to feed him, he'd peck at his food with some enthusiasm, but now he barely touches it unless I coax him for a long while. I'm starting to worry he's as exhausted as I am.

I wrap my arms around my knees, glancing at the iron bars that separate me from the rest of the warehouse. They call it a "room," but it's more like an oversized cage—sheet metal walls rigged up to create a makeshift enclosure, with a single door padlocked from the outside. The Russians have allowed me just enough space to walk around in circles if I wanted, but that's about it. Most times, I'm too tired to pace. My body screams for rest, but my mind can't shut off. Every time I close my eyes, my nightmares tear me back to reality, reminding me I might not survive this if they no longer need me.

I peer through a gap in the metal, scanning the dimly lit expanse of cracked concrete and rusted machinery. Heath is slouched against a battered desk in the far corner, scrolling through his phone. A permanent sneer twists his lips, and whenever his eyes flick to me, they're filled with smug disdain. He used to be so charming at the zoo, sweet-talking his way into everyone's good graces, but now he's shown his true self—cold, calculating, and cruel.

Jason, on the other hand, hovers near the Russians, trying to ingratiate himself. Sometimes he paces over to my cage, leaning in too close, whispering, "I missed you, Briar," or "Why didn't you stay with me?" His obsession makes my skin crawl. It's like he's gone off the deep end, his sanity unraveling with each passing day. Part of me wonders if he's in over his head too, just another pawn of these Russian gangsters. But that doesn't excuse what he's done.

My heart pounds whenever the Russians speak, especially now that they're arguing, their voices echoing in tense bursts. They're standing near Chester's cage, the parrot ruffling his feathers nervously at their raised voices. I can't understand a word of Russian, but the anger is plain as day—sharp gestures, narrowed eyes, clipped tones. One of them is a tall, hulking man with a shaved head; he's in Jason's face, while another—slimmer but with a snake-like intensity—flails his arms at Heath. The rest of the Russian crew watch from a distance, guns occasionally glinting in the weak light.

It's been like this all morning, harsh words snapping between them, followed by tense silence, then another round of angry debate. Chester squawks softly, but none of them pay him any mind. They're too absorbed in whatever argument is roiling through their organization. *It must be bad*, I think, swallowing hard. *They're on edge.*

My stomach twists. If they're fighting among themselves, it probably means the plan—whatever twisted scheme they had for Chester—isn't going smoothly. And if it's not going smoothly, if they can't sell him or leverage him... *what will they do with us?* My worst fear is that once Chester's of no use, I'll become disposable. They've been making it painfully clear that my only purpose is to keep him alive and healthy so he can fetch a high price, or be traded for something even more sinister. If that plan falls through, they won't need me at all.

I hug my knees tighter, wishing Orion would somehow burst through the doors, guns blazing, to save Chester and me. *Orion.* The thought of him sends a fresh wave of pain through my chest. I clung to anger for a while—how he lied, how he said he didn't care—but I can't deny how badly I want to see him. Even if what he said was true, if he really has no feelings, I still need him. If anyone can take on these guys, it's him. But I might be deluding myself. *He's not coming*, the dark voice in my mind insists. *He doesn't care.*

Yet there's another part of me, a tiny flicker of hope, that refuses to let go of the memory of his arms around me, the earnest look in his eyes when he promised he'd protect me. That memory is all that's keeping me from collapsing into despair.

A clamoring crash makes me jump. One of the Russians has slammed a metal bar against the floor, the reverberation echoing through the warehouse. Jason flinches, backing away with hands raised in a placating gesture. The tall Russian stalks off toward the shadows, muttering curses under his breath. From the fragments of English I catch—*"no money,"* *"Chekov,"* *"this is insane"*—I piece together that things are spiraling out of control. That doesn't bode well for me or Chester.

My eyes drift to the poor parrot. His normally bright feathers are subdued, his eyes half-lidded. The Russians gave me a cheap bag of birdseed to feed him, but it's not his usual diet, and it shows. He misses the fresh fruits, the varied nuts, the familiar voices of trainers who cared for him. My heart clenches at the sight of him so withdrawn.

"Hang on," I whisper under my breath, forcing myself to believe we'll both get out of this. My lips tremble as I stare at the overhead lights, flickering in a pattern that's become my only indicator of time passing. *Three flickers means it's likely night-time*, I told myself yesterday, but I can't be sure. For all I know, days and nights blend together here.

Sleep hasn't been an option. Even if I manage to drift off, the nightmares come roaring in. Scenes of Jason cornering me in dark hallways, Orion's face twisting in betrayal, Chester's terrified squawks echoing in my mind. I jolt awake in a cold sweat, heart hammering, sure that someone's pointing a gun at me. Sometimes I think I hear Orion calling my name, but it's just a cruel trick of my imagination. The insomnia wears on me, leaving me frazzled and weak, yet too anxious to rest.

Heath's grating voice pulls me out of my thoughts. He's stalking toward my cage now, phone in hand. Without warning, he bangs on the metal bars, making me flinch. "How's the bird?" he demands, not even glancing at me. There's no respect, no concern. It's like I'm an afterthought.

I force myself upright. "He's lethargic," I answer, voice croaking. "He needs proper food, a better environment—"

"He'll be fine," Heath cuts me off, tapping something on his phone. Probably checking messages for updates on wherever this deal is supposed to happen. "And you—don't even think about trying anything. We've got eyes on you." He sneers, then jerks his chin at Chester's cage. "This'll all be over soon enough."

One way or another, he doesn't have to say. I swallow hard, suppressing the urge to spit back some defiance. It wouldn't help. I'm too exhausted to muster anything more than a weary glare.

Heath stomps away, and my shoulders sag. Jason's across the warehouse, chatting in a hushed tone with a smaller Russian guy I haven't seen before. Obsession laces his eyes whenever he glances my way, but he hasn't tried to get close today. Maybe the Russians told him to keep his distance. I don't know. I almost prefer his absence—his attempts at conversation only remind me of how twisted he's become, how I once saw him as sweet.

A soft chirp from Chester draws my attention back to him. I crawl over to the edge of his cage, reaching through the gap in the metal. "Hey, buddy," I coo, my voice cracking. He tilts his head, and for a moment, I see a flicker of recognition. But he stays put on his perch, feathers drooping. My chest aches with guilt—*I can't even help him like I want to.* All I can do is beg the Russians for better supplies, hope they don't decide it's too expensive or time-consuming.

Fear gnaws at me. The Russians' argument keeps cycling, and from the tension in the air, I sense they're on the brink of making some decision—whether it's about Chester's sale or me. I close my eyes for a moment, breath shaking. *If they can't sell Chester... if this deal goes bad... they'll have no use for either of us.*

A wave of cold sweeps over me, chilling me to my bones. *I can't die here*, I think, the words a desperate mantra. *I won't.* Even if I have no idea how to get out, I refuse to give in to complete despair. I imagine Orion's face, summoning the memory of his warmth, and cling to that sliver of hope. Maybe he lied, maybe he really doesn't care—but he's my last chance.

"I'm sorry, Chester," I whisper, forcing myself to stay calm. "We'll find a way."

He blinks at me, shifting just enough that it seems like he's listening. My heart squeezes, and for a moment, I dare to imagine a rescue, an escape. If Orion or anyone shows up, I vow to fight with every scrap of will I have left. I refuse to let this be the end for either of us.

Chapter 27

Orion

I crouch against the splintered wall of a run-down building, heart pounding beneath my Kevlar vest. My breath comes in steady, deliberate pulls as I glance around the makeshift command post we've assembled. It's dimly lit, the only illumination coming from a portable lamp on the floor and the screens of our scattered devices. Dean stands at the center, issuing orders into his comm, while Riggs, Gunner, Asher, and Maverick double-check weapons. The tension is thick enough to choke on.

We're less than a block away from a dingy warehouse, the place we believe Briar—and Chester—are being held. It's taken days of chasing leads and a massive favor involving satellite imagery, but now we know exactly where they are. The overhead shots show a sprawling compound with multiple entrances, more than a dozen armed men, and a handful of vehicles parked near the loading docks. And inside, somewhere in the back, I'm told there's a section cordoned off by makeshift walls. That's where they've got Briar.

Gunner stands beside me, tablet in hand, flicking between images. "Twelve men, plus Jason and Heath," he murmurs, dark eyes scanning the final feed we managed to get. "Not counting any stragglers who might not show up on the thermal scans."

I nod, jaw clenched. "Any sign of bigger players? The Bratva father or anything like that?"

Gunner shakes his head. "Doesn't look like Yuri is there. Guess he really did cut ties with his sons. But these guys aren't amateurs. They've got trucks, probable arms shipments, and enough coverage to hold off a small army."

Dean steps over, adjusting the earpiece in his comm. "All right, listen up," he says, voice tense. He's in full tactical mode now, and the rest of us gather around him. "We've confirmed the back corner of the warehouse is sealed off, probably where Briar and the bird are kept. The info we got from that overhead pass shows minimal movement in that area—likely just a guard or two. Our main trouble is the front."

Riggs, who's built like a tank, folds his arms. "So we go in quiet through the west side, slip past the outer perimeter."

Maverick nods, tapping a stylus on the screen of his phone. "If we can neutralize the roving guard near the loading dock, we'll have a relatively clear path to the interior. Then we split up—some of us draw attention at the front, the rest push to the back to secure Briar and Chester."

"Yeah, about that attention at the front," Gunner interjects. "That's where the majority of these guys are clustered. We've gotta be ready for a firefight. They won't hesitate to shoot if they sense we're a threat."

A slow burn of anger flares in my chest. *Let them shoot.* My only concern is getting Briar out alive. The last few days, I've hardly slept, images of her frightened face hounding every spare moment. Hell, I can barely think about anything else. Jason, that bastard, and Heath, the traitor who waltzed into the zoo. *They're going down*, no question.

Dean catches the look on my face. He puts a hand on my shoulder. "Stay focused," he says quietly. "Don't let rage drive you. The mission is to get her out, not to rack up a body count."

I give a curt nod, swallowing back the fury. "Understood."

Asher, new to the team but already fitting in like he's been around forever, sets a couple of rifles on the rickety table. "Everyone check your gear. We go in five. Comm lines on channel three. We keep chatter to a minimum. Two teams: Dean, Riggs, and me in the front, Orion and Gunner take the west side. Maverick, you run external overwatch with the drone. You see trouble, you call it in."

We each acknowledge, doing quick re-checks: magazine, chamber, safety, earpiece, vest. The metallic clack of loading weapons is a cold comfort. I run a hand over the front pocket of my vest, where I keep a photo of Briar. It's one of the photos she had in her memento box, and I snatched it when I went home to grab Jeb. It's wrinkled and worn from being held so often, but it's the only tangible reminder I have of her smile.

Gunner notices. He quirks an eyebrow. "You really care about her, huh?"

My throat tightens. "Yeah," is all I manage. I can't afford to say anything more right now.

Saving What's Mine

He just nods once, understanding in his eyes. Then he slaps a fresh mag into his rifle. "All right, let's do this."

We head out into the night, sticking to the shadows as we approach the warehouse. The air is stagnant, carrying the faint stench of garbage from the nearby alleyways. My boots make barely a whisper against the cracked pavement. I keep my weapon pointed at the ground but ready. My senses sharpen—every scrape of metal, every distant voice, every flickering light stands out like a siren.

We split into our teams. Dean, Riggs, and Asher slip around the north side, heading for the main entrance. Gunner and I duck behind a stack of shipping pallets by the west side fence. Maverick is tucked somewhere overhead, vantage unknown, but I can hear the faint hum of a small drone he's guiding. My heart pounds relentlessly, adrenaline surging.

Through a gap in the fence, I spot a lone guard patrolling by a side door. He's armed with what looks like an AK, strolling with a bored slump. Gunner locks eyes with me, nods. We creep around, hugging the wall. The guard stops, checks his phone, and in that second, Gunner lunges. A swift elbow to the neck, gun pressed to the guard's temple, muffling any scream. The guard slumps as I knock him out with the butt of the gun. We drag him behind a dumpster, zip-tying his hands. I sweep the area—clear for now.

"Maverick, one guard down at west side," I whisper into my mic. "Moving in."

"Copy," comes his hushed reply. "Dean's about to breach front entrance. Wait for his go."

We flatten ourselves against the warehouse's corrugated metal wall. My grip on the rifle tightens, my palms sweating inside my gloves. A dull roar of voices filters through the structure, men laughing, cursing in Russian. The sweet tang of success is overshadowed by the sour taste of dread—Briar's so close, but still far from safe.

The comm crackles. "Breach on three. Three... two... one." Dean's voice signals over the channel. Then an explosion of noise erupts from the front—shouting, gunfire, the clang of metal. They've made contact.

"That's our cue," Gunner hisses. We shove open the side door. It groans on rusty hinges, revealing a dimly lit corridor stacked with crates. My heart leaps into my throat.

We move fast, rifles up, scanning every corner. The staccato of bullets rattles somewhere deeper in the building. Muffled shouts. We step over a toppled box of ammo, the smell of gunpowder heavy in the air. Two men appear at the far end of the corridor, weapons raised. Gunner drops to one knee, firing a short burst. One man goes down, the other dives behind a crate. I press myself against the wall, inch closer, and lob a flashbang around the corner.

Bang! The hallway glows white for an instant, and the man stumbles out, disoriented. I close the gap, butt of my rifle slamming into his shoulder. He crumples, and Gunner strips him of his weapon.

We push on. My ears ring, my senses hyper-focused. "Maverick," I rasp out, "any sign of Briar?"

"Check the north corner, enclosed area," he responds, panting. "Dean's team is pinned down near the front. Hurry."

Gunner and I hurry toward the north corner, passing a row of dusty windows. Sudden gunfire erupts behind us—a guard tries to flank, bullet ricochets whining overhead. Gunner returns fire, forcing the guard to duck for cover. We press ourselves behind a support column.

I grit my teeth, chest heaving. *Focus on Briar.* I peer around the column, catch a glimpse of the guard's arm. Another short burst from my rifle, and the threat goes silent. My pulse roars like thunder in my ears.

"Let's move," Gunner mutters, reloading. We navigate a maze of crates, following Maverick's direction. The air is thick with dust and the acrid smell of gunpowder, stinging my eyes. A doorway appears at the end of the passage, blocked by a makeshift barrier of wooden pallets. Light flickers from beyond.

I throw my shoulder into the pallets, shoving them aside. My mind screams *Briar* with every heartbeat. The door behind them is unlocked, just a cheap metal latch. I kick it open.

Inside is a small, partitioned area—a miniature prison cell made of plywood and corrugated metal. Dim lights hang from overhead cords. And there, in a cage-like enclosure, I see her: Briar, huddled on the floor, hair disheveled, face etched with exhaustion. Relief floods me like a tidal wave.

But there's no time to savor it—Heath stands guard, weapon in hand. The second we crash in, he whips around, eyes wild. "Don't move!" he yells, swinging the gun up.

I don't hesitate. A single shot cracks from my rifle, catching him in the arm. He reels, dropping his gun with a yelp of pain, collapsing to the floor. Gunner keeps his rifle trained on him, ready if he tries anything else.

My feet slam against the concrete as I cross the distance to Briar. She flinches, eyes blinking in confusion. "Orion?" she croaks, voice shaking.

I tear at the lock on the enclosure, forcing it open. "Yeah, it's me. You're safe," I gasp, arms wrapping around her. She's trembling, cold, and thin from days of captivity. Guilt stabs me for not finding her sooner, but relief eclipses everything else. "I've got you. Let's get you out of here."

Beyond the partition, more gunfire pops, echoing through the warehouse. Gunner curses into his comm, signaling we've retrieved Briar. *We still need Chester,* my brain reminds me, scanning the room. In a smaller cage near the back, the green shape of a parrot shuffles. That must be Chester, ruffling his wings in distress.

I grit my teeth, adrenaline still pumping. "Gunner, grab the bird," I bark, pulling Briar against my side. She can barely stand, but her arms cling to me like she's afraid I'll vanish. "We're going home."

Gunner nods, dashing for Chester's cage. Heath groans on the floor, clutching his bleeding arm, but I keep my rifle aimed at him in case he tries anything else. I secure Briar's weight against me, half-carrying her. The mission isn't over until we're outside, safely away from the chaos. But with her fragile warmth pressed against me, I feel the knots in my chest uncoil, replaced by fierce determination. *I won't let her out of my sight again.*

Time to get out—twelve men, or maybe more, but we have one goal: *Extract Briar and Chester.* The firefight still rages somewhere deeper in the building. I adjust my hold on Briar. "Dean, we got her and the bird. Moving out west side. Cover us."

"Roger," Dean's voice crackles. "We'll clear a path."

Gunfire cracks in the distance, and I steel myself for what might be the hardest part: the escape. But I don't falter. Because I have Briar now, safe in my arms, and I'm not letting go.

Chapter 28

Briar

I don't have words for the relief flooding me as Orion's strong arms close around me. One second, I'm huddled on the cold warehouse floor, my entire body trembling from days of hunger, worry, and hopelessness—and the next, he's here, warm and solid, pulling me free of this makeshift cage. My pulse pounds in my ears, too loud for me to hear anything but the steady drumming of my own heart. I cling to him, shaking, trying to convince myself this is real and not another twisted dream.

He leans close, breath ragged. "I've got you," he whispers, his gaze fierce. Even through my dazed state, I can see the raw determination in his eyes. Everything in me wants to collapse into him, let him carry me away from this nightmare. Chester, my mind whispers, remember Chester. But Orion's already calling to Gunner—someone else on his team—to grab the parrot's cage.

It's a blur of noise around us: bursts of gunfire somewhere in the warehouse, ricochets whining off metal beams, the angry shouts of men. My legs feel like jelly, and I can barely stand on my own. Orion's supporting most of my weight as we make our way toward a side exit. Each step seems to take forever. My lungs burn with each breath, stale air and the thick smell of gunpowder choking me. But I'm alive. *I'm alive because Orion found me.*

We're nearly to the door—just a few more feet. I see Gunner ahead, rifle raised, Chester's cage dangling from his other hand, the poor bird squawking in panic. My head swims, body screaming for rest. *Just a little further.* That's when it happens.

A crack of gunfire splits the air in a sharper, deadlier tone. Something smacks into Orion, and the world lurches beneath me. He lets out a strangled gasp, his hold on me faltering. I stare up at him, confusion and horror mingling in my chest. I see the dark stain blossoming across his shirt, a bullet wound on his side. *No, no, no.*

"Orion!" I scream, grabbing for him as he collapses. We both hit the ground hard, his weight crushing into me for a heartbeat before he rolls off, leaving me stunned and winded. My entire body shakes, adrenaline surging. *Not Orion,* I beg silently. *Don't take him from me.*

All around, the chaos intensifies. I hear Gunner roaring something into his comm, and I catch glimpses of more Russians spilling out from behind crates, muzzle flashes lighting the air. I scramble to get a hold of Orion, but strong hands yank me up from behind.

"No!" I shriek, thrashing. But Jason—he's back, or maybe it's Heath, I can't even see. My vision blurs with tears and rage. They're dragging me away from Orion, who's still on the ground. I catch a last, haunting glimpse of him, eyes half-

Saving What's Mine

lidded, blood staining his vest. Fear claws at me, worse than anything I've felt since this began. *He can't be dead. He can't be.*

I'm shoved into a waiting car, Jason's voice barking orders. Everything is a haze of noise and chaos. I'm flung across the back seat, my head slamming into the door, jarring my senses. The vehicle lurches forward, tires squealing on the concrete. Another burst of gunfire rings out, this time so close it rattles the windows. The men curse in Russian or something close to it, returning fire with short bursts of their own. I bury my face in my arms, trying to steady my breathing, *trying not to choke on the terror.*

All I can think is: *Orion is shot.* My mind replays the moment—the snap of the bullet, his agonized gasp. Is he alive? *Please, let him be alive.* A sob tears from my throat, but no one in the car shows me any sympathy. I can feel their hostility radiating like a heat wave.

We speed away, the car rattling as we blow through some barricade or fence. The gunfire behind us grows distant, muffled. I can't tell who's winning or losing, only that I'm trapped again. I squeeze my eyes shut, wishing I could rewind time just five minutes to when Orion held me.

Suddenly, more shots ring out from the front. The men in the car shout, the driver jerks the wheel. We fishtail, slamming sideways into something—the impact sends me sprawling against the door. There's a flurry of curses, the windshield cracks, and I hear bullets pinging off metal. *Someone's attacking the car.*

"Get us out of here!" Jason yells, voice nearly drowned by the roar of the engine.

But it's too late. Through the fractured windshield, I see headlights bearing down on us. Another vehicle cuts us off, screeching to a halt, men pouring out with guns drawn. Their silhouettes are too shadowy for me to make out details, but from the way they move, I sense *professional training. Obviously they're Orion's men?*

The driver tries to accelerate, but a volley of bullets rips through the hood. Steam and smoke billow, and the engine dies in a horrible grinding wail. The car shakes as more rounds pepper the side. The men beside me shove open their doors, lurching out to return fire, leaving me momentarily unguarded. My heart hammers. I consider diving out, but fear roots me in place. The gunshots are relentless, deafening.

Suddenly, the back door flies open, and a stranger grabs me. I recoil, fighting, but he yells, "I'm Asher, I'm with Orion's team!" His voice is urgent, breathless. I glimpse his face in the flickering headlights—young, sharp eyes, fierce determination. *Another savior?*

I let him haul me out, tears blinding me. He thrusts me toward a nearby truck, barking, "Get down!" The chaos of gunfire and shouting echoes all around, and I half crawl, half stumble into the truck's cab. Asher dives in behind me, slamming the door. I'm shaking so badly I can hardly breathe.

He twists the key, the engine roars, and we peel away from the broken mess of the other car. The back window's shot out, glass glittering across the seat. My ears ring from the relentless barrage. I press myself down, arms over my head, tears streaking my face. *Please let Orion be alive, please let Orion be alive.* My mantra pulses with every beat of my heart.

Asher yells at me to stay down, and I comply, curling up on the floorboard. The truck swerves wildly, tires squealing against pavement. We must be weaving through side streets or alleys. My stomach lurches with each abrupt turn, but I hang on, trying not to panic. *We're escaping. That's something.*

After what feels like an eternity, the engine's whine settles, and the gunfire fades behind us. My breathing is ragged, tears still burning my eyes. Asher glances down at me, jaw clenched. "You okay?" he asks, voice tight.

I shake my head, my throat too constricted to speak. *How can I be okay? Orion's shot. He might be... he might...* I can't even finish the thought. I choke out a sob. "Is Orion... is he..."

Asher grimaces, eyes flicking to the road. "I don't know," he admits, frustration evident. "Comms went down. Dean's team is still at the warehouse." He swallows, gaze full of sympathy. "I'm sorry. But we had to get you out of there."

His words land like punches to my gut. My brain reels. *Why is this happening?* Tears stream down my cheeks, and I press my forehead against the edge of the seat. *Orion, please, be alive. Please.*

Asher drives on in grim silence, weaving through back roads at high speed. My skin prickles with the cold air rushing through the bullet-riddled window. Eventually, he pulls off onto a secluded street, trees looming overhead. The headlights illuminate an old cabin-like structure, the windows dark.

"We're here," he mutters, killing the engine. "Safe house. Let's go."

He helps me out of the truck, quickly guiding me toward the door. My knees threaten to buckle, exhaustion and grief crashing over me. *Days of captivity,* then the adrenaline rush of near-freedom, only to have Orion ripped away in a flash of gunfire. My mind feels shredded.

Inside, the place is small but secure-looking, with heavy locks on every door and window. Asher flips on a single lamp, throwing a warm glow across a modest living area. There's no one else here. He leads me to a sofa, gently easing me down.

For a moment, he hovers, like he's not sure whether to console me or check the perimeter.

"Stay here," he says at last, voice firm but kind. "I need to confirm the property's clear, then get back on comms with Dean. I promise I'll tell you anything I find out about Orion the second I know."

I nod numbly, wrapping my arms around myself. My body still shakes, heart racing with leftover terror. Every instinct screams that I should be out there searching for Orion, but I'm too weak to fight, too emotionally spent. Asher slips away, his footsteps heavy on the floorboards as he checks doors and windows.

Alone in the flickering lamplight, I bury my face in my hands, tears hot and unrelenting. *Is he alive?* The question loops in my mind. *He has to be.* Because if Orion's gone, if I came this close to freedom only to lose him, I don't know how I'll survive that. My chest aches with a grief that might swallow me whole.

The last few days—being held captive, watching Chester waste away, the bullet slamming into Orion's side—have shredded any illusions of safety I once had. Now, this safe house might be my refuge, but it feels like a fragile bubble waiting to burst. *I just want to know he's okay.*

I drag in a ragged breath, pressing my back against the sofa cushions, and stare at the door where Asher disappeared. *He'll make contact with the team*, I remind myself. He'll let me know if Orion's condition is stable, if the others made it out alive. Until then, all I can do is tremble in this terrible limbo—half rescued, half destroyed by the fear that Orion was taken from me in that single explosive moment.

So I wait, heart pounding, mind racing, trying to hold onto hope. Because if there's one thing left to cling to in this whirlwind of madness, it's the desperate belief that Orion Locke isn't gone. That somehow, he'll pull through, and I'll see him again. *He can't die now,* I think, clenching my fists against the sofa cushions. *Not after all we've been through.*

But until I hear those words—*He's alive*—I can't breathe easy. All I can do is pray, shaking, exhausted, and fighting the urge to scream at the unfairness of it all.

Chapter 29

Orion

I'm slumped against the cold concrete, the world narrowed to a pinprick of agony in my side. The metallic smell of my own blood chokes me as I fight to stay conscious. Every instinct in me screams to stand, to go after Briar, but my body won't obey.

I try to raise my head, scanning the shadows where Jason disappeared with her. A hiss of frustration claws its way out of my throat. *Briar.* My heart pounds with the rage of a cornered animal. She was right there, in my arms. Now she's gone again, snatched away.

"Let me—go," I grind out, struggling to push off the floor. My vision wavers.

Gunner's hand clamps down on my shoulder. "Easy, Orion." He's kneeling at my side, looking me straight in the eyes. "You're hit bad, man."

I want to shove him off, want to scream that we can't waste time here, but he presses me back. Pain lances through my abdomen, stealing my breath. Dark red blossoms across my vest—too far right to be anything but a gut shot. *Shit.*

Dean and Riggs come tearing around the corner, both wide-eyed when they see me sprawled on the ground, blood pooling beneath me. Chester's cage rattles in Gunner's grip, the poor parrot squawking softly. I blink, hazy, trying to piece together the last seconds. Gunshots, Briar's scream, her fingers slipping away from mine...

"Orion," Dean says, crouching and placing a firm hand over the wound. He peels back a corner of my vest. "Damn," he mutters under his breath. "We need to get him out of here now. Blood's dark—looks like the liver's hit."

A fresh wave of pain steals my voice. My vision flickers, but I force my lips to move. "Briar," I whisper, throat raw. "They took her."

"Shh," Riggs cuts in, pressing a bandage to my side. I hiss at the sting, but he doesn't let up. "We'll find her. You have to let us handle this, boss."

"Delta team's en route," Dean adds, voice grim. "We'll stop the Russians. Right now, we gotta get you medical attention."

"No," I protest, trying again to push myself up. Another lance of fire rips through my torso, and I choke on a curse. *Damn it. Damn this body for failing me.*

"Gunner, help me lift him," Dean orders. Gunner carefully sets Chester's cage down, and I catch a glimpse of the bird, trembling, feathers ruffled. The poor thing. Everything has gone to hell.

Gunner and Dean hoist me upright, and my world spins. For a second, I'm floating, my legs useless. Then I'm draped across

Riggs' broad shoulder, Gunner clearing the path ahead. My mind fights the darkness creeping in at the edges. *Focus, Orion. Don't black out.*

"Delta's five minutes out," Gunner says into his comm. "They'll finish this. We gotta get Orion gone, stat."

I clench my jaw, heart pounding in frustration. *No. I should be going after Briar, not bleeding out like a rookie.*

We leave into a hail of gunfire somewhere in the distance, but all I can do is feel the slick warmth of blood seeping into my clothes. *Useless,* my mind hisses, fury tangling with desperation. The men hurry me into a waiting SUV, Chester's cage jammed in the backseat. The door slams, and we screech away.

Dean and Gunner do what they can to stabilize me, talking fast about pressure, blood loss, calling a hospital for immediate trauma support. The words blur together as we lurch around corners. I glimpse the flicker of streetlights, hear the beep of a phone dialing.

"Hang on," Dean mutters, pressing hard on my side. The pain steals my breath again. "We're almost there."

"Briar—" I rasp, forcing my eyelids up. I can't see anything but the shape of Dean's face, shadowed in the passing lights.

He doesn't answer. *Damn it.* I grab his wrist. "Tell me," I insist, my voice cracking.

His expression softens, but he stays silent. "Focus on yourself, Orion."

A curse slips between my teeth, but there's nothing I can do. My body feels like lead, warmth draining away. I slip in and out of consciousness, snatches of city noise mixing with the roar of my pulse. *Stay awake*, I order myself, but the darkness is relentless.

The next thing I know, I'm in a hallway that reeks of antiseptic. Florescent lights glare overhead. My vest is gone, replaced by cold air prickling against my skin. Hands grip my limbs, voices shouting. *Doctors?* I can't focus enough to see. I blink, and Dean's face appears, yelling something. Then he's shoved aside.

"Nine-millimeter gunshot wound, possible liver damage—he's lost a lot of blood," someone says, words clipped. A nurse? "Take him straight to OR. Clear the corridor!"

More movement, a gurney rattling over linoleum. My entire side burns like liquid fire. I try to speak, form the word *Briar*, but only a ragged gasp comes out.

A bright white overhead light blinds me, and my eyelids flutter shut. *Don't pass out*, I scream in my head, but I can't fight the undertow.

When consciousness flares up again, everything is fuzzy—like I'm suspended in warm water. The beep of machines and the hush of medical staff drift by. A nurse leans over me, adjusts an IV, then disappears. I can't move my arms, or maybe I just don't have the energy.

"Where—where is she?" I manage, or think I do. My voice is weak, hoarse. No one answers.

Time blurs. I slip under again, only to resurface to find Dean by my bed, the overhead lights dimmed. He's talking in a low voice on the phone, words like *Delta, warehouse, Russians* floating by. I groan, trying to grab his attention.

He hushes me gently, stepping closer. "Don't speak," he murmurs. "You made it through surgery, but you need rest."

My heart throbs with panic. *No. They need to tell me about Briar.* I mouth her name, but Dean just shakes his head. "Rest."

A flare of agony blooms in my side, and I can't hold back a hiss. Dean presses a button, and a soothing wave of medication fogs my brain again, dragging me under before I can protest. The world fades to black.

I come to in short bursts: nurses checking tubes, a doctor shining a light in my eyes, the steady beep-beep of monitors. Each time, I try to ask about Briar—if she's safe, if she got away, if we have any word at all—but no one gives me a straight answer.

"All that matters is you get better," one nurse says gently, brushing hair from my forehead. "You can't help anyone if you're dead."

Her logic stings. Guilt rakes through me. *I shouldn't be here in a hospital bed. I should be on the streets, hunting down Jason and Heath, tearing the Russians apart until Briar is safe in my arms.*

Every time the pain meds drag me under, I dream of Briar's face—pale, tear-streaked, eyes wide with terror as she disappears behind a veil of gunfire. The nightmares twist into memories of the warehouse, the moment the bullet slammed into me. I jolt awake in a cold sweat, only to find myself anchored to IV lines and monitors. *Useless.*

I'm going crazy, pinned here, powerless. My entire being thrums with a single need: find Briar. The steady beeping of the monitors can't drown out my hammering pulse. *She's out there, in danger. I'm stuck here, patched up like a worthless invalid.*

I grit my teeth, ignoring the throbbing in my side, vowing that the second I can stand, I'm leaving this place. Bullet hole or not, I'm going to find her. Because if there's one thing I can't bear, it's the thought of Briar out there alone, believing I might be dead, while I'm in this bed, chained by tubes and doctors.

Hang on, Briar, I think, my eyelids sliding shut again. *I'm coming.*

Chapter 30

Briar

It's been four days since the gunfire, four days since Asher shoved me into his truck and slammed on the gas, four days since I saw Orion bleed out in front of me. Yet in some ways, it feels like it was only minutes ago. I still can't get the image of him collapsing, that dark red pool of blood staining the ground, out of my head. Even now, in this quiet safe house, the memory chases me through every waking hour. I'm pissed I can't see him. I know he's at the hospital, and every hour on the hour I ask if I can visit. It's always the same answer. *"Not until he's stable."*

I'm pacing in the small living room, glancing at the front door with every second that ticks by. The rotating group of men on watch—Orion's team, apparently—have kept me here, insisting I'm not safe until the rest of the Russians are caught. A handful of them, including Jason, managed to slip away during the raid. Word is the others were either captured or shot. But that doesn't lessen my anxiety. *Jason's still out there.* My mind plays his face over and over, that unhinged desperation in his eyes.

Gunner spent one entire day here, cleaning his guns at the kitchen table while I tried to read a magazine, the tension thick as we both pretended normalcy. He's brusque but not unkind. Then Ranger arrived the next day, a charming grin in place, and opened the door with Jeb in tow. I gasped when I saw Jeb fluttering his wings, squawking a half-formed greeting. I rushed to him, loving the fact that I had my bird with me now.

I learned more about each man as they drifted in and out: how some of them had once been in the military together, how Dean formed this security firm that tackled high-risk operations. It distracts me from the fact that Orion's in the hospital, in surgery and recovery for days now, fighting to mend a bullet wound that nicked his liver. Lucky, they say. Lucky it didn't kill him. But that thought alone makes my chest tighten.

Today, it's Asher on watch, the one who pulled me from the van and got me here in one piece. He's kinder than I expected a special-ops guy to be—gentle in how he moves, calm in how he speaks. We're sitting in the kitchen, sharing a plate of scrambled eggs I attempted to cook, when his phone buzzes. He glances at the screen, eyes flicking with what looks like relief.

"Good news?" I ask, trying not to look too eager.

Asher nods. "It's Dean. Orion's awake and stable. He asked if you want to visit."

My heart lurches. "He—he wants to see me?"

"Obviously." Asher rubs the back of his neck.

Emotions swell inside me—an uneasy mix of joy, anxiety, and a raw ache I can't quite put into words. I force a breath. "Please. Can we go now?"

Asher's already standing, gathering his keys. "We'll have to be quick. You're still not a hundred percent in the clear with the Russians. But I think it's important."

We drive in relative silence. My thoughts spiral the entire way: *What if Orion hates me for leaving the safe house that day?* What if he resents that I ended up in the Russians' hands again because of my foolishness? And then the more pressing fear: what if he's still in pain, hurt beyond what the doctors can fix?

The hospital is a stark white structure, cold and clinical. Asher parks in a restricted bay, flashing credentials that Dean must have arranged. I clutch my jacket against me, following him through the corridors, heart hammering. Nurses and doctors pass in a blur. My chest feels tight, my steps heavy.

Finally, Asher stops outside a private room. The door's closed, a small sign reading *Authorized Personnel Only*. "I'll wait out here," he says, offering an encouraging nod. "Take your time."

I swallow hard, pushing the door open. The room is dim, a single overhead light and the soft glow of machines. A wave of antiseptic hits me, and I blink against the sting of tears when I see Orion in the bed, propped up, bandages swathing his side. He looks pale, his lips thin, but there's still a fierce glint in his eyes. My heart twists painfully.

This brave, *brave* man. He's shuffling a deck of playing cards in his hands and he stops when he sees me. "Briar," he says, voice hoarse. He tries to shift upright, wincing as he does.

I rush forward, stopping at the edge of the bed. My first impulse is to throw myself into his arms, but I hold back, afraid of hurting him. "Orion," I manage, tears prickling. "You—you're okay. Thank God."

He offers a faint, lopsided grin. "I've been better." His tone is subdued, breath shallow. "But I'll live."

My gaze drifts to the strong man in the hospital gown, the IV lines in his arm, the monitors tracking his vitals. Anger flares inside me—at Jason, at Heath, at the Russians. At myself. *If I hadn't left that day...*

"Sit," Orion says, interrupting my swirling thoughts. It's not really a request; it's an alpha command, soft but insistent. He pats the side of the bed. "Sit, Briar. We need to talk."

My emotions churn, but I comply, gingerly lowering myself onto the mattress near his hip. His presence is overwhelming, even injured like this, and the memory of him hitting the ground with blood pouring from his side flashes through my mind. I blink it away.

Orion's gaze bores into me. There's a storm there—anger, confusion, and something deeper. "Why did you leave the safe house that day?" he asks, voice raw. "You could've—" He breaks off, grimacing. "You *did* end up in danger." He winces again. "Is it because you overheard me on the phone?"

I look away, shame burning my cheeks. The white sheets beneath my fingers feel cold. "Orion, I—I can't..."

He inhales, nostrils flaring. "Briar, please. Just tell me."

My jaw clenches. Tears sting behind my eyelids again, and for a moment, I consider lying. But this is Orion—if anyone deserves the truth, it's him. I raise my eyes to meet his, my voice trembling. "I overheard you on the phone with Dean. You told him..." I swallow, "that you had no feelings for me."

His face falls with my words, darkening his expression. "I'm so sorry you heard that."

I nod, a shaky breath escaping. "You said... you didn't care about me. That I was just a job. It hurt. So I left. I thought I was just complicating things. Also, I saw the picture of Jason at the zoo, and thought..." my words fall away.

Orion's hands curl into fists. Slowly, he lifts one hand to brush against my arm, as if he needs the contact. "I never meant it," he says, voice trembling with anger—anger at himself, maybe. "That was a lie I fed Dean so he wouldn't pull me off your watch. There's a rule against getting close to a client. I was worried he'd see how I felt and reassign me."

My heart thuds. "You... lied to him so you could stay with me?"

His face contorts with frustration. "Briar, I'm sorry. I never wanted you to overhear that. I told Dean I didn't care so he wouldn't question my judgment, wouldn't split us up. But I *do* care. More than I should."

Tears slip down my cheeks, but this time they carry a fragile mix of relief and lingering hurt. "Why wouldn't you just tell me that?"

He grimaces, shifting slightly. The monitors beep in protest as he moves. "Because I was trying to do my job—*protect* you. I didn't want you thinking I was crossing a line. And I sure as hell didn't want Dean to reassign me."

A shaky laugh escapes my lips, half-sob, half-disbelief. *All this heartbreak because of some twisted sense of duty.*

Orion's hand slides further up my arm, thumb brushing away my tears. "You scared the hell out of me," he mutters, eyes searching mine. "When you left, and then you got taken... I nearly lost my mind. And then they shot me, and I—I couldn't protect you."

I press my hand over his, my throat tight with emotion. "I was so afraid you'd died," I admit, voice breaking. "Every night, I couldn't sleep, wondering if I'd made the worst mistake of my life by walking out."

His jaw sets. "Don't blame yourself. If I'd told you the truth from the start…" He trails off, pain flickering in his eyes. "Look, I don't know what happens next, but you have to believe me: I never meant those words. I've had feelings for you from the moment I realized you were more than just a client."

My breath hitches. If my heart could leap out of my chest, it would. Orion's gaze is so intense, so raw, that for a second I can't speak. Finally, I manage, "I believe you."

He exhales, relief flashing across his face. Slowly, he tugs at my hand until it rests over the sheet, atop his. The tension in the room eases, replaced by an unspoken promise hovering between us. Even with IV lines and hospital beeps, even with his bandaged side and the fear that Russians are still lurking, there's a sense of rightness in this moment.

Careful not to jostle his injury, I lean forward, pressing my forehead against his. He smells like antiseptic and faintly of the cologne he always wears, the one that lulled me into security every time he held me. A soft whimper escapes me, half relief, half heartache, but Orion's other arm circles around my shoulders, pulling me close.

We sit like that, hearts pounding in tandem, as the chaos of the outside world remains at bay. Eventually, he shifts, wincing at the pain, but he keeps me near. His breath ghosts across my cheek.

"There's still danger," he murmurs, "still Russians out there. Jason… I want to keep you safe, but I need you to trust me. Never doubt me again, all right? No matter what you overhear me say."

My lips quiver with a watery smile. "I won't. Next time, I'll ask you straight up."

A faint chuckle rumbles in his chest. Then he winces, a reminder that he's not out of the woods yet. We both know our problems haven't magically vanished. Jason's still at large, the Russians aren't fully dealt with, and Orion's stuck in a hospital bed for who knows how long. But for the first time, I'm not lost in confusion over where we stand.

We're together, whatever that means in this dangerous world. And I'll hold on to that truth as long as it takes to bring us both home.

Chapter 31

Orion

It's a strange feeling, stepping out of a hospital. I've had my fair share of injuries. Yet, as I limp through the double doors, a warm breeze greets me, carrying the promise of freedom—and Briar's hand is in mine, fingers intertwined, like an anchor that keeps me steady despite the twinge in my side.

Asher, Dean, and Ranger stand off to one side of the pickup loop, faces unreadable behind their stoic, protective postures. Each of them holds bags, flowers, or random gifts brought by well-wishers and team members over the past week. Briar insists on carrying my jacket, even though I'm perfectly capable, but one look at her determined expression tells me not to argue. I've learned—painfully, sometimes—that beneath her quiet exterior is a fierce spirit I can't help but admire.

"Ready, boss?" Dean asks, crossing his arms. He's got that slight crease between his brows that says he's still worried about me. And, to be fair, I'm not 100 percent. My side throbs with each step, the healing wound wrapped beneath layers of gauze, but I'm done lying in a hospital bed with tubes and monitors. I need to be *doing* something—protecting Briar, ensuring the leftover loose ends of this nightmare get tied off.

"Yeah," I say, offering a slight nod. "I'm good."

Briar's hand squeezes mine, and I glance down, catching her tentative smile. That simple gesture—her fingers in mine—is enough to remind me why I need to keep going. *I nearly lost her once.* I'm not about to let that happen again.

Ranger steps forward, clearing his throat. "We got the car ready. Safe house is still prepped. Figured you'd want to stay there until we nail Jason down."

"Yeah," I reply. "We'll stay put until the team finishes things." The only person still running free is Jason, and from what Dean's told me, he's got the entire country looking for him. Vlad and Dimitri—two of the Russian masterminds behind Chester's kidnapping—are behind bars, turned over to the FBI. It's just Jason, a rogue with too many grudges and a twisted obsession with Briar. It won't be long before he slips up. Then this will all be over.

Dean gestures toward the black SUV idling at the curb. "Let's get you home." The word "home" sounds foreign on his lips, but I appreciate it. Even if the safe house is just a temporary fortress, it means security—somewhere Briar can rest without looking over her shoulder every second.

We pile into the SUV, Asher driving with his usual calm focus, Dean riding shotgun, and Ranger jammed in the back with Briar and me. The drive is quiet, punctuated only by my team checking in with each other about procedures and sightings. Briar leans against my arm, her head resting carefully on my shoulder so as not to disturb the bandage at my side. That simple warmth melts the tension coiled in my chest.

When we reach the safe house, the place Briar's been staying, Asher pulls into the driveway with smooth precision. It's a modest, single-story cabin tucked behind tall hedges. Ranger and Dean hop out first, scanning the perimeter before giving the all-clear. Then they help me out, though I grit my teeth at the fuss. My side twinges, but I push through, not wanting Briar to think I'm more hurt than I am.

"You sure you're good?" Dean presses, always the overprotective dad of the group.

I grip his shoulder in reassurance. "I'm good. Thanks for everything. All of you."

With that, they unload the bags—mostly medical supplies, clothes for Briar, and groceries. Then, after a round of firm nods and a mutual understanding that we'll keep in close contact, the three men head off, leaving Briar and me alone.

The house feels quiet—peaceful, almost—once the door shuts behind them. Soft light filters through blinds, illuminating a cozy living room with a worn couch, a small TV, and a coffee table piled with mail. Briar sets my jacket on the arm of the couch, giving the place a cursory glance. Jeb, still in his cage, squawks as if expecting an explanation for our sudden silence.

Briar helps me ease onto the couch, her gentle touch making my pulse flutter. "You sure you're okay?" she asks, eyes brimming with concern.

"Better than okay," I murmur, meeting her gaze. "I'm alive, and you're here. That's all that matters."

"Jeb here too." The bird squawks.

I glance over at him. "Yes, Jeb's here too."

Briar sighs, crossing her arms. "You're lucky," she says, "The bullet barely missed your liver."

"It nicked it," I correct with a wry smile. "Believe me, the doctors reminded me of how close it was—over and over."

Her expression softens, worry flickering in her eyes. "I was so scared I'd lose you."

I pat the seat beside me in invitation. She doesn't hesitate, settling in, curling up so her legs are tucked under her. I wrap an arm around her shoulders, feeling the tension slowly dissolve. Outside, the distant hum of leaves rustling through trees and the chirp of cicadas remind me that life goes on, even after bullets and bloodshed.

We lapse into a comfortable quiet, leaning against each other. The television sits dark, the house still, but it's a cocoon of safety compared to everything we've endured. My mind wanders: *Where do we go from here? What happens once Jason's caught and we can put the ghosts of this nightmare to rest?*

"I can't wait to go home," Briar says softly, voicing my thoughts. "I want my normal life back. The birds at the zoo, my routines, and…" She glances up at me, cheeks reddening. "I know everything changed between us, but I… I want something normal with you, too."

My heart swells. *Me, too, sweetheart.* I shift, wincing as I adjust against the cushion, then turn to face her fully. "I, uh… about that. I don't want you going back to your old place alone." The alpha in me bristles at the thought of her living anywhere else, especially with Jason still on the loose. "I can't stand the idea of you being out of my sight, especially right now."

Her eyes widen, and I hurry to clarify, "I'm not trying to be overbearing, I just—well, I love you, Briar. And I don't want to lose you again."

She blinks, emotions flashing across her face—surprise, relief, maybe a flicker of amusement. I cup her cheek gently, thumb brushing against her skin. "I was thinking…" I swallow, suddenly nervous. "Once we can leave the safe house, I want you to move in with me. You and Jeb. My place is secure; it's big enough for all of us. I mean, it's no zoo aviary, but we'll manage."

Tears gather in her eyes, glistening in the dim lamplight. She laughs, a watery, joy-filled sound. "You're serious?"

I nod, heart hammering. "Dead serious. I want you there. Always."

Her arms loop around my neck, careful to avoid my wound. She leans in, resting her forehead against mine. "Yes," she whispers, choking back a sob. "Yes, Orion. Of course."

Relief crashes over me like a tidal wave. I tighten my hold, inhaling the faint floral scent of her hair, the presence that's become essential to me. Jeb squawks a disgruntled sound, like he's either jealous or demanding to be included.

Briar laughs, pulling back just enough to glance at the bird. "You're invited too, Jeb," she says.

I press a soft kiss to her temple, a surge of gratitude coursing through me. *She said yes.* Even with a bullet wound still healing, Russians at large, and Jason haunting the shadows, this moment feels like the first real step into a future I never thought I'd allow myself: one built on love, trust, and a fierce determination to keep each other safe.

"Welcome home," I whisper, tucking her beneath my chin. And for the first time in a long time, I dare to believe that life —our life—can be more than just missions and danger. It can be us, together, carving out something real.

Chapter 32

Briar

It's late, and the safe house is wrapped in darkness. The steady rhythm of Orion's breathing beside me has lulled me into a light sleep, one I'm desperately grateful for after the last few weeks of chaos. But something stirs me—a flicker of unease skittering down my spine. I blink away the haze of dreams, taking a moment to register my surroundings. Orion's arms are draped around me, protective even in slumber.

I carefully ease out from under his arm, not wanting to wake him. He needs his rest—his side still bandaged from that damn bullet. The idea that he nearly died keeps me awake some nights. *Not tonight*, I think, slipping my feet onto the floor. I'm just thirsty, that's all.

The wooden boards creak under my step as I pad into the hallway, arms folded against the slight chill. The safe house is quiet, shadows stretching across walls and floors under the faint glow of the streetlamp outside. Jeb's soft rustle sounds from the living room, but he doesn't stir.

In the kitchen, I flick on the small overhead light above the stove, bathing the counters in a soft, yellowish glow. I reach for a glass, trying not to dwell on the feeling that something is... off. Maybe the safe house's hush is messing with me, or the memory of all we've been through has me on edge.

I open the fridge and grab a water bottle, unscrewing the cap for a sip. That's when I sense movement behind me—a subtle shift of air, a presence lurking just on the edge of my vision. My heart hammers as I spin around.

"Jason," I manage to whisper, my voice paralyzed somewhere between shock and terror. He's standing there, mere steps away, eyes gleaming with an unsettling hunger. *He found us.*

I take a breath to scream, but he lunges forward, clapping a strong hand over my mouth. I drop the water bottle, the plastic clattering to the floor, water spilling across the tiles. A muffled cry escapes my throat, hands flailing to push him off, but he's stronger than I remember, or maybe it's the adrenaline coursing through his veins.

"Shh," he hisses, his free arm locking around my waist. "Don't make a sound."

My mind races. *How did he get in?* The safe house was locked, with extra security Orion's team set up. Did Jason manage to bypass them all? But I can't focus on that—I'm too busy fighting, thrashing my legs and twisting my hips, desperate to break free or at least alert Orion. He must hear the struggle, must wake up. *Orion, please wake up.*

Jason jerks his head toward the back door, dragging me across the kitchen. My socked feet slide helplessly on the puddle of spilled water. I try to dig my heels in, but he's relentless, forcing me to shuffle backward until we hit the threshold.

The cold night air washes over me as Jason yanks open the door, hauling me outside. My fists beat at his chest, nails scratching wildly at his arm, but he doesn't relent. When I manage a muffled cry, he clamps his hand tighter over my mouth, nearly cutting off my air. My lungs burn as I fight to breathe.

I catch a glimpse of the yard—a patchy lawn, a battered fence, the moon casting pale light across the grass. Everything looks so normal, so calm, except for the storm of panic roaring through me.

"Let me go," I try to shout, but it comes out garbled against his palm. My heart is slamming in my chest so hard I swear it's bruising my ribs.

He lowers his mouth near my ear. "Don't make this worse, Briar," he snarls, voice filled with twisted desperation. His hand slides from my mouth to my jaw, gripping it firmly as he pulls me away from the house.

I open my mouth, intending to scream Orion's name, but before I can, Jason clamps down again, suffocating any sound. I drive my elbow into his ribs, a burst of triumph flaring when I feel him grunt. But he keeps hold, dragging me further into the darkness.

My mind whirls with dread. *Orion, please.* If he doesn't wake soon, I'll be gone again—dragged off by this madman who's already stolen too much from me. I thrash harder, ignoring the tears burning my eyes. This can't be happening. *We were safe.* We were finally safe.

But Jason's iron grip says otherwise, and the night swallows my muffled screams as he drags me away.

My heart is pounding so hard I swear it's going to burst out of my chest. Jason's grip on my arm is bruising, his fingers digging into the flesh above my elbow. My teeth are clenched, and I force myself to speak through the searing panic.

"How did you even find me?" I manage to ask, fighting the tremor in my voice.

Jason's lips curl into a sneer. "I knew Orion had been shot. Figured he'd end up at a hospital, and eventually you'd show up there too." His eyes gleam with twisted satisfaction. "You basically delivered yourself right back into my hands."

My stomach twists. I try to yank away, but his hold is like a vice. "You're sick," I spit, voice trembling with adrenaline. "You can't keep doing this."

He huffs a dry laugh, tugging me closer. The stench of stale sweat and desperation clings to him, making my stomach turn. "Can't I?" he asks, low and cruel. "I loved you, Briar, and you walked away. You belong with me."

Rage surges up my throat. I lunge backward, trying to tear free, but he jerks me so hard I nearly lose my balance. My heart hammers. *Orion.* He must have heard something—he has to be on his way. I cling to that hope like a lifeline.

Before I can form another word, a presence emerges from behind a nearby tree. The moonlight cuts across Orion's tall frame, his gun leveled at Jason, unwavering. I almost sag with relief at the sight of him, bruised and bandaged but every bit the alpha protector I've come to trust.

"Let her go," Orion growls. His tone is lethal, deep, and commanding. "You're not taking Briar anywhere."

Jason's grip falters, and for a split second, I see fear flicker in his eyes. He recovers quickly, though, yanking me in front of him like a shield. My pulse spikes, but Orion doesn't lower his weapon.

"Put the gun down," Jason barks, jaw tight. "Or I'll snap her neck."

Orion's eyes fix on me, the silent message clear: *Hold on. I've got you.* He steps forward, slow, precise, ignoring the pain I know must be lancing through his healing side. "This ends now," he warns, his voice a low rumble. "You're not escaping."

Jason shifts, his grip loosening a fraction as he glances around, maybe looking for a way out. In that heartbeat of hesitation, I remember what Orion showed me about self-defense—aim for the instep. Summoning every scrap of courage, I slam my foot down on Jason's ankle, driving my heel into his vulnerable spot.

He yelps in pain, reflexively letting go. I twist free, scrambling out of his reach. Before Jason can even retaliate, Orion's finger tightens on the trigger. The muzzle flash lights the night, and my ears ring as gunfire shatters the tense silence.

Jason staggers, eyes wide, then collapses onto the grass. A single ragged breath escapes him before he goes still. I stand there, chest heaving, heart racing, time frozen in the aftermath. It's over. *It's finally over.*

I turn to Orion, tears welling up as the magnitude of what just happened slams into me. He's already lowering his weapon, exhaling a shaky breath. Despite his injuries, despite everything, he's here, and he saved me.

We lock eyes. My knees nearly give out, but Orion catches me before I fall. His arms fold around me, warmth radiating from him in a rush of relief. I bury my face in his shoulder, trembling as the realization sinks in—Jason's gone. He can't hurt me anymore.

The night air feels suddenly colder, the moonlight glaring on the motionless figure on the ground. But Orion's presence steadies me, his heartbeat thudding reassuringly against my ear.

"It's over," he murmurs, pressing a careful kiss to my temple. His voice shakes, just a little. "He can't take you from me ever again."

And for the first time in what seems like forever, I feel safe— truly, finally safe.

Epilogue

Orion

A warm summer sun spills across my back porch, the light catching on the rim of an iced tea pitcher and reflecting in bright patches on the worn wooden boards. I suck in a deep breath, enjoying the lingering aroma of freshly mowed grass, and then return my attention to the grill. The sizzle of hot dogs and the occasional flare of tiny flames fill me with an odd sense of contentment—an anchor grounding me in this moment.

It's been a few months since everything happened. A few months since the gunfire, the hospital stay, and that final confrontation that nearly cost me everything I cared about. But now, as I stand here grilling hot dogs in my own backyard, the smell of charcoal and spiced meat mingling with the laughter drifting through the open screen door, it all feels a world away.

Saving What's Mine

Briar's moved in with me, and though we've had our share of adjustments—my tidy habits versus her sudden bursts of creative clutter, Jeb's unpredictable chatter in the early mornings—it's better than I could've dreamed. She's here. She's safe. And that's all I could ever really want.

Chester was returned to the zoo, and continues to engage with his adoring fans. They're all happy he's back, and he gained about two million more followers from the whole ordeal.

"Yo, Orion!" Riggs calls from behind me, leaning against the porch rail. He's holding a bottle of beer, wearing a grin that crinkles the corners of his eyes. "How're those dogs looking?"

I glance at the ten hot dogs sizzling away. "They look about done. You see Dean's face if I burn them?" I smirk, flipping another patty. "He'd never let me hear the end of it."

Riggs chuckles, knocking back a swig from his beer. "He might make you run laps around the block."

"Or reassign me to cooking duty full-time," I tease. Even the thought of official assignments sends a ripple of relief through me, because the last few months have been blessedly quiet. The Russians and Heath are in custody, Jason's no longer a threat, and the rest of us have returned to normal routines—whatever normal means for a bunch of protective detail guys.

From inside the house, I hear a burst of laughter, punctuated by the distinctive squawk of Jeb's voice. That bird's grown more talkative by the day, apparently thrilled to have so much company around. He's become the unintentional life of every gathering.

Riggs nods toward the open patio door. "Sounds like Jeb's entertaining the masses again."

I can't help the grin that surfaces. "He's a show-off. Next time we have a big get-together, I'm half expecting him to break out a stand-up comedy routine."

Riggs arches an eyebrow. "Couldn't be worse than some of Gunner's jokes."

We share a laugh. Then the squeak of the screen door signals new arrivals to the porch. I glance over my shoulder and see Dean stepping out, hand in hand with Sophia. She's beaming, dressed in a breezy sundress, her dark hair pinned up in a loose bun. Dean's got that relaxed look of a man who's left a thousand worries behind. The difference from a few months ago is night and day—he's let himself enjoy life again.

"Everything okay in there?" I ask, nodding toward the house.

Sophia answers with a radiant smile. "Everything's great. Ranger was telling Tory about his last assignment in the Bahamas, and Jeb keeps repeating the word 'Bahamas' in the funniest accent. Gunner's about ready to throttle him if he says it one more time."

Dean slips an arm around Sophia's waist, giving her a playful squeeze. "We're going to set the table. If those dogs are ready, we can bring them in."

I poke one of the hot dogs with my tongs, listening to the juice sizzle. "Yep, just a minute or two more. You guys mind grabbing the buns and condiments?"

"On it," Dean says, turning back into the house with Sophia.

The screen door clacks shut, and Riggs steps forward to help me pull the hot dogs off. We slide them onto a large platter that Briar insisted we get—white porcelain, no chips around the edges—one of many little upgrades to the place since she moved in. I used to live a strictly functional life: minimal furnishings, no decorative nonsense. But now there are splashes of color in every room, pictures on the walls, a new throw blanket across the couch. Every time I see these little touches of her, a quiet joy sparks inside me.

Platter in hand, I nod for Riggs to open the door. We head inside, where the living room is in the midst of some chaotic conversation. Jeb is perched on the back of a chair, repeating "Bah-hah-mas!" in a singsong voice that's part parrot, part comedic impression. Ranger stands near him, arms crossed, grinning. Beside Ranger is Tory, the petite blonde who overcame her own set of challenges—some of which I only half know, involving a security mission that went sideways. She's wearing a bright smile, amused by the spectacle.

Across the room, Gunner sprawls on the couch, rolling his eyes while Maverick and Briar chat animatedly next to him. The moment we walk in with the hot dogs, the smell must hit them because the conversation halts, replaced by appreciative murmurs.

Briar looks up, and our eyes lock. Her smile is instant, brightening every corner of my heart. She bounds over to me, pressing a quick kiss to my cheek. "Smells amazing," she says, her voice low enough that only I hear the approval in her tone.

"Have to keep you well-fed," I murmur back, ignoring the gentle teasing glances from our friends. I never used to do small talk or flirty banter, but with Briar, it's as easy as breathing.

She giggles, guiding me toward the dining table, which has been extended to accommodate the entire group. Bowls of salad, chips, a tray of condiments, and a pitcher of iced tea line the center. Dean sets down a basket of warm buns, and Sophia places a stack of plates at one end. Within seconds, the once-quiet table is a flurry of activity as we all gather around, pulling out chairs and passing around dishes.

"All right, all right," Ranger calls out, raising his voice to be heard above the hustle. "Let's get a seat before Jeb decides to sample everything." He gently shoos Jeb off the back of a chair, and the bird flutters to a smaller perch in the corner, squawking in mild protest.

We manage to cram around the table, a cozy sort of chaos. Dean at the head, Sophia beside him, then Maverick, Gunner, Ranger, Tory, Briar, and me. Riggs, who always picks the most awkward seat, ends up at the far corner near Jeb. The bird eyes him as though planning a sneak attack.

A lull settles as we dig in. Paper plates crinkle, and plastic cups rustle. The aroma of fresh-grilled beef mingles with the crisp tang of salad dressing. There's a sense of relief in the air, that intangible weight lifted from all our shoulders.

Mid-meal, I glance across at Gunner, who's wearing an expression of thinly veiled disgust. He picks at the label on his beer bottle. Maverick arches an eyebrow. "Something on your mind, Gunner?"

Gunner huffs. "The new assignment. Dean stuck me with bodyguard duty for that Hollywood actress, Scarlett something. I'm not looking forward to babysitting some pampered starlet."

At that, Tory laughs softly. "You think it's going to be that bad?"

He shoots her a half-glare. "I'm an ex-Marine, not a glorified fashion accessory. The job starts in a week—two months in Los Angeles, trailing after this actress at red carpet events and swanky parties." He shudders. "Doesn't seem like my scene."

Saving What's Mine

Ranger chuckles, nudging him with an elbow. "C'mon, maybe you'll like it. All those fancy parties and free drinks. Might even see some big-name celebrities. Hell, you might end up on the front page of a magazine."

Gunner's face twists like someone just made him eat a lemon. "I'd rather babysit Jeb in a hurricane."

"Bah-hah-mas!" Jeb exclaims from his perch, as if weighing in on the conversation. We can't help but burst into laughter, the tension melting away in an instant.

Dean clears his throat, pretending to be serious. "Look, we all have to take the occasional assignment that's not exactly a perfect fit. Just try not to scare the poor woman with your scowl."

"Asher might be more suited for that job," Maverick says. "He's got the calm, quiet thing going on. He can handle starlets, no problem."

Gunner levels a scowl at them. "At least I won't have to deal with your wisecracks. I'll be on the west coast, far away from this crew."

Riggs, who's been silent, chimes in with a smirk. "Send pictures, or we'll never believe it's real."

The table breaks into another round of laughter, and I smile, letting the conversation wash over me. This is what we fought for—these moments of camaraderie, free from fear or bullets or kidnappings. My gaze shifts to Briar, who's nibbling on a chip while surveying the group with a contented expression. She catches me looking and raises an eyebrow in question.

I lean closer, letting the chatter fade into the background. "How're you holding up?" I ask softly, mindful of her past anxieties.

Her green eyes shine with warmth. "I'm good," she answers, resting a hand on mine under the table. "Happy."

A wave of affection swells in my chest. *God, I love her.* The thought is so strong I can't help the surge of pride that follows—pride that she chose me, that we survived all that chaos and still found each other intact.

Across the table, Dean pushes back his chair and stands. The group grows quiet, expecting some sort of announcement. Dean's always been the leader, the anchor for us. He clears his throat, glancing around.

"I just want to say," he begins, "it's good to have all of us here, healthy and safe. Lincoln, Asher, and Boone are definitely missed, but their jobs are still going strong and they're in the thick of it now. However, we've seen some dark days, but nights like this remind me why we do what we do—to protect the people who matter, and to keep living even after the worst storms."

A flicker of emotion passes over his features, and Sophia slips her hand into his. The rest of us nod, murmuring our agreement. I feel Briar squeeze my fingers again, an unspoken vow that we're in this together.

"Now," Dean continues, forcing a lighter tone, "I'm going to excuse myself to rummage through Orion's fridge. I need another drink, and there's bound to be dessert around here. Right, Sophia?"

Sophia laughs. "We brought homemade cupcakes. Double chocolate, your favorite."

A general groan of delight ripples around the table. I catch Gunner rolling his eyes again, but the corner of his mouth quirks up. Maverick chuckles, patting his stomach. "Well, we might have to waddle out of here."

We continue feasting, the conversation weaving from topic to topic—Ranger and Tory's upcoming trip to the mountains, Maverick's new side hobby designing custom drone attachments, Riggs's plan to visit family overseas. Even Jeb gets a mention, though mostly to complain about his 5 a.m. squawking. Briar volunteers an impassioned defense of the bird, claiming he's just "energetically curious." We all grin and humor her.

Eventually, the plates clear, the drinks run low, and we drift into the backyard to sprawl on lawn chairs, the sky overhead streaked with oranges and purples from the setting sun. Jeb waddles around on the grass, pecking at random spots. Ranger keeps an eye on him, calling out, "Don't you dare take flight and vanish, you little thief." Jeb merely cocks his head, squawks "Bah-hah-mas!" once more, and flutters closer.

I settle onto a cushioned outdoor sofa, Briar tucked beside me. She leans her head against my shoulder, and I drape an arm around her. Her hair smells like citrus shampoo and sunshine. The rest of the crew lounge around, finishing off the last of the iced tea or cracking open new bottles of beer. A comfortable silence envelops us, punctuated by the chirping of crickets and the occasional whir of a passing car in the distance.

When darkness finally settles, Dean and Sophia start gathering their things. Gunner stands, picking at his phone, no doubt checking for the next dreaded Hollywood assignment. Maverick and Riggs chat quietly about tomorrow's training schedule. Ranger and Tory slip inside to wash a few dishes, and the muffled sound of running water filters through the open windows.

Briar shifts in my arms, her lips grazing my ear. "Ready for them to go so we can have some alone time?"

My heart stutters at her soft tone. *Alone time.* After everything, that concept feels sacred. I nod, pressing my mouth to her forehead. "More than ready."

As if on cue, the final goodbyes are said. Maverick, who was quiet most of the evening, offers a handshake and a grin, referencing an early morning briefing with Dean. Ranger and Tory linger a bit, exchanging a warm look with me and Briar. Then, with Jeb safely back on his perch, we're left alone at last.

We migrate back into the house, flipping off a few lights until only the living room lamp casts a gentle glow. The remains of the evening's feast clutter the table, but it can wait. I guide Briar to the couch, and we sink into the cushions, the hush of night settling around us.

"You did good tonight," she whispers, tracing a fingertip along the collar of my shirt. "You always do. Making everyone feel safe."

I shrug, a little self-conscious. "They're family, in their own way."

She nods, eyes reflecting the warm light. "A big, protective, kinda crazy family," she amends with a grin.

We laugh, letting that notion sink in. For a moment, I recall the day I almost lost her, the bullet in my side, the endless hospital nights. My chest tightens with a flood of gratitude that she's here, that we survived. Slowly, I cup her cheek.

"I love you, you know," I say, voice thick with emotion. "Not a day goes by where I don't realize how lucky I am."

Her gaze softens, tears glistening at the corners of her eyes. "I love you too," she breathes, leaning in. Our lips meet, a soft, lingering kiss that conveys more than words ever could—a quiet vow, a promise of tomorrow.

Saving What's Mine

When we part, she curls closer, resting her head on my shoulder. I skim my fingers up and down her arm. The hum of the air conditioner clicks on, stirring the curtains slightly. Jeb mutters something from the other room, but it's subdued now that the crowd's gone.

"What do you think happens next?" she asks softly, perhaps uncertain about the future now that the immediate danger has passed.

I take a slow breath. "We keep living," I say simply. "Jason's gone, the Russians are done for, and we've got a new normal. We watch out for each other, chase away nightmares if they pop up, and build something real here. Day by day."

She nods against me. "Yeah. I like that plan."

We settle into a contented quiet, the weight of the last few months lifting bit by bit. The living room lamp casts shadows that dance across the walls, and I hold onto Briar, my heart full in a way I never imagined possible.

Suddenly, Jeb flutters in, squawking what sounds like "Goodnight!" We exchange amused glances. Briar giggles, sliding off the couch to guide him back to his perch. I watch her, my chest tight with the kind of happiness that's both terrifying and exhilarating in its intensity.

This is it, I think. *This is what I wanted.* A home, a life, and someone to share it with. Even if the next mission or crisis calls me away for a while, I know where my heart will remain —right here, with Briar. There's no question about it.

She returns, curling into my side again, and I press a kiss to her hair. Outside, the night sky stretches infinite and peaceful, unbroken by threats. Inside, warmth and laughter linger, even after the lights dim, forging a memory I'll carry forever. And I vow that nothing will take this peace from us again.

Bonus Epilogue

Briar

It's been a few weeks since our big cookout, and life is finally settling into the kind of steady rhythm I've always craved. I'm up before dawn most mornings, greeting the birds at the zoo and going over show scripts with the newly expanded avian team—**my** team, now that Marcie promoted me to bird trainer. The title still feels surreal on my tongue: *Bird Trainer.* A year ago, it was a distant dream. Now it's my everyday life.

But today is even more special. Today is the first performance of a brand-new show I pitched to Marcie—a magic extravaganza featuring Orion as the magician and Jeb as his "assistant." I know, it sounds a little crazy: a trained security specialist turned magician, teamed up with a mischievous African Grey parrot. Marcie's eyebrows nearly hit the roof when I first proposed it. But Orion and I practiced for weeks, and Jeb's comedic timing is so spot-on that even I can't stop laughing during our rehearsals. And Orion's helped him get over his stage fright.

Bonus Epilogue

Now, I'm leaning against the backstage railing, heart thudding with a mix of nerves and excitement. The zoo's small amphitheater is packed—families with wide-eyed kids, young couples on dates, older folks who come to the zoo just for the bird shows. The sun is high overhead, but the staff has set up big umbrellas for shade, and there's a constant breeze rustling the palm trees lining the back of the stage.

Marcie stands beside me, clipboard in hand, scanning the audience with that critical gaze of hers. "Looks like a full house," she mutters, half to herself, half to me.

I nod, taking a steadying breath. "Yep. Fingers crossed everything goes smoothly."

She shoots me a sharp grin. "It will, *Bird Trainer.*"

I snort softly, my stomach fluttering. I'm about to respond, but an eruption of applause from the stands signals that the show is about to start. We exchange a final glance, and then I slip around the side of the stage, mind racing with last-minute checks: *Are Orion's props ready? Did Jeb get enough warm-up time? Did we feed him enough so he's not cranky?*

From my hidden vantage, I watch the show's intro video flash across a large screen. It's a montage of exotic birds, swirling colors, and upbeat music that the zoo's marketing team whipped up last week. Then the lights shift, and an announcer booms over the speakers: "Ladies and gentlemen, welcome to our brand-new Magic in Flight spectacle! Please put your hands together for our resident magician... **Orion Locke**... and his talented co-star... **Jeb** the African Grey!"

The crowd bursts into cheers, and I feel a wave of pride wash over me. Orion steps onto the stage, tall and confident, wearing a fitted black jacket, jeans, and the slightest hint of a smirk. He's come a long way from bullet wounds and bodyguard gear. Now, with a deck of cards in one hand and a small

Bonus Epilogue

top hat perched on a stand nearby, he cuts a striking figure. The sun glints off his dark hair, and I recall countless nights watching him practice those card tricks in secret, never imagining he'd one day perform them in front of an audience.

"All right, everybody," Orion's voice echoes warmly, projected by the mic clipped to his lapel. "I'm not your typical magician —but I've got a not-so-typical helper, too. Meet Jeb!"

On cue, Jeb flutters out from the side, perched on a little rolling stand. The crowd gasps and giggles as the African Grey greets them with a squawk, then a surprisingly clear "Hello, everyone!" He's been practicing that line for days.

Orion's grin widens. "Care to pick a card, Jeb?"

He fans out a deck in front of the bird, who cocks his head, mutters something that sounds suspiciously like "Bah-hah-mas," a leftover from Ranger's tall tales, then pecks at the center card. Orion flips it to show the audience—an Ace of Hearts—and slides it back into the deck.

"Now, ladies and gentlemen," Orion continues, "keep your eyes on Jeb. He's going to help me find that exact card again."

The crowd murmurs, enthralled. In typical comedic fashion, Jeb leans forward, plucks a random card from the deck with his beak, and flings it onto the stage floor. Orion bends to pick it up, revealing... the Ace of Hearts. Applause erupts, the kids in the front row bouncing in excitement. But Jeb isn't done— he squawks, and Orion plays along like he's listening to the bird's instructions.

"Oh, you want to do one more trick?" Orion says, raising an eyebrow. He lifts the top hat, which the audience can see is empty. With a flourish, he sets it on the ground, taps it thrice with a wand, then tips it over. A flurry of bright confetti rains out, revealing a small plush parrot toy that Orion *swears* wasn't inside before. The crowd howls with delight. Jeb, apparently miffed at the sudden confetti storm, ruffles his feathers and says, "What the—?" in his squeaky approximation of Orion's voice, sending the audience into hysterics.

I can't help laughing softly from the sidelines, heart brimming with pride and warmth. *We did it*, I think, chest light. Orion's so at ease in front of the crowd, and Jeb is a total ham, soaking up every ounce of attention. As the act continues, Orion transitions to illusions involving small hoops, bright silks, and Jeb's impeccable comedic timing. At one point, Jeb "steals" Orion's wand, flying just a foot above the stage while holding it in his beak, and the children in the front row nearly fall over with laughter.

The final trick is a showstopper: Orion pretends to vanish Jeb in a big, glittering box. Everyone gasps when Orion opens the box to reveal it empty. The stage lights dim, suspense thick in the air. Then a spotlight appears on the back of the amphitheater, illuminating Jeb perched on a technician's booth, bobbing his head like he owns the place. The crowd *explodes* in cheers.

I swallow the lump in my throat, overwhelmed by the joy in the amphitheater. This is my job now—helping these amazing birds shine, entertaining and educating people, and, apparently, staging magic shows that highlight Orion's secret talent. I can't believe how far we've come.

The show wraps with a thunderous round of applause. Orion takes a bow, then nods toward Jeb, who dips his head in what looks like a respectful acknowledgment but is probably just him wanting a treat. People file out, chatting excitedly, several kids begging their parents to let them see the show again tomorrow. My heart soars.

Bonus Epilogue

As the last visitors trickle away, I step onto the stage from behind the curtain, crossing toward Orion. He's gently coaxing Jeb into stepping onto his forearm, passing him off to one of our fellow trainers so Jeb can rest and get some well-earned snacks. The instant he sees me, Orion's face lights up, eyes warm.

We meet in the middle of the stage, the amphitheater almost empty now. "That was incredible," I say, voice trembling with excitement. "You two had them in the palm of your hand."

Orion sets a hand on my hip, leaning in to press a quick, tender kiss to my forehead. "Couldn't have done it without you. Or Jeb," he adds with a grin.

I glance offstage where Jeb is happily chattering away at one of the zoo staff, no doubt babbling about who-knows-what. "I think he's expecting a five-star dinner after that performance."

Orion chuckles. "He'll get it. We owe him big time." Then his gaze slides back to me. "And you too, Bird Trainer. That was your idea, your vision. I'm just following your lead."

Warmth floods my chest, and I slide my arms around his waist. "I'm so proud of you," I whisper, letting my head rest against his chest.

He squeezes me gently, voice a low rumble. "I love this. I love *you*, and the life we're building."

My heart flutters, remembering how uncertain everything was not so long ago—Jason's threats, the Russians, the nights I wondered if we'd even survive. Now, we're standing on the stage of my *new job*, living together without fear. The contrast is dizzying in the best way.

"Thank you for always believing in me," I say softly, pulling back enough to look him in the eye. "Before... I never thought

I'd have a life like this. Or a show that merges magic and bird training, for God's sake."

He chuckles, tipping my chin up for a light kiss. "You're unstoppable, Briar. Soon enough, you'll be running the entire zoo."

I grin, cheeks flushing at the compliment. "Let's focus on the next few shows first, huh?"

He smirks. "Deal. I can handle that."

We linger there, letting the stage lights dim to a faint glow. The staff milling around understand we need this moment—there's no immediate call to shuffle us off. My mind wanders, imagining a future of bigger bird shows, maybe even a traveling act if Marcie gets ambitious. But for now, we'll keep it simple: daily magic sets featuring Orion and Jeb, wowing the crowds. And behind the scenes, we'll keep building this life we've fought so hard for.

I slip my hand into Orion's. "Think Jeb will still do the card tricks in tomorrow's show, or do we need to up our game?"

He laughs, steering me gently toward the backstage area. "He might get bored and try to juggle. Or maybe vanish on me for real. That bird's ambition knows no bounds."

I picture that: Jeb tossing Orion's wand into the audience mid-performance. The mental image alone has me snickering. "We'll have to watch him carefully. But hey, at least the audience loves him."

Orion nods. "True. He's a star, all right." Then his tone shifts, growing softer. "Just remember, you're the real star here, Briar. You're the one behind the scenes making it all happen."

I tighten my grip on his hand, gratitude brimming in my chest. "Couldn't do it without you," I whisper. "You're my partner—in magic, birds, and everything else."

His eyes crinkle at the corners, that familiar warmth I've come to associate with his love shining through. "Always."

The amphitheater empties out entirely, leaving us in a quiet hush broken only by the last echoes of staff chatter. We meander backstage, where Jeb is perched contentedly, munching on grapes in a little treat bowl. He lifts a wing, babbling, "Good show, good show!"—one of the new lines we taught him last week. Orion ruffles the feathers on his head, beaming.

Then Orion slips an arm around my waist, guiding me toward the exit. "How about we celebrate?" he suggests, voice low. "Pick up dinner on the way home, maybe open that bottle of wine we've been saving?"

I lean into him, pressing a kiss to his jaw. "I'd like that. Let's do it."

In that moment, the swirl of uncertain tomorrows and half-remembered fears fades. All I feel is the steady reassurance of Orion by my side, the soft flutter of love in my chest, and the knowledge that while life is never guaranteed to be easy, we've found the kind of happiness most people only dream about.

As we step out into the last golden rays of the setting sun, I glance back at the empty stage one final time, thinking of how it looked with Orion and Jeb in the spotlight, the crowd laughing and applauding. We've both traveled a long, dangerous road to get here. And with each day that passes, each show, each quiet dinner at home, I realize just how precious it all is. And how lucky we are to have it.

Bonus Epilogue

Clinging to his arm, I savor the present. Whatever the future holds—more illusions, more exotic birds, or maybe even a brand-new act featuring a parrot stand-up routine—one thing's for sure: we'll face it together, with laughter, magic, and a heart as full as I ever dared to hope.

Sneak Peek of Guarding What's Mine

Chapter One
Boone

Today promises to be a good day. Not only do I get to travel for work—a perk I'm always excited about—but I'll also have a chance to escape to my cabin tucked away in the Tennessee woods just outside of Nashville. That place has been my sanctuary since I left the military. Something about the pine-scented air, the hush of the forest, and the satisfaction of chopping your own firewood speaks to a part of me that Saint Pierce's salty breeze never quite reaches.

This upcoming job is exactly what I need. Dean hinted last week there might be an assignment near Nashville, and he knew I'd be perfect for it—maybe because I'm ex-military and more than capable of handling tough situations, or maybe it's because I look the part. My beard's grown in thick and full lately, and I have to say, even though I'm more used to deserts and jungles than mountains, I've embraced the rugged look. The grizzly mountain man look.

I flash a quick grin to the blonde receptionist behind the front desk in the gleaming lobby of Maddox Securities, perched on the thirtieth floor of one of the tallest buildings in Saint Pierce. Then I step into the elevator. As I ride up, I can't stop myself from picturing the Tennessee wilderness, the crisp air, and the logs stacked neatly beside my cabin's porch. It's exactly what I need—a reprieve from Saint Pierce's relentless heat and an excuse to indulge in the kind of hands-on work that makes me feel alive.

When the elevator doors glide open, I stroll into the sleek, glass-walled conference room. "I'm here," I announce, rubbing a hand over my beard, letting a slow grin spread across my face. "The meeting can begin now."

A few of the guys chuckle, and I drop into a seat, nodding at Ranger. His expression is tight, like something's weighing him down. I remember what he told me last week—about his sister—and my tone shifts as I murmur, "Sorry to hear about your sister."

He gives me a brusque nod. "It's fine."

But I can see from the tense line of his jaw that it's anything but fine. Greta's a good woman. The thought of her hurting over some scumbag's betrayal sets my teeth on edge. I fold my arms over my chest, the protective instinct I honed in the Marines kicking up a notch. "If you need me to knock that motherfucker out," I offer, letting my voice go cold, "just say the word."

Ranger's gaze flicks to mine, appreciation in his eyes. "Thanks, Boone. I'll keep that in mind."

Across the table, Lincoln raises an eyebrow. "Knock who out?"

Ranger explains how his sister's long-term boyfriend cheated on her, leaving her heartbroken—and with little faith left in men. The reminder pulls at a part of me that's hardwired to protect the people I care about. Greta's off-limits when it comes to heartbreak, at least if I have a say in the matter.

I push a breath through my nose, cracking my knuckles as I consider the possibilities. Nothing makes my blood boil like someone who preys on a woman's trust. Moments like this take me back to my military days—guarding bases, escorting civilians through danger zones. I've seen enough ugliness in the world to know you can't stand by when someone you care about is in trouble.

"She's been devastated ever since," Ranger mutters, his voice low and pained. He laces his fingers together on the table, as though trying to keep himself calm. "It's probably why I'll never fall in love."

I feel a pang of sympathy twist in my chest for his sister, but I also get where Ranger's coming from. If I had a drink in hand, I'd raise it to toast that sentiment. I'm about to agree when Dean clears his throat.

"Love isn't all bad," he says, in that confident way he has of looking on the bright side.

A laugh escapes me. "I'm surprised you're even here, Dean," I tease, my tone lighter than the tension in the room. "Figured you'd still be holed up with your girl."

Dean's expression softens immediately. He starts talking about Sophia—this woman who turned his entire life upside down. The story is wild, even by our standards: the job was supposed to be a simple extraction, kidnap one of the Four Families' daughters, only for him to discover Sophia in her place at the last moment. Suddenly, he found himself pretending to be married to her, all so he could lure out Bishop Blackstone, a notorious mob boss. And now here Dean is, grinning like a fool because he's clearly head over heels.

"I've never seen him like this," Ranger whispers, nudging me. And he's right. Dean's happiness is so obvious it practically fills the room.

Then the door bangs open, interrupting the moment. Orion staggers in, his hair disheveled like he just tumbled out of bed. Honestly, knowing him, he probably did. He yawns, settles into a chair, and props his feet up on the table—unapologetically Orion.

I turn back to Ranger, who's rubbing the back of his neck. Seeing the hint of worry in his eyes reminds me why I'm closest to him out of everyone in the group. He's solid. Dependable. And he's the reason I'm even here. We met a couple of years ago. As soon as we both got out of the military, Ranger talked to Dean on my behalf, and got me this job at Maddox Securities.

It was exactly what I needed at the time—an outlet for that military readiness that never really leaves you, but without all the red tape. Dean built Maddox Securities from scratch, first dealing in high-tech security systems before branching into personal security. Now, he—and by extension, all of us—have flown around the globe, working with mafia families and all sorts of clients most people wouldn't touch with a ten-foot pole.

Of course, we keep our mouths shut about the specifics. That's part of the deal. Anyone who can afford the high price tag of Maddox Securities wants the best, and the best requires absolute discretion. We're a tight-knit, elite group, which suits me just fine. I'd rather keep my head down, do the job, and get paid well for it than deal with the nine-to-five grind.

Still, I can't help but notice the faint slump in Ranger's shoulders whenever someone brings up his sister. I remind myself that when push comes to shove, I've got his back—both on the clock and off. It's just who I am.

"Why do you schedule these meetings so early in the morning?" Orion complains the instant he drags himself through the door. His voice is a low grumble, and he slumps into a chair like his bones barely hold him up.

Dean looks at his watch and shakes his head. "It's nine a.m. That's hardly the crack of dawn." He chuckles, clearly amused at Orion's theatrics.

Ignoring Dean, Orion presses his forehead against the polished cherry-wood table, letting out a long groan. I arch an eyebrow at the sight.

"Rough night?" I ask, my tone playful, though I already know exactly why he's so wiped—and unfortunately, it's not because he got lucky. Given how dedicated Orion is, he probably spent half the night chasing down leads or combing through files on our latest client. Still, I can't help wishing he'd had a more enjoyable reason for the dark circles under his eyes. The guy deserves a break. Hell, we all do.

But he only grunts in reply, which sends a ripple of laughter through the rest of us.

A moment later, Asher enters, his dark eyes flicking around the table, quietly taking in the scene. He's our newest recruit, and I don't know much about him yet—other than the fact that he's as sharp as any of us, and Dean seems to trust him implicitly. That's more than enough to put him in my good graces.

Dean clears his throat, gathering everyone's attention. "Thanks for being here. I know the past couple of months have been rough with me on the hunt for Bishop." His gaze drops to the stack of papers in front of him. He flips through them, the seriousness of his expression taking hold of the room. "I can't thank you all enough for the roles you played in tracking him down. Hopefully, now we'll have a little peace."

I nod in agreement. It's no secret that Lincoln and Isabel ran themselves ragged to keep things running smoothly while Dean was away. We all did our part, but those two especially carried a heavy load.

Dean continues, "And I owe Isabel a lot, too. She's been a huge help. Having a sister who's also a part of this operation is...well, I'm damn lucky." He smiles briefly, then glances at Lincoln. There's a flicker of something there—appreciation, maybe gratitude. I wonder if he'll acknowledge the extra mile Lincoln went. Or if there's something else going on behind the scenes.

Before I can dwell on it, Dean's all business again. "All right. Now that the dust has settled, I've got some new assignments to hand out. Let's get to it."

My pulse stirs. Nashville. I already know that's where I'm headed, but I try to keep my eagerness under wraps. I haven't been to my Tennessee cabin in too long, and just the thought of breathing in that crisp mountain air has me itching to head out.

Dean shuffles another stack of folders and picks one off the top. "Ranger, I'll start with you." He hands Ranger a slim file. "This is Tory Ann."

Ranger opens the folder, his brow furrowing as he scans the contents. "Is she attending the summit?"

Dean shakes his head. "No, her father—Frederick Malser—is the one attending. He's a world-renowned scientist and one of the keynote speakers at the G-Summit this weekend. He'll

Sneak Peek of Guarding What's Mine

have his own personal security detail, so he wants separate coverage for his daughter."

Ranger arches an eyebrow. "Why not just let his own team watch over her, too?"

It's a fair question, and one that makes me lean in, interested to hear the explanation. Dean folds his arms, preparing to elaborate, and I can't help but notice how the tension in the room builds again—like we're all bracing for whatever surprise might come next.

"Frederick's been receiving threats related to his presentation at the Summit," Dean explains, tapping the file on the table. "He doesn't want anyone knowing his daughter will be in town. He wants to keep it all under wraps—especially since he isn't completely sure he can trust everyone on his own security detail."

Ranger grimaces. "That sucks."

Dean nods in agreement before continuing. "You'll take his daughter to the safe house: SEASHELL, and keep her there until the Summit is over. Minimal contact, minimal movement."

"Sounds good," Ranger mutters, though his expression suggests he knows it won't be that simple.

Dean's gaze slides over to Orion, who's half-dozing in his chair. I give the leg of his chair a good kick to jolt him awake.

"Orion," Dean says, "this is for you. Her name's Briar Green —the daughter of socialite Minnie Green. She has an ex-boyfriend stalking her. Her mother wants to ensure she's safe going to and from work."

"Ex-boyfriend?" Orion echoes, lifting his head. He flips through the file, eyes still heavy with fatigue. "Can't I just beat him senseless, scare the hell out of him, and call it a day?"

Dean's lips twitch with a hint of a smile. "It's never that simple, my friend. We need a more…subtle approach this time." He slides the folder fully in front of Orion.

"It never is," Orion grumbles, but he seems more alert now, scanning the details of his assignment.

From the corner of my eye, I notice Dean glance at Lincoln. Dean mentioned earlier that Lincoln already has his assignment, but there's a flicker of tension between them that piques my curiosity. Something else is going on there, but it's not my place to pry—yet.

Finally, Dean turns to me. I straighten up, anticipation coursing through my veins. "Boone," Dean says, sliding a manila folder across the table. "Here's yours. I gave you a quick preview last week, but now we have more details."

My pulse quickens as I pick up the file. Nashville. I'm already picturing my cabin nestled in the Tennessee woods. But the photo clipped to the first page stops me in my tracks. A woman's face—delicate features, fiery amber eyes, and hair a shade of red that practically smolders off the page.

"Wow," I breathe, before I can stop myself. "Who's this?"

"Aubree Ryan," Dean responds, leaning back in his chair. "She's got a stalker, too. We don't know who it is yet, but it sounds serious. She needs to get out of Nashville until we can figure out who's behind it."

I glance at the photo again, something tightening low in my gut. It's unexpected—this surge of protectiveness. I've guarded plenty of women before without blinking an eye. But there's something about Aubree that's already under my skin.

"Right," I say, clearing my throat. "I'll take her to my cabin nearby. That should keep her off the radar."

"Good." Dean snaps another file shut. "We'll coordinate the details, but you'll head out as soon as you can."

I barely hear him. My mind's already drifting to that tiny stretch of forest I call home, imagining what it'll be like to have this striking, vulnerable woman tucked away with me—hidden from the rest of the world.

What's wrong with me? This isn't the first time I've protected someone. Yet the sight of Aubree's photo has my thoughts scattering in a way they never have before.

I let out a low breath. Has it really been that long since I let anyone get close? Because one look at her, and I can feel my carefully constructed walls start to shift. And that…well, that might be a problem.

I swallow hard and force my features into a neutral mask, hoping Dean doesn't notice the spark of interest flaring inside me. It's not exactly professional to react to an assignment this way. But, damn it, seeing Aubree Ryan's photo triggered something I wasn't expecting—a twist of protectiveness mixed with an undeniable attraction.

This is fucked up, I tell myself. *Keep it together, Boone.*

I glance across the room at Orion, who's also flipping through his file with a furrowed brow. It's always something new with that guy, and by the way his eyes widen slightly, I can tell his current assignment isn't a walk in the park either. I make a mental note to check on him later, see if he needs anything.

Dean dismisses the meeting, and we all file out of the conference room. I catch a glimpse of Asher being asked to stay behind, probably for a private update on his own job.

Sneak Peek of Guarding What's Mine

Once we're in the hallway, I run a hand over my beard and smirk at my friends. "We all need to catch up soon," I say, remembering the last time we hung out. It ended in far too much whiskey and just enough laughs. "Last time was a damn good time."

Orion yawns, but there's a mischievous light in his eyes. "Maybe once I'm done protecting a girl from her psycho ex, we can do a guys-only poker night."

Ranger chuckles. "I'm definitely in."

Of course he is. Ranger kills it at poker; the man's practically a human lie detector. I still remember losing five hundred bucks the last time we squared off. Stubborn pride and a poor bluff are a lethal combination.

"I'd love some more free money," Ranger says, crossing his arms with a smug grin.

"No way I'm playing with you again," Lincoln cuts in. He shakes his head like he's still nursing that old wound. "Besides, my own assignment isn't exactly a cakewalk."

He shoots a quick glance down the hall, and I can't help but wonder if his job has something to do with the big meeting Dean had earlier. Ranger cuffs him lightly on the shoulder.

"Yeah, I figured," Ranger says. "Dean asked to see you before all of us earlier. What's going on?"

Lincoln blows out a breath. "It's Isabel," he admits, lowering his voice. "She's been threatened."

A heavy silence settles over us. Isabel is Dean's sister, and as long as I've been with Maddox Securities, I know one thing: family is off-limits. That makes whoever is messing with her a dead man walking.

"Who is it?" I ask quietly.

Sneak Peek of Guarding What's Mine

Lincoln shakes his head. "We're not sure yet. Dean has a few leads, so while he's looking into it, I'm basically glued to Isabel's side."

"Good luck," Orion says with a half-laugh. "You know how she gets when she's pissed."

We all nod in agreement. Isabel's not a woman you want to cross. And sure enough, the rapid click of stilettos against marble tiles echoes down the hallway. She comes into view, her gaze locked onto Lincoln like a heat-seeking missile. The fury in her eyes says she's well aware of this new 'protection detail,' and she's not happy about it.

Before she can level her wrath at the rest of us, we scramble to make ourselves scarce. I head for the elevators, shaking my head with a mix of amusement and pity for Lincoln.

That's life at Maddox Securities—constant danger, complicated assignments, and sometimes a little heartbreak. But we stick together, even when we're butting heads or chasing down leads.

Stepping into the elevator, I think of the folder tucked under my arm and the redhead who's about to turn my life upside down. I need to get a flight and meet Aubree Ryan. Keep her safe. Keep my head on straight.

I let out a slow, steadying breath. It's time to handle business, the way I always do—like a professional. Even if my gut twists every time I remember those fiery amber eyes.

Meet Boone and Aubree in Guarding What's Mine, Book #3 in the Men of Maddox Security.
CLICK HERE to snag your copy! Guarding What's Mine releases March 11th, 2025!

Patreon

Calling All Romance Lovers!

Ready for exclusive perks, behind-the-scenes access, and swoon-worthy surprises? Join **Logan Chance's Patreon** today!

Here's what you'll get:

- **Sticker of the Month Club** – Collect your favorite characters and moments in adorable sticker form.

- **Signed Paperbacks** – Delivered straight to your door, just for you.

- **Exclusive Giveaways** – Win books, swag, and more.

- **Bonus Content** – Unreleased scenes, steamy extras, and secrets from your favorite stories.

- **Character Interviews** – Get to know Logan's characters like never before.

- **Sneak Peeks** – Be the first to dive into upcoming books and projects.

Patreon

And that's just the beginning! There's SO MUCH MORE! Logan's Patreon is packed with romance reader delights you won't want to miss.

Sign up now and get access to all the swoony goodies today!

CLICK HERE, or visit www.patreon.com/loganchance

Your next favorite romance moment is waiting for you.

About the Author

Logan Chance is a USA Today bestselling author who specializes in high-octane romantic suspense with a touch of humor (or more). Known for weaving intense, pulse-pounding plots with sizzling chemistry, Logan's novels captivate readers from the first page. He was nominated for Best Debut Author Goodreads Choice Awards in 2016. He crafts tales filled with steamy romance, gripping twists, and heart-stopping action.

When he's not writing, Logan can often be found watching great movies, devouring his ever-growing TBR pile, or brainstorming his next captivating series. He currently resides in South Florida, where he continues to pen stories that keep readers on the edge of their seats—and always craving more.

Also by Logan Chance

Men of Maddox Security
PROTECTING WHAT'S MINE
SAVING WHAT'S MINE
GUARDING WHAT'S MINE
TAKING WHAT'S MINE
DEFENDING WHAT'S MINE

The Moore Brothers, coming soon
Moore Than A Bosshole
Moore Than A Booty Call
Moore Than A Single Dad
Moore Than A Frenemy
Moore Than A Fake Date

The Magnolia Ridge Series

DON'T FALL FOR YOUR BEST FRIEND, Paxton and Hartford's Story

DON'T FALL FOR YOUR BROTHER'S BEST FRIEND, Anya and Griffin's Story

DON'T FALL FOR YOUR GRUMPY NEIGHBOR, Shepherd and Felicity's Story

DON'T FALL FOR YOUR FAKE BOYFRIEND, Brock and Willow's Story

DON'T FALL FOR YOUR EX-BOYFRIEND'S BROTHER, Tripp and Millie's Story

DON'T FALL FOR YOUR GRUMPY HUSBAND, Callum and Violet's Story

The Gods Of Saint Pierce

SAY MY NAME

CROSS MY HEART

CLOSE YOUR EYES

ON YOUR KNEES

Magnolia Point

TEMPTING MR. SCROOGE

LATTE BE DESIRED

THE UMPIRE STRIKES BACK

The Taken Series

TAKEN BY MY BEST FRIEND

MARRIED TO MY ENEMY (BOOK ONE)

MARRIED TO MY ENEMY (BOOK TWO)

STOLEN BY THE BOSS

ABDUCTED BY MY FATHER'S BEST FRIEND

CAPTURED BY THE CRIMINAL

Men Of Ruthless Corp.

SOLD TO THE HITMAN (As featured in the hit Netflix Movie: *Hitman* starring Glen Powell)

Harmony Hills Series

RUIN'S REVENGE

STEP-SANTA

HOLIDAY HIDEOUT

HATED BY MY ROOMMATE

HARD RIDE

The Trifecta Series

HOT VEGAS NIGHTS

DIRTY VEGAS NIGHTS

FILTHY VEGAS NIGHTS

Vampire Romance

Wicked Matrimony: A Vampire Romance

A Never Say Never Novel

NEVER KISS A STRANGER

The Playboy Series

PLAYBOY

HEARTBREAKER

STUCK

LOVE DOCTOR

The Me Series

DATE ME

STUDY ME

SAVE ME

BREAK ME

Sexy Standalones

THE NEWLYFEDS

COLD HEARTED BACHELOR

Holiday Romance Stories

FAKING IT WITH MR. STEELE

A VERY MERRY ALPHA CHRISTMAS COLLECTION

MERRY PUCKING CHRISTMAS

Steamy Duet

THE BOSS DUET

Box Sets

A VERY MERRY ALPHA CHRISTMAS COLLECTION

ME: THE COMPLETE SERIES

FAKE IT BABY ONE MORE TIME

THE TRIFECTA SERIES: COMPLETE BOX SET

THE PLAYBOY COMPLETE COLLECTION

FILTHY ROMANCE COLLECTION

THE TAKEN SERIES BOX SET: BOOKS 1-3

THE TAKEN SERIES BOX SET BOOKS 4-6

Made in the USA
Las Vegas, NV
21 March 2025